WIND CALLED

THE WITCHES OF MINGUS MOUNTAIN - BOOK 4

CHRISTINE POPE

WIND CALLED

Published by Dark Valentine Press

Cover design by Indie Author Services

Ebook formatting by Indie Author Services

1

"YOU'RE REALLY GOING THROUGH WITH THIS," Bellamy McAllister's father Kirby said, and she somehow managed to prevent herself from rolling her eyes. It wasn't that she was annoyed with him for caring. No, what irritated her was how he'd been like a dog with a bone about this whole thing, and even now, when she was getting ready to load her stuff into her car, he didn't seem able to let it go.

"Dad, we've been over this, like, a million times," she replied as she zipped up her overnight bag. "It's not even permanent. I'm just house sitting until the place is sold, and then I'll be right back in Jerome."

Or maybe Cottonwood or Clarkdale, depending on what was available when she was looking for a place to land. That day could be a month or six months from now —impossible to say for sure, since she had no idea how quickly the sprawling ranch property she'd lucked into would be off the market.

"We're not supposed to live in Sedona," her father said, a factoid he'd also helpfully brought up a rough dozen times over the past few weeks.

And yes, it was true enough that witch-kind weren't supposed to spend too much time in Sedona. The McAllisters and the Wilcoxes had managed to hammer out an agreement more than a hundred years earlier that neither witch clan should lay claim to Sedona's red rocks…which supposedly possessed their own power…so no one from either clan had ever lived there full time, although magical folk certainly visited to shop or dine or hike. Frankly, Bellamy thought all the talk about Sedona's mystical powers was mostly a bunch of hooey designed to bilk tourists out of money for vortex tours when they came here to achieve their version of enlightenment, so she wasn't about to let herself be too troubled by the way she was ignoring a century-plus of tradition.

"The ranch isn't even inside Sedona's city limits," she said, unperturbed. "So I don't think I'm breaking any rules. Besides, staying there makes my commute a lot easier."

Only a month earlier, she'd gotten an awesome job as assistant manager at Sedona

Vines, a wine bar in West Sedona, and although she'd been thrilled by the step up in responsibility and pay, she had to admit that commuting there from Jerome five days a week had been kind of a pain. Now she'd only have to drive ten minutes to get to work, and she was going to enjoy every second of it, even as she understood her current situation wasn't going to last forever.

Her father frowned. Although he was pushing fifty now, he still looked as boyish as ever, with wavy brown hair and laughing blue eyes. Bellamy knew she didn't resemble him very much, with her coppery hair and gray eyes, and assumed she must have taken after the woman who'd donated her egg to the process and also acted as a surrogate. The red hair was definitely a McAllister thing, though, and she figured the recessive gene had shown up in her after skipping a couple of generations.

"I'm still not sure I like it," her father said slowly, and she stepped away from the bed so she could go over to him and give him a quick hug.

"I had to move out sometime," she replied, which was only the truth. It had been easy to remain at home while she was getting her enology certification at Yavapai Community College down the hill, but no one could have expected her to live in the apartment over the candy shop forever. The place was a decent size, just a hair over eighteen hundred square feet, and yet being here with her two dads, she'd thought it was starting to feel a little tight.

Time to grow up and move on. She was twenty-two, after all.

Her father cracked a grin. Her other dad Jordan was downstairs watching the store so Kirby could say goodbye to Bellamy since she and Jordan had already shared a goodbye breakfast earlier that day, but she knew Kirby couldn't linger here in the apartment forever, not on a busy August day with lots of tourists hitting the former mining town.

"You're right, of course," he said. "You're sure you don't want any help taking this stuff over to the new place?"

He'd already made that offer multiple times, and her answer was still the same.

"I'm good," she replied, even as she sent him a smile she hoped would communicate her gratitude despite not needing the assistance. "Bree's going to take some of the bulkier things, since she has a bigger car."

A huge gas-powered Suburban that was a hulking relic from the time before smaller, more efficient vehicles. But Brianna McAllister was always hauling a bunch of instruments and amplifiers and whatnot from one gig to another and needed the room, and she'd offered to help

Bellamy move her things since Bree was going to be playing at one of the resorts in West Sedona that evening anyway.

Kirby seemed to realize any additional arguments he put forth would also get shot down, so he shrugged, saying, "Well, it looks like you've got it all figured out. You make sure to call if you need anything, though, okay?"

"I will," she promised.

The doorbell at the back entrance to the flat rang then, and Bellamy sent her father a smile. "Gotta go."

"But you'll be back for dinner on Sunday."

"Wouldn't miss it," she said.

Seeming to understand that it was time for him to go, he ducked his head at her before heading downstairs, and Bellamy hurried over to the door to let in her friend.

Bree was about ten months older than Bellamy and spectacularly blonde, with the kind of looks that always seemed to lead to at least one person each day asking her whether she was a model or an actress. Those inquiries seemed to embarrass her more than anything else, although she did her best to act as if there wasn't anything out of the ordinary about her looks.

Of course, the people asking could have no way of knowing that her amazing beauty was a gift from a father who just happened to be an otherworldly creature summoned to this plane to be the consort of the de la Paz clan's *prima* more than two decades ago.

Not that Bree's mother Hayley was exactly a slouch in the looks department, either, but still, it was Levi who'd contributed the most to his daughter's genetic makeup.

"Ready?" Bree asked as she stepped inside the apartment. No point in her looking around, not when the two women had been friends since they were little girls and the flat where Bellamy had grown up was almost as familiar to Brianna as her own house.

"As I'll ever be," Bellamy said, reaching for her overnight bag so she could sling it over her shoulder. "I want to make a quick getaway before my dad tries to come up with yet another reason why I shouldn't be living in Sedona."

Bree grinned and grasped a couple of suitcases. "Well, it is kind of breaking tradition."

"Yeah, and Angela and Connor cleared it, so there's nothing to worry about."

Because after Bellamy had gotten to talking with that one patron at Sedona Vines and he'd told her he was looking for someone to be a caretaker at his house while it was on the market, she'd made sure to speak to her clan's *prima* and her consort, just to make sure she wouldn't be stepping on any toes by going to live at the ranch.

Both Connor and Angela had agreed that, while the tradition might have had some merit back in the day, neither of them could think of a single reason why it wouldn't be okay for Bellamy to live in red rock country for a while, especially since the situation wasn't permanent.

And if the leaders of both the McAllister and Wilcox clans couldn't come up with a reason for her not to hang out in Sedona for a few weeks or months or whatever, then she didn't see why she should turn down the chance to live in the lap of luxury for a bit.

This reassurance seemed to be all Bree needed to hear, because she nodded and said, "Sounds good to me. Then let's get going—I have to be at Enchantment by five to set up."

The two women headed down the back stairs, where they loaded Bellamy's suitcases into the cavernous cargo compartment in the Suburban. In direct contrast, her own vehicle was a small Fiat convertible, something she absolutely loved zipping around in with the top down but wasn't exactly the best thing in the world for trans-porting her wardrobe.

Once everything was loaded in the big Chevy, Bree closed the hatch. "I'll follow you over there," she said.

"Okay," Bellamy replied, then paused. Although they'd been good friends for most of their lives, she knew Bree had been dancing around her own issues this summer, and she wondered whether she should bring it up now or pretend the whole thing hadn't happened.

Well, sometimes you just had to go for broke.

"So…you're really for sure not going back to college?"

Bree's full mouth set, and she paused for a second to look around them. They were utterly alone back here, in the small carve-out designated as parking for the apartment over the candy store, but it was clear she didn't want anyone overhearing them.

"If I were going to head back to Flagstaff, I should have been doing it by now," she said lightly. "Classes start on Monday. But no—I tried college, and it just wasn't for me. It's fine. I'll figure something out."

Although her expression seemed casual enough, Bellamy could practically sense the tension radiating off her friend. No one could ever accuse Levi McAllister of being a hard-ass, not when he'd always seemed like one of the most open and accepting people she'd ever met, but Bellamy had a feeling he'd still given his only daughter some grief over dropping out of college, and she knew Hayley had, since she'd overheard her friend's mother talking about it with her dad Jordan only a week ago.

Well, not her circus. Her job as Bree's friend was to be supportive, and she supposed eventually this would all blow over. Honestly, she had no idea how much of a difference a degree would even have made for her friend—she'd still play her gigs around the Verde Valley and teach guitar and piano and voice on the side. A diploma wasn't going to change any of that.

"Let's go," she said. "And if you have time, I'll give you a tour of the new house."

Marc Trujillo's eyes opened, straining against the darkness. For just the barest moment, he couldn't remember where he was…until he realized he was lying in his bed in the house he'd bought a little less than a year earlier, in the Sam Hughes historic neighborhood near the University of Arizona campus in Tucson. Cool air from the vents above his bed caressed his face, and he knew he should have been comfortable enough despite the blazing August heat that lingered long after the sun had gone down.

And yet….

He sat up and looked around. Pale green numerals glowed from the clock at his bedside, telling him it was a little past one in the morning. Everything was utterly quiet.

Well, except for the pounding of his heart.

Very little of the dream remained. Only that sense of foreboding, like a distant rumble of thunder on the horizon.

And the woman.

Her back had been to him, so all he'd seen was lush coppery hair blowing in the wind. However, even though his mother had hair nearly that shade, he didn't think she was the woman he'd seen in his dream.

And while most people would have dismissed it, telling themselves they'd had a nightmare, Marc knew this latest dream was something more than that.

Much more.

Witchy tradition held that seers tended to be women, and his mother Caitlin had that gift. But when Marc was around eleven and he'd started to have dreams that came true, his family began to realize her oldest child had inherited that talent, even if it was very rare for a man to be a seer.

Most of the time, his visions weren't of anything terribly unsettling, although he'd dreamed of the *prima's* daughter getting into a car accident on prom night a couple of years ago, thanks to a rare and catastrophic failure of the vehicle's self-driving mechanism. But Rosa had been fine, although the SUV she'd been riding in was a total loss.

This dream, however…it worried him, even if there hadn't been anything about it that should have caused such disquiet. Only the red-haired woman standing with her back to him, and vague shapes in the distance that made him think of Sedona's red rocks.

Well, he would talk it over with his mother tomorrow. Caitlin McAllister had been dealing with prophetic dreams for most of her lifetime, and if she didn't have any helpful advice to offer, then no one would.

With any luck, it would turn out to be nothing at all.

Holding that thought in his mind, Marc rolled over onto his side, pulled in a few measured breaths, and told himself to go to sleep.

Unfortunately, his mother only seemed troubled when he recounted the dream to her. They sat in the living room of the house where Marc had grown up, with its breathtaking vistas of the Catalina Foothills beyond a wall of glass that gave the space such a sensation of light and air, while the swimming pool sparkled a cool blue-green under the bright August sun. Even though the patio was shaded and had multiple ceiling fans, it was still far too hot to sit outside, so they remained indoors, drinking iced tea and discussing the dream that had awoken him the night before.

"She had red hair, but you don't think it was me," Caitlin McAllister said. A few threads of silver had started to show in her copper-hued locks, but her face was still fresh and youthful, and she didn't really look old enough to have a son who would be turning twenty-four in less than a month.

He shook his head. "No, she seemed taller. And although her hair was red, it was a couple of shades darker than yours."

Yes, after he'd thought about it, he realized the dream-woman's hair had been a dark copper, not the paler, almost strawberry blonde shade his mother had always sported. Marc had no reason to believe she'd ever helped it along with any sort of dye, or she probably would have been covering up those silvery strands that had begun to make their appearance over the last six months or so.

"A witch?" his mother asked, and he shrugged.

"I don't know for sure. But…maybe."

"Well, a red-haired witch would be part of my clan," she said. "We always had a redhead sprouting here and there, although there are a lot more McAllisters who're blonde or have light brown hair. I suppose I can ask Angela who in the clan has red hair—I've been kind of out of touch down here in Tucson, and haven't been paying much attention to what's going on with the McAllisters."

No, Caitlin McAllister had made her choice decades earlier to go and live among the de la Paz clan, and although their family had traveled north here and there to visit and check in, their last trip had been several years earlier, just as he was about to start his final year of college. She'd never seemed too worried about missing Jerome, which made sense.

Her life was here, after all.

But something told Marc it was probably foolish to be bothering the *prima* about a dream that didn't even have any real details, just a general sense of foreboding. And although everyone agreed that his talent was real, it still didn't mean that some of his dreams weren't just that—dreams and nothing more.

Before he could say anything in reply, though, his mother gave a shake of her head, looking rueful. "I swear, I don't know where my brain is these days. I don't need to contact Angela—I'll just give your grandmother a call. She's got her finger on the pulse of all things McAllister, maybe even more than the *prima* does."

Marc supposed his mother was right about that. Tricia McAllister had been a clan elder since before he was even born, and she lived in Jerome full time rather than dividing the months between the touristy former mining town and Flagstaff, the way Angela and Connor did, doing their best to split their time evenly between their two witch families. Maybe if you sat down and calculated the numbers, they probably spent more days in Jerome, but still, they didn't live the entire year in any one place.

"Sure," he said, trying to sound unconcerned about the whole thing. Although he'd been dealing with dreams and visions for the past thirteen years, he still didn't feel entirely comfortable with the concept, partly because even in witch clans, people tended to look at those sorts of gifts with some serious side-eye.

Especially when they came from a man.

His mother probably knew all too well what he was thinking, but she looked utterly at ease as she got up and went into the kitchen, where she'd left her cell phone sitting on the countertop. As she walked back to resume her seat in the living room, she was already typing away.

It seemed nothing too pressing must have been happening in Jerome, since her phone pinged a moment later. His mother gazed down at the screen and nodded.

"Your grandmother says the clan has a few redheads right now, but only one who would be around the right age."

Marc didn't know if he could even have assigned an age to the woman he'd seen in his dream, considering how she'd been turned away from him. Still, she was obviously an adult, not a child, which he supposed could narrow things down a bit.

"Who's that?" he asked. Maybe it was a bit strange that he knew so little about his relatives in Jerome, but his family just hadn't visited there all that often.

His mother smiled.

"Her name is Bellamy."

2

THE GROUP OF TOURISTS HURRIED OUT OF
Sedona Vines so they could climb into their bus
and head to their next destination—which
sounded as if it was going to be Javelina Leap over
in Page Springs—and Bellamy let out a relieved
breath. Although she supposed she should be glad
for the business, it was always a lot of extra work
when one of the tour buses stopped by, since
everyone wanted to cram in the maximum
amount of wine tasting before they went on to the
next stop on their route.

Honestly, she wasn't sure why they even came
to the wine bar at all, since it wasn't a winery, per
se, only a place where vintages from all over the
world, not just the Verde Valley, were available.
On the other hand, Sedona was pretty short on
actual wineries, since they tended to be clustered

in Cottonwood and Page Springs and yes, in Jerome.

Before this, she'd worked at Caduceus Cellars just a couple of doors down from McAllister Mercantile, where she'd also picked up some part-time hours, but after she got her enology certificate in June, she'd moved on to bigger and better things. It had been a little hard to accept that she wouldn't be pulling shifts at the store anymore, but with Seth McAllister now settled down in Jerome following his trips in time with Devynn Rowe, the two of them were pretty much running the shop these days. In 1926, his immediate family had managed the place, and Rachel McAllister, the current owner, had decreed that she was giving the whole thing over to Seth to handle.

At any rate, they didn't need her to work a few hours here and a few hours there anymore, which was why Bellamy had jumped at the chance to take over the assistant manager job at Sedona Vines when the position became available. While she adored Jerome and would never seriously think about living anywhere except the Verde Valley, she had to admit it was something of a relief to be working in a place where no one knew all that much about her except that she was a McAllister, just like so many other denizens of the area.

And even though her dads weren't totally

thrilled about the whole Sedona thing, she knew they were happy she'd found a job that so neatly dovetailed with her education and her interests. While she was getting her enology certification, she'd taken many classes on making wine, of course, and probably could have gotten work at one of the wineries in the area. However, although she loved learning about the science involved in winemaking, she'd never had much desire to actually create her own vintages.

No, she was much more into talking about wine, suggesting varieties and blends that she thought would tempt a customer's palate, leaning into the mystique of the whole thing. It was just fine with her if she never again had to be up at the crack of dawn harvesting the grapes so they'd be picked at the peak of perfection…or nervously eyeing the weather when a late frost threatened the delicate buds.

Much better to enjoy the product of those labors rather than having to agonize over every single bump in the road.

A few more customers came in, and she chatted them up, asking them whether they liked white or red, dry or sweet. They had a good crowd this particular Saturday afternoon, just enough to have a nice ebb and flow without things getting too crazy. Of course, as the day bled into evening, they'd get busier, with people coming in to amuse themselves before they headed off for dinner.

Or just stayed here. While Sedona Vines didn't have a full kitchen, they had snacks and charcuterie boards that were big enough to substitute for a meal, and plenty of people hung around and nibbled and drank rather than going in search of some real food. The space had been set up to invite people to linger, with its mixture of round bar-height tables and chairs and conversation areas with comfy couches, not to mention the welcoming reclaimed-wood bar, so they often had clients who stayed there for hours and hours.

There would be live music later, too. Bree played here sometimes, although not tonight, since the group on the calendar today was a husband and wife duo from Missouri who'd been making the circuit for the past couple of years. They always offered a good time, though, so Bellamy couldn't let herself miss Brianna too much, especially when she knew her gigs at Enchantment tended to earn her bigger tips.

She hoped her friend was okay, though. Even if Bree was trying to act as though it was no big deal that she'd completely upended her family's expectations for her, Bellamy knew she was still probably second-guessing herself, trying to decide if she'd made an impulsive decision that would come back to bite her in the ass when she least expected it.

Well, if that happened, Bellamy knew she'd offer a sympathetic ear whenever Bree needed one.

And then the door opened again, and for a moment, a tall figure was silhouetted against the warm light of the setting sun. Bellamy found her eyes narrowing as she looked at the newcomer, whose features slowly resolved themselves once he was well inside and not so backlit.

Hot damn, he was gorgeous. While handsome strangers came to the wine bar on a fairly regular basis, they usually weren't alone. No, someone who looked like that generally had a date hanging on his arm.

That wasn't all, though. When he got closer to the bar, a brief ringing in her ears told Bellamy the stranger was just as much witch-kind as she was, and although she was a little startled, it wasn't as if this sort of thing hadn't happened before.

In fact, her first thought was that he must be a Wilcox, since he was dark enough, but somehow, she didn't think so. Although she couldn't claim to have met every twenty-something guy in the Wilcox family, enough of them came to visit Jerome that a good percentage were immediately recognizable to her.

No, the stranger was probably a member of the de la Paz clan who'd come up to the Verde

Valley for a change of scenery. Although they didn't visit these parts as often as the Wilcoxes did, it wasn't as though having a de la Paz warlock drop in out of nowhere was completely out of the ordinary, either.

Even if she was pretty sure this guy was the best-looking de la Paz she'd ever seen.

He came straight for her, his stride purposeful, which seemed to indicate that he wasn't here solely to get a drink or pick up a couple of bottles of wine. No, he stopped on the other side of the bar and gave a quick glance around, as if to make sure no one was paying them any particular attention, before saying, "Bellamy McAllister?"

"Who's asking?" she returned with a smile. Yes, the guy was gorgeous, but she wasn't going to give it all away without getting some idea as to his reason for being here.

His expression remained serious. "My name is Marc Trujillo. There's something I'd like to talk to you about…in private."

She felt her eyebrows lift, although she wouldn't allow her smile to waver. No one seemed to have listened to their exchange, but there were still plenty of people clustered near the bar and the tall tables set up close by, so no way in the world could anyone view this as a situation where they had even a modicum of privacy.

"Can it wait?" she asked. "We're kind of busy right now."

Marc Trujillo's dark gaze swept their immediate environs as though to count all the customers gathered inside the wine bar, and he gave a reluctant nod. "I suppose so. When can you take a break?"

Since she was the assistant manager, she could go on a break pretty much anytime she wanted. However, she was new enough here that she didn't want to take advantage or make the other employees think she was willing to bend the rules as long as doing so benefited her in some way.

"Half an hour," she replied, since that was when she'd already planned to take her break.

He didn't look overly thrilled by that reply, but at least he didn't protest.

"Okay," he said. "What've you got for a dry rosé?"

She recited the options, then poured him a glass of the wine he'd ordered. Apparently resigned to waiting until she was ready, he took the glass out onto the patio. It was blazing hot today, hovering just under a hundred degrees, but she supposed that if he really was a de la Paz and therefore from Phoenix or Tucson or points in between, then he knew a little something about hot weather.

The next half hour was busier than she'd

expected, but eventually she was able to murmur to Pierce, the other guy working the bar that afternoon, that she was taking her break and would be back in fifteen. Thoughts of a glass of rosé tempted her, although she did her best to resist them. She was working, and even if she was currently on her break, that didn't mean she should start drinking.

Marc Trujillo sat at a table over to one side, where the spreading branches of a large cottonwood tree did a decent job of shielding that section of the patio from the hot sun. As soon as she approached, he set down his glass of wine—she was a little surprised that he hadn't finished it yet, and guessed he'd been nursing the drink to make it last until she came out to meet him—and stood, then pulled out a chair for her.

"Thanks," she said, settling herself in the seat. Good-looking and polite?

She could definitely deal with that.

"Visiting from down south?" she asked once he'd settled himself in his chair, and he nodded.

"From Tucson."

He was a long way from home, then. Although the McAllisters headed into Phoenix all the time to go shopping or run other errands, not nearly as many of them made it as far as Tucson, which was more than a three-hour drive from Jerome.

"Come up to see the red rocks?"

She'd essayed another smile as she asked the question, but his expression remained serious.

"No, I came here to see you."

For a second or two, she could only stare back at him, trying to figure out if he was making some kind of joke. But no, those dark eyes with their fringe of heavy lashes were sober, without even a single glint to tell her he was teasing.

"Me?" she said, then went on, "I don't even know you."

"No, you don't," he said calmly. "Look, this is probably going to sound totally strange, but…I had a dream about you. Or at least, I had a dream with a red-haired woman in it, and my grandmother told me there was only one redhead in Jerome who would have been the right age."

Even to someone who'd grown up in a witch clan and therefore had had to roll with some pretty crazy punches over the years, this all sounded as if it had come right out of left field.

"Who's your grandmother?" Bellamy asked, figuring it was easier to pose that question than try to pick apart the more problematic elements of Marc Trujillo's comments.

"Tricia McAllister."

Okay, that made a little more sense. Tricia had been an elder the entire time Bellamy was alive, but her daughter Caitlin had married a de la Paz warlock and settled in Tucson more than twenty years ago. They visited Jerome every once in a blue moon, but certainly not enough that Bellamy would have even run into Marc.

And Caitlin was a seer.

Did that mean Marc had inherited something of his mother's talent? If he'd really had some sort of dream where he'd seen Bellamy, then she supposed that might make some sense, even though she'd always heard that men usually weren't seers.

On the other hand, she had a feeling that he wouldn't have driven all this way if he didn't have some kind of talent in that department.

"What was in the dream?" she asked.

Did she even want to know?

But she'd already asked the question, which meant she needed to sit here and listen to the answer.

"I'm not sure," he said, and his mouth tightened. She had the impression that he wasn't too thrilled by the position his talent had put him in, knowing that what he said must often sound ridiculous to anyone who hadn't experienced the same visions he had. "That is, the dream was more about…impressions, I guess. Like something was really wrong, even if I can't say exactly what."

Well, this was getting better and better.

"'Wrong' how?" she asked, doing her best to sound neutral and not at all judge-y.

"I don't know," he replied. Those dark eyes met hers, and even though Bellamy really didn't like his reason for being here and liked even less that he'd felt the need to drop everything and drive a couple of hundred miles so he could talk to her in person, a small thrill went down her back.

He was so *very* good-looking…and utterly unlike any of the McAllister warlocks she'd grown up with.

Before she could say anything, he went on, "I suppose I wanted to come here to make sure you were all right."

Bellamy found herself smiling again. "You could have called."

"Maybe," he allowed, and his lips quirked in response to her smile, as if he knew how odd all this looked on the surface. "But this talent of mine…it likes to experience things in person. I wanted to know if there was anything near you that might explain why I would get such a sensation of foreboding from my dream."

"And is there?" she asked as she leaned against the back of her chair…and wished she'd grabbed that glass of rosé after all.

"Not that I'm aware of," Marc replied. He paused there, his gaze moving around the patio. It wasn't quite dark enough yet for the bistro lights strung overhead to have been switched on, but the sun had dropped sufficiently toward the western horizon that it was no longer reflected in the waterfall and small pond that occupied one corner of the wine bar's outdoor area. More than half the tables were occupied by laughing, chattering groups despite the heat, and all in all, it should have been a cheerful, welcoming space.

Why, then, did a shiver want to move its way down her back?

Power of suggestion, she told herself. Nothing dark lingered here. It was just a place where people gathered to drink and hang out, nothing more.

"Are your dreams ever wrong?" she asked, and immediately, Marc shook his dark head.

"No," he said. "Sometimes it takes me a bit to figure out what they're trying to tell me, but they've never given me incorrect information."

Hmm. Bellamy didn't much like the sound of that, not when she'd been the focus of one of those dreams.

Or at least, Marc seemed to think she was the person he'd seen, even though he'd admitted that he hadn't seen her face and therefore the dream-woman could have been some other redhead.

"Maybe it wasn't me at all," she said. "I mean, I can see why you might think it was a witch in your dream, but since the woman's back was to you, how can you know for sure?"

His fingers tapped against the side of his stemless glass. Less than a quarter inch of the rosé remained, so pale that you couldn't tell what color it had once been.

"I suppose I can't," he replied, his tone frank. "But my dreams have always been about my clan and the people in it. I don't seem to have visions about civilians, for whatever reason."

Well, there was something. Bellamy supposed it would have been kind of disruptive to continually be interrupted by images of plane crashes and house fires and what-have-you. The de la Paz clan was very large—maybe even bigger than the Wilcox clan, although she wasn't sure whether anyone had ever done a census comparing the two —so she guessed there was plenty going on among that particular witch family to keep Marc's seer gift hopping.

She almost pointed out that she wasn't a member of his clan but realized that sort of comment would be disingenuous at best. Yes, he'd been raised among the de la Pazes, but he was still a McAllister on his mother's side, and that meant he had plenty of connection to Jerome and the people who lived there, even if he'd grown up hundreds of miles away.

Which also meant she should probably be

taking this seriously…although she really didn't want to.

"Well," she said, doing her best to keep her tone cheerful, "I suppose you can consider me warned. But my life's pretty boring. I don't think there's much chance of me getting into any kind of trouble."

Marc's dark eyes had taken on an amused glint when she uttered the word "boring"—it wasn't the sort of adjective one would generally use when describing the life of a witch or warlock—but he didn't try to contradict her.

"Maybe it's nothing," he said. "On the other hand, I don't usually have a dream like this when there's no there, there, if you know what I mean. Has anything unusual been happening among the McAllisters lately?"

Bellamy wanted to say there hadn't, but again, she didn't know for sure whether such a statement would be completely accurate. After all, it wasn't every day when you had someone from more than a hundred years in the past take up residence in your hometown.

However, she found it hard to believe that this had anything to do with Seth McAllister and Devynn Rowe. Ever since they'd gotten back to the mid-twenty-first century, they'd been living quietly in the bungalow that had originally been his—Margot Wilcox, who owned the place, had given it to them, saying that Seth had owned it first and therefore he should get it back —and had taken over running McAllister Mercantile so Rachel could finally enjoy the retirement she'd been pondering for at least the past ten years.

Absolutely nothing there to send a dark, foreboding dream to Marc Trujillo, something powerful enough that he'd been compelled to drive hundreds of miles so he could talk to her in person.

Except….

No, she really didn't want to talk about the magical object Seth and Devynn had brought back from the past. Bellamy knew about it because Devynn had shown the bronze amulet with its cabochon garnet to her before locking it back up in its safe, the kind with a biometric lock so no one except Devynn and Seth could open it, but she'd said the elders wanted to keep the thing on the down-low. Honestly, most people in the clan didn't know the artifact even existed.

Which meant it probably wasn't a good idea to mention the amulet now. It sounded immensely powerful—it seemed to have the intrinsic ability to strengthen a witch or warlock's gifts, similar to Bree's mother's talent but even stronger—and since the elders wanted to keep the object a secret, blabbing about it to a de la Paz warlock who'd just appeared in their territory was something Bellamy knew she shouldn't do.

"Everything's been pretty chill," she said, wishing more than ever that she'd brought a glass of wine out here with her. She didn't like lying, but she also knew some matters needed to stay within the clan…no matter how handsome and appealing her visitor might be.

As soon as the words left her lips, though, an odd, sharp wind swept across the patio, catching at her loose hair and causing several napkins and other odds and ends at the other tables to swirl into the air. The patrons jumped up from their chairs to grab the flotsam and jetsam, and a moment later, the wind subsided as if it had never been.

Marc's eyes had narrowed as soon as the wind blew over the space, but Bellamy held her tongue. Yes, her gift was controlling the wind—or at least, calling a breeze here and there—and yet she knew she hadn't summoned the mischievous little wind that had caused such minor havoc just a moment earlier.

Or at least, she didn't think she had. Her talent was a small one at best, but she'd never had it get away from her before.

His lips parted, and she wondered what she would say if he asked her point-blank whether she'd had anything to do with that strange gust of wind.

To her relief, though, he only said, "Well, I suppose that's a good thing. God knows we've had enough excitement to last our clans for decades."

That was for sure. True, a lot of what had gone down lately had happened over in New Mexico and not here in Arizona, but Bellamy had a feeling the de la Pazes were still smarting over the way a bunch of their grimoires had been stolen by the dark warlock Simon Escobar and used in his quest for domination over all the witch clans of the Southwest. Luckily, the grimoires were now back in their proper owners' hands—well, in the hands of their *prima,* anyway, who'd built an addition to her house to contain them, an addition protected by probably every shielding spell they could think of—and yet the whole incident had put everyone on edge, even though Simon was now safely dead and buried.

"True," she agreed, and glanced down at her watch. She'd been out here for fifteen minutes, so technically, her break was over and she needed to get back to work.

Marc must have guessed why she was checking the time, because he said, "I won't keep you. Maybe this was all a bunch of nothing."

"Are your visions usually a 'bunch of nothing'?" Bellamy asked, genuinely curious.

His mouth tightened. "No. But that doesn't mean I don't make a mistake from time to time."

He sounded casual enough as he said those words, telling her he wasn't worried about admitting he wasn't infallible. After some of the guys she'd dated, men who felt like they needed to be right about every single thing all the time, she had to admit it was a refreshing change.

Not that she was dating Marc Trujillo, of course. No, best as she could tell, they seemed to be two ships passing in the night and nothing more.

"Well," she said as she got up from her seat, "I guess you can let me know if you have any more weird dreams. Are you staying here in Sedona?"

"No," he replied at once. "I got a hotel room in Cottonwood. Everything was pretty booked up, but they had a last-minute cancellation."

Lucky for him, she knew, since a lot of people were trying to squeeze in one last family trip before their kids had to go back to school. Briefly, she wondered why he hadn't stayed with Tricia; the elder's house was a big Victorian up on Paradise Lane, only slightly smaller than the home Angela and Connor shared, so Bellamy knew there was plenty of room.

Most likely, he hadn't wanted to impose. She didn't know anything about the guy, but even their brief acquaintance seemed to signal that he was someone who didn't like to make much of a fuss.

"That's good," she said. "I guess enjoy the rest of your time in the Verde Valley."

"I will."

She gave him a smile she knew was limp at best, but what else was she supposed to say? It was time for her to get back to work, and, as far as she could tell, this whole thing had been a wild-goose chase and nothing more.

After all, there was certainly nothing interesting going on in her life.

Even if she kind of wished there were.

3

HE SUPPOSED HE SHOULD HAVE PREPARED himself for the possibility that she would be pretty.

No, he thought as he pulled out of Sedona Vines' gravel-paved parking lot and headed back toward Cottonwood. *Not just pretty.*

Beautiful, with that rich coppery hair and those clear gray eyes, the full mouth that mostly had been quirked with amusement but at the same time promised all sorts of lush delights.

He shouldn't be thinking about her mouth, though…or anything else, really, except why his talent had tried to tell him something was going on with Bellamy McAllister.

Exactly what, he had no idea, because she'd said that her life was pretty darn boring, with nothing to indicate why his gift had zeroed in on her, for whatever reason.

And yet…what had been going on with that strange gust of wind that had blown through the patio at the wine bar, catching her long red hair and sending the other patrons' cocktail napkins swirling all over the place?

Bellamy had looked almost guilty when it happened.

Was that her gift? Working with the wind?

Maybe, but even if that were the case, he could tell she hadn't meant for the breeze to play such havoc on the patio.

He would have asked, except it was generally etiquette among members of the various witch clans not to inquire as to a person's magical gifts, and instead to wait for them to volunteer that information when they thought the time was right.

Clearly, Bellamy hadn't felt the need to tell him that much about herself.

Frowning, he found himself passing his hotel in Old Town Cottonwood and continuing along 89A as it went through tiny Clarkdale and then began climbing the hill to Jerome. Although his mother had let his grandmother know he was coming to the Verde Valley, he hadn't reached out to Tricia yet, since he wasn't sure when he'd be able to swing by.

But with his conversation with Bellamy pretty much a bust, he figured it might be a good idea to talk to his grandmother and see if she had any insights to offer about the troubling dream… vision…he'd had.

Far more traffic was coming down the hill than going up it, signaling that most of the tourists seemed to view Jerome as a day destination rather than a place where they planned to hang out and sample the nightlife.

Was there even any nightlife in Jerome? He had the vague idea that there were a couple of bars on Main Street, places that might have live music, but obviously, his parents wouldn't have taken him and his little sister Lucy to those sorts of venues when they were here visiting the grandparents.

He had to hope Tricia wouldn't mind too much if he dropped in so close to dinner.

But of course she welcomed him with a hug and said she hoped he would stay to eat, so that seemed to be the end of that. His grandfather didn't seem to be anywhere around, though, and she only smiled and shook her head when he asked.

"Oh, he and a couple of his friends are up by Williams, doing some quail hunting," she explained. "That's why I made a big pot of soup—

I figured I'd eat it over the next couple of days until he gets back."

"I don't want to eat up all your stash—" Marc began, but she only smiled and shook her head.

"It's fine," she told him. "And I made some bread, too. A growing boy like you needs to eat."

Now it was his turn to smile. "I think my growing days are kind of behind me now."

Good thing, too, since he'd shot up six inches his sophomore year of high school and the experience had been excruciating, to say the least. But now he topped his father's six foot two by almost half an inch, so all those worries that he was going to turn out to be a runt had been mercifully left by the wayside.

"Your mother told me you had one of your dreams," Tricia said as they headed into the dining room. A warm, rich aroma drifted in from the kitchen, and his stomach rumbled.

Whatever that soup was, it smelled delicious.

"I did," he replied. "That was why I went to talk to Bellamy, since she seemed to be the only person in the McAllister clan with the right color hair."

Even as the words left his mouth, he thought how foolish they sounded.

But Tricia didn't seem to think they were foolish, and instead frowned slightly. He knew from old family photos that her hair had once been the same coppery blonde shade as her daughter's, but now her sleek bob was pure white. However, like Caitlin, her skin barely bore any lines at all, only a few crow's feet around her eyes and another line right in the middle of her brows, probably etched there after managing the McAllister clan's business for the past twenty-plus years.

"Yes, we don't have a lot of redheads right now," his grandmother said. "Well, Lisbeth's daughter, but she's only seven, so she couldn't have been the woman in your dream." She paused there, and added, "You go ahead and take a seat. I'll have the food out in just a minute."

"Do you need any help?"

"No, I'm fine," Tricia assured him. "You just sit tight."

Feeling a little awkward—even though he knew any more offers of assistance would only be met with additional refusals—Marc sat down at the dining room table, which was covered by a cheerful flowered tablecloth. As far as he'd been able to tell, that table was never bare, since it always had worn a seasonally appropriate cloth the few times his family had come to Jerome for the holidays.

His grandmother came back out with some flatware and a bowl of heavy cream-glazed stoneware, along with a cloth napkin that matched the tablecloth. "There you go," she said, putting the place setting in front of him. "Would you like a glass of wine, or is water okay?"

"Water is fine," he replied. That one glass of rosé hadn't had much of an effect on him, but he still didn't think it was a good idea to have anything else tonight, not when he still had no idea exactly what had been going on with that damn dream.

His grandmother smiled at him before returning to the kitchen. Soon enough, she had a tureen of soup sitting on the table, along with a loaf of gorgeously crusty bread and some butter.

"I know it's a little silly to be having soup on such a hot day," she said as she ladled some into his bowl. "But I just got a craving for green chile corn chowder, and since your grandfather wasn't here to tease me about it, I made a big pot anyway."

"It smells amazing," Marc said. Corn chowder was his favorite soup, so he thought it positively providential that his grandmother had whipped up a batch today.

And no, she wasn't a seer like her daughter and her grandson, but she was still a powerful witch, and maybe she'd somehow known this was just what the doctor had ordered.

"What did Bellamy have to say?" she asked after they'd helped themselves to soup and bread, and taken a couple of bites.

Marc found his mouth twisting. "Not a whole heck of a lot. She said there hasn't been anything of real note going on in the clan, and she couldn't figure out why I would have a dream with her in it."

His grandmother had just buttered another slice of bread, but she set it down on her plate as he made that comment, her expression now thoughtful.

"Oh, we've had a little excitement," she said. "A witch named Devynn Rowe—she's a Wilcox, but was working here at the mercantile—traveled in time and came back with a fiancé from 1926, Seth McAllister. Turns out he was one of the family who owned the store back then, so he's basically running things now."

Well, that was something. Not many witches had the gift of time travel, but to return to the present day with a significant other in tow?

He wondered why Bellamy hadn't said anything about that. Maybe she'd thought it wasn't the sort of thing that would have any bearing on his dreams.

After all, he'd dreamed about her, not this Devynn Rowe person.

"But I assume Seth being here is a good thing for the McAllister clan," Marc said.

"Oh, it is," Tricia assured him. "And he and Devynn are very happy. Still, it's a little out of the ordinary, even if I can't see how it would have anything to do with that dream you had."

He couldn't see it, either.

"Does Bellamy control the wind?" he asked next, thinking he should try to clear up that one small mystery. "When we were talking on the patio at Sedona Vines, this weird breeze came up out of nowhere. She didn't say anything, but...."

He let the words trail off, even as his grandmother frowned.

"Yes, that's her talent," Tricia said. "But I've never heard of her losing control of it. In fact, she's never really used it all that much, except to call in a breeze when some of the clan's children wanted to fly their kites and the day was too calm. It's one of those magical talents that exists but doesn't seem to have a lot of practical use."

No, he supposed not. Sure, maybe back in the day, witches and warlocks of the past had used such a gift to turn the sails of a windmill to grind their grain or whatever, but it wasn't the sort of thing anyone would have needed for a long, long time.

Then again, how useful was his own talent? It had sent him signals now and then that allowed him to see something of the future, but they had never been anything remotely earth-shattering. Honestly, if it really wanted to be of some help, then it should have warned him that Simon

Escobar was going to steal those grimoires from the various de la Paz clan members who had them stashed in their houses.

But his gift hadn't told him a damn thing.

"I'm sure there's a completely rational explanation for what happened," Tricia went on. "It might not have been Bellamy's talent at all. Sedona can get some odd winds, probably because of all those red rock canyons. We just don't know that much about it because the McAllisters have never lived there." A pause, and her brows drew together. "Even if Bellamy is living in Sedona at the moment."

"She is?" Marc replied, a little startled. Despite growing up in de la Paz territory, he knew that Sedona had always been a kind of neutral ground in between the McAllister and Wilcox lands.

"Yes," his grandmother said, and helped herself to a spoonful of corn chowder. "Not permanently," she added, as though she needed to clarify the situation so he wouldn't think they were being utterly reckless. "But some rich man who owns a ranch in West Sedona wanted someone to live there while he was trying to sell the place, and Bellamy agreed to be his caretaker. I assume she'll be back in Jerome once the ranch is sold—or maybe Cottonwood or Clarkdale. Housing in Jerome is always at a premium."

Marc could see that. The tiny former mining

town had fewer than five hundred full-time residents, and that meant competition was fierce whenever a house or flat became available. Nothing he would ever have to worry about, of course, not when the de la Paz clan had all of southern Arizona to choose from when it came to living spaces, but he supposed he could see why Bellamy might have wanted to have something of an adventure and camp out in Sedona for a while.

If nothing else, it would seriously reduce her commute.

"Well, I guess it wasn't anything important," he said, then reached for the butter so he could cut off another chunk and put it on his plate.

"Probably not," his grandmother agreed.

A warm wind—one Bellamy hadn't summoned—caught at her loose hair as she stood under a waxing moon. It was nearly one o'clock in the morning, and she knew she should go to bed, even if she had the day off tomorrow...well, today, since it was now technically Sunday.

But an odd restlessness had caught hold of her after she pulled into the huge four-bay garage and entered the ranch house, one she didn't think would be assuaged by making herself a cup of chamomile tea and watching a few YouTube videos until she'd finally convinced herself it was time to go to bed.

That was why she'd poured some water and gone out into the courtyard so she could stand there and look at the stars. The ranch sat on more than five acres of extremely valuable land—part of the reason why it was listed for a little over seven million dollars—but the courtyard offered a much more intimate space, with an outdoor kitchen off to one side of the covered patio and a modern fountain of granite and brazed bronze in the center. A series of metal wind sculptures ornamented the flowerbeds, and they now moved lazily in the night breeze, never going completely still.

Even though Sedona Vines had been jumping this Saturday night—a tour bus with a bridal party had pulled up only a few minutes after the band got started—Bellamy hadn't been quite able to put Marc Trujillo out of her mind. She tried to tell herself that of course she would be on edge after a man who claimed to be a seer told her she'd been the central element in a foreboding dream, but she guessed it was something a little more than that.

He was way too attractive for his own good.

Well, for her good, anyway. Unlike a lot of handsome men she'd met, he didn't seem to have much of an opinion regarding his appearance. In fact, he'd seemed almost diffident when speaking to her, as if he didn't quite know how she was going to react to what he was saying.

That made some sense, she supposed. No one liked to hear they'd been part of someone's dark vision, even if the person having the dream in question looked like a male model.

But no…that wasn't quite right. Marc Trujillo was definitely gorgeous, but he didn't give off that aura of being way too full of himself like the few models she'd run across while working the wine tasting rooms.

Not that it mattered if he was the handsomest guy in the world, as well as the most self-effacing. He'd come here to see if his dream had any merit, and she'd pretty much shot him down. Maybe he'd hang around for a few days so he could spend some time with his McAllister relations, but there wasn't any reason why he should seek her out again.

Unless he had another dream, of course.

Bellamy frowned and glanced up at the moon. It continued to sail serenely overhead, just a day or two past the halfway mark, and she guessed it wasn't going to give her any answers.

Almost without thinking, she raised a hand, and immediately the warm, gentle breeze that had been playing with the loose ends of her hair strengthened, turning into a real wind, one that wanted to whip those strands into her face. Across the courtyard, the spinning of the metal sculptures increased, one of them creaking just the slightest bit with the movement.

She'd need to hit that with some graphite lubricant tomorrow. It wouldn't do to have those things squeaking all over the place during the home's next showing…whenever that was. So far, the realtor representing the listing hadn't reached out to tell her that anyone wanted to look at the place.

Then again, Bellamy had only gotten here yesterday afternoon, and although the property was divine, buyers who qualified for that kind of mortgage…or had that kind of cash just lying around…weren't exactly thick on the ground. It could take months to get the place sold, which was why Ike Davidson had wanted her living here in the interim. Yes, the house had an elaborate security system, but she could see why he'd needed to make sure the property wouldn't stand empty all those months.

As quickly as it had come, the wind she'd summoned died down, and she shook her head. She'd had to consciously call the breeze, which meant she wasn't quite sure what had happened at Sedona Vines when she was talking to Marc Trujillo. Even when she was a ten-year-old kid with her powers just waking up, she'd never made the wind come without thinking about it first, so she didn't quite know what to make of that odd little display at the wine bar.

Maybe it hadn't been her powers at all. A coincidence, nothing more.

That would be the easiest thing, wouldn't it?

Well, she'd figure it out in the morning…or wouldn't, depending on whether she achieved some sort of illumination overnight. At least it would be a quiet day, one in which she didn't plan to do anything more momentous than the laundry and maybe a quick trip into town to hit the Safeway and Whole Foods. Once upon a time, she wouldn't have dreamed of shopping at what her friends called "Whole Paycheck" unless she knew she couldn't find what she was looking for anywhere else, but now that she was pulling in an assistant manager's salary in addition to getting paid an extra two grand a month to babysit the ranch, she figured a little splurge wouldn't hurt anything.

Maybe she would dream about Marc Trujillo.

4

He dreamed again that night.

This time, Bellamy stood outside under a black sky studded with stars, her warm-toned hair bleached pale by the gibbous moon that floated overhead. She didn't seem to be in any particular distress, and yet the scene still felt vaguely menacing, as if some threat lurked in the shadows at the edges of his vision, something he thought he should be able to recognize but which remained tantalizingly obscure.

For one moment, her eyes met his, and then she shook her head.

Warning him off?

Telling him he was barking up the wrong tree?

He didn't know. In a way, it was strange that he stood there in that moon-pale courtyard with her, water from the fountain glistening in the moonlight, because in every other prophetic dream he'd ever had, he hadn't been present at all, was instead some sort of detached observer.

Maybe this wasn't a vision, though.

Maybe it was just an ordinary garden-variety dream. He had those all the time, after all, far more frequently than the ones that tapped into his seer powers.

And he knew he'd be lying to himself if he didn't admit that Bellamy McAllister had made quite an impact on him.

In his dream, she turned away and headed into the house, passing through a set of enormous bifold doors that created a wall of glass on that side of the home. He began to follow—only to walk into something small but very solid, sitting squat and square on the terra-cotta pavers.

The object was a safe approximately a foot square. A red light blinked on its face, telling him it had some kind of biometric lock engaged.

Why in the world would he be dreaming about a safe?

He didn't know, and when he walked around the thing so he could go into the house in search of Bellamy, the dream fell away, and he found himself lying in bed and staring up at the ceiling. For a second or two, he couldn't quite remember where he was.

Right—his hotel room in Cottonwood. He'd

had dinner with his grandmother, then driven down here, watched some TV, and gone to bed much earlier than he normally would have. Maybe he could blame the early evening on being tired after his long drive, but he thought there was probably more going on here than simple weariness.

However, more than a decade of dealing with meaningful dreams had told him he should do his best to analyze what he'd seen, even if on the surface, it didn't seem to make a whole hell of a lot of sense.

He'd seen the moon as he was driving down the hill to his hotel, so he knew what he'd glimpsed in his dream was a direct reflection of its current phase. And although he obviously had never visited the ranch Bellamy was caretaking, he had no reason to believe that the courtyard and the wall of glass were anything but a reflection of reality.

Why had she been standing out there, gazing up at the moon? Had she been restless after her shift at Sedona Vines, and had gone out to feel the warm desert wind and ground herself before going to bed?

Had she been thinking about him?

That, he thought, was flattering himself. She'd been friendly but brisk when they met, and hadn't shown any sign that she'd been impressed by him at all. No, if anything, she'd been almost dismissive, as if she knew she needed to humor him but didn't think there was anything about his dream of her that merited any particular concern.

Maybe there wasn't. Maybe all this had been a wild goose chase and nothing more. He'd come up here on a weekend, but because he had his own landscape design business and could set his own hours—and because August was a slow time in Tucson, thanks to the unrelenting heat—it didn't really matter if he lingered in the Verde Valley for a few days, trying to get to the bottom of all his odd dreams.

If there was even a bottom to get to.

But there had been that safe....

In his experience, if something so out of place appeared in one of his dreams, then it carried much more significance than the object intrinsically possessed. Also, it had blocked him from following Bellamy into the house, which seemed to signal it was something that might cause a problem between them.

If he even saw her again, which right now seemed kind of iffy.

Well, he'd talk to his grandmother tomorrow and see if she had any insights as to what the safe might have meant. Maybe it was nothing.

And maybe it was everything.

Groceries had been bought, and the second load of laundry was already chugging away in the washing machine. Bellamy would never say that doing laundry was one of her favorite household tasks, but it was a lot easier to manage when the room you were doing it in was bigger than your childhood bedroom at home. The flat she'd shared with her two dads her entire life only had the equivalent of a closet with a set of stackable machines, since it had been built long before modern washers and dryers were even a thing, and while they had been efficient enough, they couldn't really compare to this large space with what felt like miles of counters and more storage than she even knew what to do with.

Well, she didn't need to do anything with it, really. She used one cupboard for her laundry supplies, and had designated another to store some candles—pretty scented candles were her one real weakness, and she almost always had one burning when she was home—and then left everything else empty. Maybe it was going to take a while to get this place sold, but in the meantime, she didn't see the point in cluttering up the house with a bunch of stuff she'd only have to move once Ike's realtor finally found a buyer.

Even though she'd kept pretty busy today, she

hadn't been able to keep herself from thinking about Marc Trujillo. He hadn't pressed her for more contact and had seemed just fine with letting her get back to work, and yet she wondered if she should simply leave things there.

What if there really had been something to his dream? She didn't want to think that some kind of danger lurked out there, just waiting to pounce, but she knew the Arizona witch clans—and the Castillos in New Mexico, who'd suffered just as much if not more—had dealt with a whole bunch of crazy over the past couple of years.

Was it foolish to think the danger was now past?

On the surface, probably. Although she hadn't been directly involved in any of it, she knew the Escobar clan in El Salvador was basically a non-threat now that it had new leadership. There was no reason to believe they would continue to reach out and try to get their hooks into any of the clans here in the U.S., not when they were attempting to rebuild after years of domination by a couple of evil leaders.

And Marc's clan had worked hard to provide a safe home for all the magical books they'd collected over the years, so there didn't seem to be much chance that anyone would be able to steal them again, not when they were now stored in the witchy equivalent of Fort Knox.

But he'd felt something all the same, something that involved Bellamy.

Which made absolutely no sense at all. She wasn't the *prima* or one of the elders, just a minor witch with a minor magical talent. There was no reason in the world why Marc's dream would have singled her out amongst all the other witches and warlocks in the McAllister clan.

Maybe she should have given him her number.

No, that was silly. He'd come up to the Verde Valley on some kind of fact-finding mission, but now he'd realized there wasn't anything to find, he'd head back to Tucson and that would be the end of it.

Besides, he knew where she worked, and therefore knew where to find her.

Except she wasn't working today…and wouldn't be back at Sedona Vines until Tuesday at noon.

Hmm.

No, she would not act all desperate and reach out to Tricia McAllister to see if she could get her grandson's phone number. She'd finish her chores and then put her feet up for a while, maybe watch TV or read a book, and she'd put Marc Trujillo out of her mind.

Good plan. Too bad the more Bellamy tried not to think about him, the more he seemed to invade her thoughts—the impossibly long eyelashes that framed his deep brown eyes, the faint scruff of dark stubble on his fine chin...the way he made a pair of faded Levi's look absolutely sinful.

Great. Just great.

She'd been sitting in the living room with a book open on her tablet, since she'd had the idea that reading might be a better way of distracting herself rather than trying to watch a show on the enormous hundred-inch TV that took up most of one wall. However, it seemed as if the more she tried to focus on the words on the electronic page before her, the more her thoughts strayed to the patio at Sedona Vines and the man who'd sat across from her at a table there.

Clearly, sheer willpower was failing her now.

She set the tablet down on the coffee table and tried to remember where Bree was playing this afternoon. Maybe it would be better to get out and think about something other than Marc Trujillo.

Unfortunately, although her friend had mentioned her schedule a few days earlier, it had completely slipped Bellamy's mind, what with getting situated at the ranch...and having Marc show up at the wine bar.

No biggie, though. It would be easy enough to check Bree's social media. She was always careful to keep it updated, mainly because she had a set of fans who liked to follow her from venue to venue, and posting her various gigs on Facebook and Instagram and TikTok was easier than trying to maintain a real website.

Bellamy reached for her tablet and took a peek at Instagram. Sure enough, Bree would be playing at Tantrum Wines in Cottonwood starting at four. Only an hour from now, so Bellamy thought she should be able to keep herself from climbing the walls in the interim…especially since it would take her about twenty-five minutes of that hour just to drive over there.

And if she should just happen to bump into Marc Trujillo once she was at the winery….

Not going to happen, she told herself. *There are at least seven tasting rooms over there, so the chances of him being at Tantrum are pretty low.*

If he'd even hung around at all. She thought it very possible that he'd already packed it in and headed back to Tucson, since she hadn't given him any useful information and there didn't seem to be much point to him staying in the Verde Valley. Besides, tomorrow was Monday, and she assumed he would have to be back at work.

Or maybe not. He hadn't mentioned anything about what he did for a living, but a high proportion of witches and warlocks owned their own businesses, just because it was easier that way. It was also possible that he lived off the stipend he got from the de la Paz clan and didn't work at all. Bellamy didn't have a clear idea as to exactly how much they paid, but they were a large and prosperous family, and probably allotted more to the family stipends than the McAllisters did.

You're just going to hang out and watch your friend play, she told herself. *It's something you've done a hundred times before. Even if by some miracle you do bump into Marc, no one's going to think you're stalking him.*

At least, she hoped not.

Marc had texted his grandmother in the early afternoon, well after lunch so she wouldn't think he was angling for another free meal. He'd slept in much later than expected, not that big a deal since he'd booked the room for three nights. Maybe he wouldn't see any reason to stay here that long, but in the meantime, it was nice to know that he didn't have to rush to get out of Cottonwood.

Tricia, of course, had been happy to see him again—although once he described the dream he'd had of Bellamy, his grandmother's welcoming smile faded immediately.

"You saw a safe in your dream?" she asked,

and he nodded, then reached for the glass of iced tea she'd poured him just a few minutes earlier.

"Yes," he said, then took a sip of tea. "It was sitting in the courtyard of the house I dreamed about. I think the home was supposed to represent the place where Bellamy is staying right now, but obviously, I've never seen it, so I have no idea whether my dream was accurate or not. But the safe was blocking my way when I tried to follow her into the house."

For a moment, his grandmother didn't say anything, only sat there with a frown creasing her brow and her fingers wrapped around the glass, now sweating slightly, that she held.

"And she didn't mention it to you when you spoke," she said.

Now it was Marc's turn to frown. "So…the safe is a real thing?" he asked. "Not just some kind of metaphor?"

Again, his grandmother was silent while a couple of seconds ticked past, as if she was weighing exactly how she should reply. But then she seemed to come to some sort of decision, because she released a breath and set her glass of iced tea down on the coaster in front of her.

"Oh, it's real," she said. "It contains an extremely valuable artifact, an amulet that Devynn Rowe and Seth McAllister brought back from the past. They encountered a warlock using it to enhance his magic—he was a performer in some kind of traveling variety troupe."

Marc had to take a moment to absorb that statement. It was the cardinal rule amongst all the witch clans that they never, ever performed feats of magic in public, since they all knew their continuing survival depended on the general population not realizing that witches and warlocks were real. Things were a little different here in Jerome, since the civilians who lived in the former mining town were let in on the secret once they'd been carefully vetted, but still, the idea of a random warlock in the past using his magic to pretend to be some sort of conjurer seemed reckless at best.

As for the amulet's existence in the first place…well, he'd never even heard of such a thing. Witches and warlocks were born with their magic and generally didn't use outward foci to work with it. They had no need to, not when their talents came to them as easily as breathing.

But then he thought of the grimoires the de la Paz clan had collected over the centuries, books filled with spells and enchantments that allowed them to concentrate their magic and make it even stronger. Was this amulet Devynn Rowe and Seth McAllister had found really all that different?

"So…it makes someone's magic more powerful?" he asked, and his grandmother nodded.

"Yes. When they were in the past, Seth used it to be able to teleport both himself and Devynn—that's his talent, although on its own, it's only strong enough for him to teleport himself—and Devynn, who has the ability to mask her witch nature, used it to shield the two of them when they were working in Wilcox territory."

A very useful item, obviously. It sounded as though Devynn and Seth had been pretty busy in the past.

But none of that probably had too much bearing on what was happening now, not when they were safely back in the twenty-first century.

"So…the amulet is locked up in a safe?"

"Yes," Tricia said. "Angela and Connor said they thought the thing could be a tempting target, so it's been kept in a biometric safe pretty much ever since Devynn and Seth returned to our time. In fact, the safe is locked up in Connor and Angela's house here, rather than at Seth and Devynn's bungalow. Both Angela and Connor—and we elders agreed—thought it was probably better to be hidden someplace where no one could interfere with it."

A good idea. Marc didn't pretend to know what kind of wards and other spells of protection had been placed on the *prima's* house, but he had to believe they were far stronger than anything

Seth and Devynn would have in the home where they were currently living.

Also, Paradise Lane was a locals-only kind of street. It sat far above the touristy parts of Jerome, and if you didn't live there or weren't visiting someone who did, there was no reason in the world to drive all the way up to the secluded neighborhood.

Still....

"Who keeps an eye on the safe when Angela and Connor aren't here?" he asked, since even he knew the *prima* and *primus* divided their time between Jerome and Flagstaff.

"The elders, of course," his grandmother replied, now looking a little more sure of herself. "Levi is the one who usually refreshes the wards, just because he's the most skilled at that kind of magic."

And probably just about any other kind of magic he needed to utilize. He looked like a man, but he wasn't...not exactly. Not for the first time, Marc had to wonder how things might have shaken out if Levi had become his cousin Zoe's consort, rather than Ethan McAllister. Zoe had created Levi out of nothing because she'd despaired at finding her soul match, but it turned out that the man who'd come to fix the mess she'd made was the one who was truly meant to be with her.

Ethan and Zoe's daughter Rosa was about to turn twenty-one and would soon begin her own consort search. Marc could only hope the process would be a lot less fraught this time.

"Does Bellamy know about the safe and the amulet?" he asked abruptly, and his grandmother frowned again.

"Yes, she does. She's very good friends with Devynn Rowe, and Devynn wouldn't have seen any reason to hide something like that from her."

Which meant that Bellamy hadn't been completely truthful when she'd told him nothing unusual had been happening in the clan lately. Marc thought that having the McAllisters come into possession of a rare and powerful magical artifact probably fell into the "unusual" category.

Then again, he supposed he couldn't be too annoyed with her for holding back that piece of information. She'd only just met him, and even though she knew he was as much a McAllister as he was a de la Paz, it wasn't as if she knew anything about him other than he had the gift of true seeing, just like his mother. Witches and warlocks understood that keeping secrets was part of their nature, and she wouldn't have been in a position to start blabbing about the amulet Devynn and Seth had brought back from the past, not when she hadn't been given permission to do so.

"If you dreamed of the safe," his grandmother went on, "then it seems the amulet must have even more significance than we thought. What, though? We're keeping it as protected as we possibly can."

It sure sounded that way. However, Marc recalled the sense of low-level foreboding that had suffused this latest dream, and couldn't help wondering if the McAllisters were doing enough to keep the thing out of unfriendly hands.

"I don't know," he said slowly. "Something about the dream felt ominous, even though I didn't see anything in particular to give that impression. And why would the amulet even be connected to Bellamy? She's not the one who found it, and she's certainly not the person who's keeping it safe."

His grandmother reached for her glass of iced tea—not, Marc thought, because she was particularly thirsty, but because she wanted to take a sip as a way of giving herself some time to think.

"No, Bellamy doesn't have any real connection to the amulet, except for being friends with the witch who found it. And in the great scheme of things, Bellamy's power really isn't that significant. Even if she wanted to use such an artifact to magnify her magic, what could it do other than summon some gale-force winds?"

And that didn't seem very useful, unless you

were trying to hold a champion kite-flying competition in Jerome or whatever.

None of this appeared to make much sense.

Marc released a breath and drank some of his iced tea, his throat suddenly dry. The thought occurred to him that his dream might not have meant anything at all, and he was grasping at straws here because he desperately wanted it all to make sense.

But no, that didn't feel right, either. If his dream had been completely random, then he wouldn't have dreamed of something that had real significance to the McAllisters.

Instead, he should have dreamed of something silly, like a purple kangaroo or a volcano that spewed hot fudge.

"Maybe I should talk to her again," he said. "She didn't have anything too helpful to offer when we spoke yesterday, but that was before I had this dream about the safe."

Now his grandmother's blue eyes—so like his mother's—had an amused twinkle in them. However, her tone was serious enough as she said, "That might be a good idea. If nothing else, you could describe the house you saw in your dream and find out whether it was an accurate representation of the place where she's staying. That would tell you whether the safe was some sort of random element or whether it really was supposed to mean something."

He hadn't thought of that angle to the problem. If the home he'd seen in his dream turned out to be exactly the same as the house Bellamy was caretaking, then he'd know his magic really had been trying to tell him something.

"Do you have Bellamy's phone number?" he asked. Only an hour earlier, he wouldn't have been caught dead asking his grandmother to give him a girl's number, but now he knew he needed to reach out to her and try to get to the bottom of this whole mess.

Tricia smiled. "Let me get it for you."

5

On that Sunday afternoon, Tantrum Wines was a bit more crowded than Bellamy had expected. Not so much that she wasn't able to snag a seat on a purple velvet couch positioned a few yards away from the spot where Bree had her chair and microphone stand set up, but just enough that Bellamy couldn't help feeling the teensiest bit guilty about taking up the whole sofa.

Well, she'd buy a couple of bottles of wine to take back with her to the house just so she wouldn't feel like an utter freeloader.

Bree had inclined her head and offered Bellamy a smile as she came in and sat down, but because she was in the middle of singing an old folk song from the seventies, something about a bayou, she wasn't about to pause and offer any kind of real conversation.

Which was fine. Bellamy knew her friend was working, and honestly, she'd only come here because she thought she might start climbing the walls if she had to go back to the house and pretend to do something productive. It wasn't like the place needed cleaning—Ike had already told her she didn't need to worry about housework, since he had someone come in once a week to make sure the house was spotless—and it was really too hot to do anything outside.

So, here she was.

She sipped some of her white blend and did her best to relax against the back of the couch. Although she would never have referred to herself as a Type A kind of personality, she also knew it still felt a little weird to know she was done with school and needed to find her rhythm when all she had to do now was work a regular nine-to-five job and not have to fit in her enology certification coursework on top of everything else.

No, now she was supposed to function like a real adult…whatever that meant.

She didn't recognize any of the faces around her, which wasn't too strange. Most locals tried to visit the various wine tasting rooms during the week when things weren't quite so busy, so she guessed most of these people were probably tourists getting in a last drink or two before they headed back down to Phoenix or wherever it was they'd come from. Cottonwood and Jerome and Sedona got lots of day-trippers, since Phoenix and its surrounding cities were only a little over an hour away, depending on where you were coming from.

But then the tasting room door opened, and Marc Trujillo walked in.

Bellamy had been in the middle of swallowing some wine when she caught sight of him, and it took everything she had to maintain her composure and not choke on the liquid as it was halfway down her throat. Somehow, though, she managed to gulp it down and even look as though she hadn't been startled out of her skin by his sudden appearance.

His eyes met hers, and he smiled even as he came over to the sofa where she sat. "Mind if I sit down?" he asked, keeping his voice pitched low so it wouldn't interfere with Bree's performance.

"No, go ahead," Bellamy replied in a murmur, and scooched over so he'd have room next to her.

Noting this new addition to the listening crowd, her friend Bree lifted an eyebrow, but it wasn't as if she could make some kind of comment, not when she was mid-song.

And Alyssa, the girl working the wine counter today, approached them and asked Marc in an undertone what he'd like to drink.

"Whatever she's having," he said, and inclined his head toward Bellamy.

Alyssa smiled and said she'd have it right out, and hurried off to pour a glass for him.

With her gone, Bellamy was all too acutely aware of how close Marc was, even though it wasn't as if he'd sat down right next to her and tried to invade her personal space or anything. Still, the sofa was small enough that he was still a lot closer than she should have been expected to handle.

As usual when she wasn't sure how she should react to a given situation, she retreated to sarcasm. "Are you stalking me?" she murmured, and Marc grinned.

"Lucky coincidence," he replied, then paused as Alyssa came back with his glass of white. "I was actually about to text you, but I thought I'd come in and have a drink first."

Bellamy wanted to lift an eyebrow at that comment—how had he even gotten her phone number? his grandmother?—but she was forced to admit that lucky coincidences tended to happen among witch-kind more often than they did with the regular population.

Besides, hadn't she been kicking herself earlier for not giving him her contact information, or at least asking for his?

"Well, you made a good choice," she said.

"The wine here is great, and you also lucked out because my friend Bree is performing today."

His gaze slid toward the other woman, who'd now moved on to another folksy song, this one by a musician from way back when named Neil Young. However, he didn't seem to be awestruck by Bree's beauty, which Bellamy had to admit was something of a relief. Never in a million years would she admit to being jealous of her friend, and yet it still started to get old whenever the two of them went out together and everyone paid attention to Bree like she was some kind of goddess descended from Mount Olympus or something.

"She's really good," he commented, but his tone was casual, almost absent. "Does she play here every weekend?"

"No," Bellamy replied. "She kind of rotates among the various tasting rooms and resorts in the area. I think she's at Tantrum maybe twice a month at the most."

"Then I suppose I got lucky," he said, but his gaze was fixed on Bellamy's face, and she got the impression that the "luck" he was talking about didn't have much to do with Bree's performance schedule. A certain warmth stirred inside her, one she couldn't ignore no matter how hard she tried.

"So, are you sticking around for a while?" she

asked next, then wanted to shake her head at herself.

Talk about sounding desperate.

"For a few more days," Marc said. He didn't appear too concerned by her question, so it didn't seem as if he thought she was being clingy. "Maybe longer, depending."

Depending on what? she thought, but decided it was probably better not to ask that question out loud. "You don't have to get back to work?"

Now he smiled, his dark eyes warming, becoming almost velvety as he gazed back at her.

Damn, he was gorgeous.

"I do landscape design," he said. "But it's my own business, so I set the schedule. Anyway, this is a slow time of year for me, thanks to the heat. I don't have anything on the calendar until the last week of August."

He didn't sound too concerned about the whole thing, but she supposed that was probably because he had his clan stipend to pay the bills and therefore didn't have to worry about any slow periods in his work schedule.

And if he wasn't even busy until the end of the month....

As best she could, she pushed that thought away. Maybe Marc Trujillo was fancy free for the next few weeks, but her own boss was expecting her at work at noon on Tuesday, so it wasn't as if she could drop everything to hang out with the handsome newcomer.

Not that he'd even shown any indication that was what he wanted from her.

"Actually," he went on, "I had something I needed to talk to you about, but I'm not sure this is the best venue."

His gaze moved past her over to the chair where Bree sat with her guitar and sang, and then on to the people who occupied the other sofas and conversation areas. Clearly, he thought this was far too public a place for whatever topic he wanted to discuss.

"Does it have anything to do with what we talked about yesterday?" Bellamy asked, and he nodded.

Since she knew he was staying at the hotel just down the street, it probably would have been simpler to suggest that they finish their glasses of wine and head over there.

However, something prompted her to say, "We could go to my place."

To her surprise, Marc didn't even hesitate, but immediately replied, "That's a good idea. It's over in Sedona, right?"

"Yes," she said. "Off Dry Creek Road. You can follow me."

"Sounds like a plan."

They both went quiet then as they finished their glasses of wine—or in Marc's case, gulped down most of it, since he'd barely started drinking his. Maybe not the smartest thing to do when they were about to drive to Sedona, but Bellamy told herself it was only one glass, not enough to make him even close to impaired.

Seeing that both their glasses were empty, Alyssa came over and asked if they wanted another round. They demurred, and Marc dug a twenty out of his wallet and handed it over, surprising Bellamy a little. She hadn't expected him to pay, not when she'd ordered her drink way before he even showed up.

But she knew protesting would only delay their departure, so instead she thanked him for picking up the tab, lifted one hand in a small wave to Bree—who inclined her head, acknowledging the goodbye—and then followed him outside.

"Are you parked at your hotel?" she asked, and he nodded.

"Do you want to meet me in the lot there? I'm driving the gray Nissan truck."

"Sounds good," she said, and then watched as he walked down the sidewalk toward his hotel, which was about a block away from the winery.

Her Fiat was parked right at the curb, so she went ahead and got inside and started the engine, then drove over to the parking lot. Sure enough, Marc was climbing into his truck as she pulled up, so she waited until he was ready and then pulled back out onto Main Street, following it until she got to Mingus Boulevard and could turn left to get back out to the highway.

Through all of this, she drove conservatively, since she didn't know how familiar he was with Cottonwood and didn't want to ditch him before they turned onto 89A and headed north toward Sedona. But he remained firmly in her rearview mirror the whole time, and soon enough, they were on the open road.

Was it crazy to have him come back to the house? After all, she barely knew the guy.

True, but he was a McAllister elder's grandson. It wasn't as if she'd picked up a total rando on the side of the road or something.

Thus having reassured herself that she wasn't bringing a serial killer back to a house that wasn't even hers, she maintained a steady pace on the highway, checking in the rearview constantly to make sure he was keeping up. Not that she guessed that would be much of a problem; his big Nissan truck obviously had a far more powerful motor than her little Fiat.

And it wasn't as if they had to drive through the heart of Sedona or anything, either. Dry Creek Road was only a little inside the town's western limits, and although they would have to wander a bit to get to the house she was caretaking, the roads weren't anywhere close to crowded out in the semi-rural neighborhood.

A pause to press the remote for the gate that opened onto the property, and then they were driving down the long gravel road that led to the house. Dust plumed out behind them; although this should have been the height of monsoon season, there hadn't been any storms for nearly a week.

Bellamy thought the dry streak might be over soon, though, because as they'd driven into Sedona, she'd noted enormous thunderheads beginning to build over the Mogollon Plateau to the east. The real question was whether they'd spill westward enough to get any rain in the Verde Valley.

Well, she supposed they'd find out as the afternoon wore on.

She touched the second remote clipped to the visor, and one of the four garage doors opened so she could pull inside. Marc seemed to realize he was on his own for parking, because he stopped in the open space off to one side and got out of his truck, then headed over to the place where she was waiting just inside the garage.

"We can go in through here," she told him as he approached, inclining her head toward the interior door that led into the kitchen.

He nodded, and soon enough they were inside, with cool air from the home's climate-control system surrounding them.

"Well, this is impressive," he said as they entered the kitchen, which had what felt like miles of soapstone counters and a set of commercial-grade stainless-steel appliances.

"It's not mine," she said quickly, thinking she needed to disabuse him of the notion that she was in any kind of financial position to afford a place like this. "I'm just playing caretaker while it's on the market."

Marc didn't appear too dismayed by this revelation. "That's a pretty good gig."

"It is," she said. "I'll admit that I'm kind of hoping the house is going to be on the market for a long while." She stopped there, thinking of the half-drunk bottle of pinot grigio she had in the refrigerator. Should she offer him a drink, or would it be better to keep this strictly business and only ask if he wanted a glass of water?

Oh, the hell with it. Today was her day off, after all.

"Some wine?" she asked next. "I've got an open bottle of pinot grigio in the fridge."

Maybe he hesitated for a fraction of a second. But then he said, "Sure. That would be great."

Bellamy went over to the cupboard and got out a couple of stemless wine glasses—Ike had told her she could use the glassware and dishes and anything else she needed, just as long as everything was cleaned and returned to the cupboards once the house was sold—then poured some white wine for her and Marc. After handing one of the glasses to him, she said, "We can go sit in the living room. It's probably too hot to be outside, even in the shade."

"Sure."

He followed her into the space in question, where his keen dark eyes seemed to take in the huge bifold glass doors that overlooked the court-yard. She had to admit that it looked inviting enough out there, with the wind sculptures turning in the breeze and the fountain in the center of the space splashing in the bright sunlight.

Well, until you actually went outside and real-ized temperatures today were just kissing the century mark.

They both sat on the big leather couch, Marc a respectful distance away. Still, Bellamy found herself far too conscious of his presence, of the way the sofa creaked when he shifted his weight, or the strong muscles of his tanned throat as he swallowed some pinot grigio.

Then he said without preamble, "I dreamed about this house last night."

She blinked at him. "What?"

"This place," he said, and waved a hand toward the sunny courtyard just beyond the bifold doors. "I'm glad you invited me here, because now I can see it was a true dream. Everything looks just the way I dreamed it."

Well, this wasn't awkward at all. Bellamy swallowed some of her wine and said, "What was in your dream?"

"You were," he said steadily. "I dreamed that you were standing out in the courtyard with the moon overhead and those wind sculptures moving in the night wind."

How in the world was she supposed to respond to that? Because what he'd just described was exactly what she'd done the night before after she got home from work, too restless to go straight to bed even though it had been well past midnight.

"That's what you wanted to talk to me about?" she asked. "To see if your dream was a true one?"

"Partly," he replied. "In the dream, I was standing out there, too, but when I tried to follow you into the house, there was a safe blocking my way."

"'A safe'?" she repeated blankly, her brain conjuring an image of a big, blocky object like something you'd see in an old Road Runner cartoon just before it got dropped on Wile E. Coyote's head.

"Yes," Marc said, and then described a shape with his hands that was much smaller, maybe twelve inches on all sides. "It was about this big, and it had a biometric lock."

Oh. She knew exactly what he was talking about, because she'd seen the thing at Devynn and Seth's bungalow before everyone in the clan had decided it would be safer if it was kept at the *prima's* house instead.

However, since Angela and Connor had made it pretty clear that they really didn't want news of the safe—and the amulet it contained—spread all over the witch community, Bellamy wasn't sure how she should respond to Marc's comment... especially since she'd already told him that nothing of any real import had happened in the McAllister clan over the past few months.

"It's okay," Marc continued, speaking a little more quickly now, as though he understood the reason for her diffidence and knew he needed to do what he could to allay any concerns she might have about discussing the sensitive subject. "My grandmother told me all about the amulet and where it came from. I suppose I'm just trying to figure out why I would dream about it."

Well, so much for that. If Tricia had thought it safe to confide in her grandson, then there wasn't much point in trying to obfuscate now.

"I have no idea," Bellamy said. "I mean, it's obvious that the amulet is powerful and would probably be dangerous if it fell into the wrong hands. But the elders and Angela and Connor have done everything they can to make sure that won't happen."

Marc gave a brief nod, but something about his expression was troubled, as though he wasn't quite sure whether all those measures would be enough.

"Did you see anything else in your dream?" she asked next, wondering if there was something he wasn't telling her, something he wanted to keep hidden.

However, his next words seemed to disabuse her of that notion.

"Not really," he replied, then lifted his glass of pinot grigio to his lips so he could swallow some. "But even though I didn't see anything concrete, something about the whole thing gave me a bad feeling, as if there was some kind of danger lurking out beyond the walls of the courtyard, even though I couldn't see it."

Bellamy's gaze moved outside. The courtyard was utterly deserted, with not even any birds sitting on the fountain as they often did so they could get a drink in the middle of what was otherwise a dry landscape. Back at home, she and her dads had bird feeders on their balcony, but she'd known better than to sully the pristine space outside the living room here with anything as messy as bird seed.

Although everything appeared quiet and serene, a chill inched its way down her back.

"What kind of danger?"

Marc shook his head. She didn't know him very well yet, but she could tell he was frustrated.

"I don't know for sure," he said. "That's the problem with these dreams or visions or whatever you want to call them. A lot of the time, they just hint at something, and then it's up to me to figure it out. In this case, though, while I totally understand why someone might want to snag that amulet and use it for their own ends, I don't have any idea who it could be. I definitely don't want to believe that it could be anyone in the Arizona witch clans."

"Or the Castillos," Bellamy said. "I mean, maybe they're not as interconnected with us as the rest of the clans here in Arizona, but still, with Angela's daughter Miranda as their *prima,* they're still much more our allies than they used to be."

Marc gave a glum nod, then reached over so he could set his glass of wine on one of the coasters on the coffee table. "The Ludlows, maybe?"

Bellamy supposed that was one possibility. Back in the day, the northern California–based clan had joined forces with Joaquin Escobar and had kidnapped Levi McAllister in an attempt to force him to become their *prima*-in-waiting's consort. None of that had worked out so well, and the son of their *prima* had even abandoned his clan so he could go to Flagstaff and marry one of the Wilcox witches there, but still, she had to admit that the Ludlows were kind of a wild card despite being pretty quiescent these past two decades.

"I don't know," she said slowly. "I mean, I hadn't heard that they've been up to any skullduggery lately, but I also haven't been paying all that much attention."

A small crease appeared between Marc's eyebrows, and then he shrugged. "I haven't heard anything, either. Everything's been pretty quiet on the California front, since the Santiagos have also been minding their own business. On the other hand, we both know that when you have a big witch clan, you sometimes have members who go rogue."

Well, that was true. Not that anything like

that had happened among the McAllisters and the Wilcoxes—or the de la Pazes—as far as she knew, but it was a big world out there, with plenty of clans who might have members among them who wanted to do whatever they could to score an advantage.

Marc sat up a little straighter, as if something had just occurred to him. "Do you know which clan the amulet came from?"

"It would have disappeared more than a hundred and fifty years ago," she pointed out, but her companion didn't appear too put off by that argument.

"Maybe so, but still, isn't it possible that someone might have just found out about it and tried to track down where it went?"

Such a possibility had never even entered Bellamy's mind, and yet she thought Marc might be on to something here.

"I guess so," she allowed. "I know the guy Seth and Devynn took it from was named Lawrence Pratt and that he came from Minnesota…I think…but I have no idea who the witch clan is in that part of the world."

"Well, I guess we'll need to ask Devynn and Seth," Marc replied without missing a beat. "Do you know where we can find them?"

Since it was Sunday and Bellamy knew her friend and her new fiancé always tried to be at the store on the weekends when it was busiest, that question was easy enough to answer. True, they'd have to drive all the way back to Jerome to talk to them, but since this was the only real lead they had, Bellamy couldn't think of anything better to do.

"Sure," she said, and added, "They're in Jerome, at McAllister Mercantile."

6

THEY DROVE TO THE FORMER MINING TOWN in Marc's pickup, even though Bellamy had protested that she could follow him so he wouldn't have to go all the way back to Sedona to take her home. He didn't care about that, though; in fact, he thought if he timed this right, they might be able to eat dinner there, someplace where they could sit and watch the sunset over the red rocks.

It sounded very romantic, even as he had to admit to himself that there hadn't been much romance in his and Bellamy's interactions.

Although he sure found himself wishing there was.

On that hot Sunday afternoon, Jerome was positively jumping, and they had to circle around and drive down to one of the lower parking lots before they could find a place to leave his truck.

However, he had to admit it was a little cooler here than it had been in Sedona or Cottonwood —and much more comfortable than it would have been in his hometown of Tucson—so he didn't mind the slog back up the hill to get to McAllister Mercantile.

It was a big storefront located at nearly the end of Main Street before the road looped back on itself and headed up toward Mingus Mountain. Although he'd driven past it multiple times—and had a vague recollection of visiting the store when he was a kid —he knew it had been a long time since he'd gone inside. From what he could tell, it was a touristy sort of place, with jewelry made by local artisans in a glass case in the center of the store, and tables with stacks of Jerome-themed T-shirts and sweatshirts and other Arizona-centric memorabilia.

A pretty woman around Bellamy's age was working behind that counter and was in the middle of showing a pair of earrings to an older couple. At the far end of the store, a brown-haired guy who looked like he was maybe around twenty-five was talking to some more tourists.

"That's Seth," Bellamy said in an undertone. "And Devynn's working the counter. I think we'll need to wait for the patrons to clear out before we can talk to either of them."

Judging by the ebb and flow of visitors in the

shop, Marc had a feeling they might be waiting a while before they got a private moment. However, since he knew that discussing witch clan business wasn't something they could do while the store had a full house, he told himself he needed to be patient.

Besides, the longer all this dragged on, the better the chance they'd get back to Sedona right in time for dinner, in which case he thought asking Bellamy if she wanted to grab something to eat with him would feel a lot more natural.

Devynn nodded at Bellamy, as if acknowledging her presence. Bellamy inclined her red head in return, signaling that she was willing to wait until Devynn had a free moment to talk.

That moment didn't come until at least ten minutes had passed, but then the tourists miraculously cleared out, and Devynn emerged from behind the counter, even as Seth walked over to join her.

"What's up?" she asked Bellamy, her gaze moving to Marc, frankly curious.

"Hi, Devynn, Seth," Bellamy said. "This is Marc Trujillo. He's visiting from Tucson—he's Tricia's grandson."

At once, Seth extended a hand. "Nice to meet you, Marc. What brings you to Jerome?"

Marc sent a sideways glance at Bellamy, and

she gave a subtle nod, as if to signal that it was okay to discuss things openly with the couple.

"Some dreams I couldn't figure out," he said. "That's my talent—I'm a seer."

Devynn's arched brows lifted slightly, and Seth looked a little taken aback. Since Marc was used to getting that reaction from other witch-folk when he revealed his gift, he wouldn't allow those responses to put him off his stride.

"We think it has something to do with the amulet," Bellamy put in, and at once, Seth and Devynn exchanged a glance.

"You know about that?" Devynn asked, and Marc nodded.

"My grandmother told me about it," he said. "My dreams have had a sense of danger, of foreboding, about them, and I can't help thinking that it might be because someone is going to try to steal the amulet."

At once, Devynn's blue-gray eyes narrowed. Although Bellamy had said her friend was a Wilcox, Marc couldn't help thinking she didn't look much like one of them, with those light-colored eyes and that mid-brown hair.

Well, her appearance wasn't anything he needed to worry about.

"It's totally protected," she said. "It's in a safe with a biometric lock that only Seth and I—well, and Angela and Connor—can open. And it's also got all kinds of wards placed on it."

"Yes," Marc replied, doing his best to sound patient, "Bellamy told me all that. But still, I don't think I'd be having these dreams if something wasn't wrong."

"We were thinking that maybe someone from the clan of the guy you took it from might have finally figured out where it went and is trying to get it back," Bellamy offered, and again, Seth and Devynn shared another weighty glance.

"That doesn't seem very likely," Seth said. "I got the impression that Lawrence Pratt never said anything to his clan about the amulet, or they would have done what they could to prevent him from using it publicly."

"But you don't know that for sure," Bellamy responded.

His shoulders lifted, and he looked over at Devynn, as if encouraging her to step in.

"No, of course we don't," she said, a frown again pulling at her brows. "All we heard is that he left the troupe he was traveling with and headed back to Duluth."

"Minnesota, right?" Bellamy asked, and Devynn nodded.

"Yes. He said the clan there was the Olsens, but obviously, since they're such a long way from Arizona, it's not as if any of the clans here have had any interactions with them." She paused there, and her eyes narrowed. "What…you think your dreams are signaling that the Olsens are sniffing around, trying to get the amulet back?"

"I honestly don't know for sure," Marc replied. "But it sounds like not many people in your clan even know the thing exists, so Bellamy and I were trying to figure out who else might have access to that information."

Even as he spoke, he thought of what a long shot the whole thing was…especially since Angela and Connor should have known if any interlopers were wandering around in their territory. Sure, Bellamy had said that Devynn could mask her witch nature, but since Marc had never even heard of such a thing until she mentioned it, he had to believe it was a very rare gift.

"It's hard to say for sure," Seth said, his tone now almost musing, as if he was trying to put the pieces together as he spoke. "We always thought that Lawrence Pratt must have done his best to keep the amulet a secret, just because if he said something about it to anyone in the Olsen clan, then they'd know he'd been using the thing to work magic in public. I don't care what witch clan you're from—everybody knows doing that is forbidden."

Yes, it was, and the sort of the activity the man probably would have done his best to conceal.

However, that didn't mean he didn't have a diary that might have been found by his descendants, or that he might not have made some sort of deathbed confession about the powerful artifact. If that were the case, though, wouldn't his heirs have come in search of the amulet decades earlier, since to them, it would have been missing for a very long time and not the several months it had actually been here in the mid-twenty-first century?

Maybe, or maybe not. Members of the witch community couldn't freely roam wherever they wanted, since it was considered proper etiquette to reach out to the *prima* of a clan to get permission to even pass through another clan's lands. Somehow Marc doubted that anyone on a quest to find a forbidden piece of magic would want to tip their hand to the local head of a witch family, especially when those leaders had access to all sorts of magic the rank and file didn't, and might be able to tell if they were being lied to.

"How accurate are your dreams?" Devynn asked then.

Next to him, Bellamy shot Marc a worried look, as though she wasn't sure whether he would take offense at such a point-blank question.

However, he could see why Devynn had asked him that. She knew nothing about him or his gifts, and probably thought there wasn't much point in getting all riled up over something that might not even be real.

"Very accurate," he said. "That is, I sometimes have to stop and figure out what they're really trying to tell me, but they've never shown me anything that was outright wrong."

"He dreamed the house I'm staying in, and he's never even been there before," Bellamy put in. "So I'm pretty sure we should take his dreams at face value."

Devynn didn't respond right away but only gazed at him for a moment, as if doing her best to take his measure by reading his expression.

"Okay," she said after a moment. "It sounds like you're the real deal. And I guess I should be glad you wanted to warn us that something might be coming down the pike. I'm just not sure what else we can really do, since we've taken all the possible precautions."

Well, other than maybe burying the safe ten feet under and hoping for the best. Marc still wasn't sure he liked the idea of the thing being kept in an unoccupied house, even if it was protected by as many wards as the McAllister elders could conjure.

Including ones cast by Levi McAllister, who wasn't exactly your garden-variety human being. Or at least, while his body was human, the spirit it contained was something utterly different, far more powerful than your regular run-of-the-mill warlock.

"Maybe that's all that's needed," Marc said. "For all I know, giving you a warning will be enough. I just wish we had a better idea of who else might know about the amulet."

Devynn's lips parted to reply, but a family group came into the store right then, mom and dad and three little kids who seemed intent on touching everything they could lay hands on, and that seemed to signal the end of the conversation.

So Bellamy said, "Thanks for the help—just let us know if you think of anything," and then headed outside with Marc following right behind.

The sun overhead was fierce, and he immediately unhooked his sunglasses from where they'd been hanging from the neck of his T-shirt and put them on, while Bellamy did the same thing as well, except that she dug them out of her purse.

Once they'd gone a few paces down the sidewalk, she said, "I'm not sure if that helped any."

His shoulders lifted. "Well, at least we know the clan Lawrence Pratt came from was the Olsens. It's too bad my talent isn't for computer hacking, because then I might be able to find out a little more about them."

"It's not mine, either," Bellamy said, although she didn't look too dismayed. "But there's a warlock in the Wilcox clan who's supposed to be a genius at that kind of thing. I can text Devynn and ask her if she can have him look into the Olsens and see if he can dig up anything useful."

Deep down, Marc had a feeling that wasn't going to accomplish much. However, since he didn't have any better ideas, he only nodded.

"That could work."

"Well, let's duck into Caduceus and grab a glass of wine, and I'll send her a text," Bellamy suggested. "The views there are incredible."

Even though they'd already shared a glass back at her house, Marc thought that sounded like a great idea.

"Sure," he said.

So they went inside and made their way to the seating area at the back of the wine tasting room, which, as she'd promised, offered a wall of windows that overlooked the Verde Valley all the way to the red rocks of Sedona and beyond.

After they both got glasses of the Chupacabra —Marc didn't think he could resist a wine with that name—Bellamy got out her phone and typed out a quick text. The reply came back almost immediately, which seemed to signal that Devynn wasn't completely overwhelmed with customers right then.

"She says she'll get Jeremy right on it," Bellamy announced after looking down at her phone's screen. "So I guess about all we can do now is just sit tight and see if he can dig up anything."

That would be the simplest outcome, of course. Not that Marc was too happy about the prospect of a clan halfway across the country trying to meddle with the Arizona witch families, but it would still be a lot easier if they could at least pin down a possible suspect.

If there was one at all. He hadn't been lying when he'd said that his dreams were never wrong, and yet sometimes the interpretation could be a little difficult to nail down.

He looked around, but the other patrons of the tasting room were clustered near the bar rather than here in the sitting area, despite the spectacular views.

"What else do you know about the amulet?" he asked.

Bellamy's lips pursed, but she seemed to realize there wasn't anyone close enough to hear what they were saying because she replied, "Not a whole lot beyond what I've already told you. I guess making those sorts of things was kind of in vogue during the Renaissance, and the people who created them poured their own life energy into the artifacts. Sounds like it was sort of a dangerous process, and some people died during the process. That might be why the practice fell by the wayside over the years."

No, he supposed a method that might deplete your life force enough to end up killing you was probably better left abandoned.

"Does anyone know how many of them are out there?"

At once, Bellamy shook her head, and her loose coppery hair slid across bare shoulders revealed by the sleeveless blue top she wore. Not for the first time, he thought of how beautiful she was...and how she appeared to be utterly oblivious to that fact.

"Honestly, I'd never even heard of the things until Devynn and Seth showed up with the one they found in the 1880s. Sounds like it was a surprise to them, too, so I have a feeling artifacts like that amulet mostly got lost in the mists of history. Probably they were mislaid or maybe fell into civilian hands, and since a civilian wouldn't even be able to sense the power they contained, they were probably treated like harmless trinkets."

Maybe that was a better outcome. Although Marc didn't really like the idea of a bunch of regular people acquiring objects they didn't understand and couldn't possibly use, at least that way, they couldn't be employed against the magical population.

"Here's hoping," he said, and drank some of his Chupacabra. It was a smooth, fruity red, a nice change from the whites he'd drunk earlier in the day. "Because I'm not sure I want to think about what it would be like if these things started popping up out of nowhere."

Bellamy grinned, a flash of white teeth against the peach-toned lip gloss she wore. "No, that would kind of suck, wouldn't it? But if that was even a possibility, you'd dream about it, wouldn't you?"

He wished it was that easy. The dreams came when they willed, and he didn't have much control over when they decided to appear. Also, it wasn't as if he had a prophetic dream every time something bad was going to happen in his clan, or otherwise his sleep would be filled with car crashes and cancer diagnoses and all the other thousand and one things that could go wrong in a person's life.

"Not necessarily," he said. "I mean, in this case, it seems like a warning of some kind, but I still can't figure out exactly what the dreams expect me to do."

"I think you've already done it," Bellamy replied, still smiling. "That is, you let your grandmother know what's going on, and I'm sure she's talked to the other elders, and to Connor and Angela, too. Forewarned is forearmed, after all."

Marc supposed she had a point there. Even so, he couldn't quite rid himself of the niggling sensation that the universe expected something more from him…despite his not knowing what the hell it was supposed to be.

Not for the first time, he found himself wishing he had a simpler gift, something like making plants grow or healing people or even just being able to soothe a crying infant, like his cousin Lorelei, who was hugely in demand as the de la Paz clan's babysitter. Something cut and dried, something tangible, rather than receiving images from beyond and doing his best to interpret exactly what they were trying to say.

Since he wasn't sure of the best way to respond to Bellamy's comment, he only nodded and then drank some more of his wine. Just as he was setting his glass down on the table in front of them, his phone buzzed from within his jeans pocket, and he hurried to pull it out.

A text from a 928 area code number, one he didn't immediately recognize.

However, the content was clear enough.

He looked up from the screen to see Bellamy watching him, brows puckered slightly, as if she somehow knew this was no ordinary text.

"It's from my grandmother," he explained.

"Someone just tried to steal the amulet from Angela and Connor's house."

7

Everyone was assembled in front of the big Victorian on Paradise Lane—the three elders, Tricia and Levi and Allegra Moss, along with Angela and Connor themselves. Their presence startled Bellamy for a moment…until she remembered that the two of them had the power of teleportation, so even though they'd been spending the summer at their house in Forest Highlands just outside Flagstaff, they could be here in the blink of an eye as soon as someone sent the alarm.

"They didn't get the amulet," Levi was explaining as they all went up the porch steps and inside the house. Nothing appeared to have been disturbed, which made Bellamy feel a little better about the situation. The home was gorgeous, with its carefully restored oak floors and understated locally made furniture and Connor's *plein air* landscapes on the walls, and she knew she'd been worried the intruder might have ransacked the place.

"But they got past your wards," Angela said. She was in her early fifties, but you'd never know it to look at her, since her dark brown hair didn't have a single trace of gray and she only had a few laugh lines in the fair skin next to her brilliant green eyes.

"They did," Tricia replied briskly. She didn't look too happy about the situation, but she also appeared ready to deal with the problem head on and try to figure out what had gone wrong. "No one should have even been able to get past the front door. But then there's that."

She pointed to the safe, which sat on a coffee table of burnished juniper in front of one of the big leather couches that dominated the living room.

Connor took a step forward, a frown of his own pulling at his brows. Like his wife, he had night-dark hair and greenish eyes, only his were a cloudy mixture of green and gray, like moss agate. "We would never have left it there."

"And you didn't," Levi said. He'd paused near the entrance to the living room, but now he approached the safe and laid one long-fingered hand on top of the little box. "It was on a shelf in the main bedroom closet. Whoever got past the wards was able to bring it this far, but then they must have realized that the magic barring the front door wouldn't allow them to remove it from the house."

"And thank goodness for that," Allegra put in. She was much older than the other two elders, nearing eighty and probably past the point where she should have retired and allowed someone a few decades younger to take over her duties. However, she seemed determined to drop in harness, and since Connor and Angela appeared to have decided it was better to let the matter go than press her to step aside, no one had seriously brought up the prospect of her replacement. Pale gaze shifting to Levi, she added, "I'm so glad we followed your advice and doubled the wards on all the doors and windows."

He didn't look very glad, however. No, he was frowning deeply, keen blue eyes sweeping the room, even though—at least as far as Bellamy could tell—there wasn't anything to see.

Well, except the safe where it incongruously sat on the coffee table.

"They must have left it there and fled," Levi said. "Whatever magic they used to get in, it probably told them that they'd tripped the alarm, so to speak, and that it would only be a matter of time before we came to investigate."

Angela had moved to the center of the living

room and stood there for a moment, arms outstretched at her sides, as though she was trying to reach out and feel the energy of the space. "I can sense frustration," she said. "But that's about it."

"Any dark magic?" Connor asked. Clearly, he hadn't forgotten about the recent incursion by an Escobar warlock into de la Paz territory, even though the McAllisters had mostly stayed out of that tussle.

The *prima's* lips pressed together, and then she shook her head. "Not that I'm able to tell. Whoever did this, their energy feels weirdly... neutral, for lack of a better word."

"That's the sense I get, too," Levi said. "Which may not mean anything at all. We could be dealing with someone who has the ability to mask their particular brand of magic."

Bellamy had never heard of a gift like that, but she'd be the first to admit she hadn't done an in-depth study of all the various types of magical talents that manifested amongst the witch clans. There were your standard ones, of course, like healing and controlling the weather and seeing the future, but odd ones popped up all the time. She'd heard that Marie Begonie, one of the Wilcox witches, had made it her life's work to catalog such things in addition to keeping track of her clan's complex genealogy, and yet Bellamy wasn't sure whether Marie had ever shared her findings with the other Arizona clans.

"Well, the important thing is that they weren't able to get the amulet," Tricia said, still sounding no-nonsense and brisk.

"No, they weren't," Angela replied, although she appeared far more troubled. "But the problem is that now they know exactly where it is."

"We can take it back to the Forest Highlands house with us," Connor suggested, but his wife immediately shook her head.

"I'm not so sure that's a good idea. We're the only witch family in the development, and I'd feel better if we had it someplace where we have some backup. No, I think we'd better come back to Jerome a little early, just to be safe."

Connor's mouth tightened slightly, but it didn't look as if he planned to argue with her on that point. Most of the time, they returned to their house here on Paradise Lane in late September now that they were far past having to worry about their kids' school schedules, which a decade ago would have dictated that they be in Jerome no later than the first week of August. Now, though, they tended to linger at the higher elevations until the summer heat began to ease and they could enjoy autumn in the Verde Valley on their own time.

All those considerations had gone out the

window, though, now that they had to worry about whether someone might make another attempt to steal the amulet. Bellamy had a hard time believing anyone would try such a thing if they were both here, just because she knew that working together, Connor and Angela were probably stronger than any other witch or warlock on the planet.

Well, at least now that the Escobars were no longer a threat.

She hoped.

"But thanks for putting all those wards in place," Angela went on. "I think we would have been dealing with a very different situation if we'd only trusted the house's regular security system to keep the amulet safe."

Right. Even though the magic that protected the house was its first line of defense, they also had an alarm they left on whenever they were going to be gone for an extended period. No one had mentioned it getting tripped, which made Bellamy believe that whoever had broken in, they'd used magic or some other means to bypass the system.

The elders nodded, although Levi still looked troubled. Because of his otherworldly origins, he tended to take more upon himself than the other two elders, and he was probably beating himself up right now that even his powerful magic hadn't been sufficient to keep the intruder away.

But it had been enough to keep the thief from escaping with his—or her—prize, and that was the most important thing.

Angela looked over at Marc then, as if really seeing him for the first time. "And thanks for putting the elders on alert," she said. "Because of what you told your grandmother, she and the others were already keeping an eye out for anything strange. I think things might have gone much worse for us if it hadn't been for that."

He gave an embarrassed hitch of his shoulders, as if he wasn't quite sure whether he'd actually provided all that much help. "No problem," he said, tone a little too casual. "I just wish my dreams could have shown me who's behind all this."

"Well, they still might," Tricia said briskly. "For now, though, I think it's enough that the feeling of foreboding you got from those dreams was real, and that something is trying to communicate that the amulet is a real target."

"Exactly," Connor chimed in. "We owe you a debt of gratitude."

"It's nothing," Marc began, but Angela shook her head.

"It's not 'nothing.' Since don't know who tried to take the amulet, we also don't know what they wanted to use it for. Maybe their reasons were totally innocuous—maybe they needed to boost their healer's abilities to cure a particularly awful case of cancer or something—but I have to believe if that was their real reason for wanting to take it, then they could have just approached us directly."

Bellamy hadn't even considered that angle to the problem, but she thought the *prima* had a point there. They also could have asked Levi's wife Hayley for assistance, since her natural-born gift offered much the same kind of magical boost that the amulet did.

Which made Bellamy think the thief's motivations for trying to steal the artifact weren't exactly pure.

"With any luck, we'll never find out," Allegra said. "Now the thief knows they can't get the safe or the amulet out of this house, so let's hope that's enough to dissuade them from making a second attempt and they'll leave us alone."

Especially since Angela and Connor would be back here, adding another layer of protection to the amulet. Still, Bellamy couldn't help thinking that maybe Devynn and Seth should have left the damn thing in the past.

Then again, if they'd done that, they wouldn't have had the power to make it back to the present day. Great-Aunt Ruby, then just the *prima*-in-waiting, had given them a magical boost as well, but Devynn had sure made it sound as if she and Seth had needed both Ruby's powers and the amulet to send them all the way into the mid-twenty-first century.

And that meant the current-day McAllister clan would have to deal with the fallout of possessing the thing whether they liked it or not.

Neither of Allegra's fellow elders nor Connor and Angela looked very sanguine at the prospect of the thief just giving up and going away, but no one seemed inclined to argue with her.

"Yes, I suppose it's no harm, no foul," Angela said. "All the same, can you elders stay here at the house while Connor and I go home and pack up? We weren't planning to come back to Jerome for at least a month, so we weren't really ready to relocate."

"For as long as you need," Tricia assured her, then looked over at her grandson. "Marc, thanks again for the heads-up, but I think we've got things under control here."

By which she probably meant that her grandson—and Bellamy—weren't really needed on the scene, and that was fine by her. Neither of them possessed the sorts of gifts that could possibly help if there was another incursion at the house while Angela and Connor were preparing for the move back to Jerome.

Better to get out from underfoot and go someplace where they could talk in private about what had just happened.

"Sure," Marc said easily. "I need to take Bellamy home anyway. I guess just text me if something else comes up."

"I will," Tricia replied, and that seemed to be that.

After saying their goodbyes, Bellamy and Marc headed down the hill to the spot where he'd left his truck parked. Both of them were silent during the walk, but she was okay with that. Once they were away from Paradise Lane, there were tourists on all sides, and it wasn't as if they could talk about anything important anyway.

Once they were in the truck and driving down 89A toward Cottonwood, though, she figured it was safe to speak up.

"That was kind of crazy."

His shoulders lifted. "I don't know. I mean, we were all halfway expecting that someone might try to make a move on the thing."

Well, when he put it that way....

"But it's a little freaky that neither the elders nor Connor and Angela could get any sense of who was behind the theft."

Marc nodded, although he kept his eyes fixed on the road. It was just curvy enough as it wound its way down the hill that not paying attention could be a recipe for disaster. Sure, he could have turned on the self-driving mechanism, but she noticed he'd kept the truck on manual, as if he wanted to focus on something other than the attempted theft of the amulet.

"That part does worry me," he said, slowing as they turned onto Clarkdale's tiny main street. "I mean, that's a pretty powerful group of witches up there. How is it possible that the person who tried to steal the amulet is so strong that they were able to hide any trace of their magic?"

"I don't know," Bellamy replied. She reached into her purse and pulled out her phone, hoping maybe she'd missed a text from Devynn letting her know Jeremy Wilcox had dug up all sorts of dirt about the Olsen witch clan that would explain who'd broken into Connor and Angela's house and tried to steal the amulet.

But she hadn't missed anything except a text from her hair salon reminding her about her appointment the week after next. The owner of the salon was a stickler about people showing up when they were supposed to, so she'd continue to receive those messages right up to the day she was scheduled to appear.

Well, at least she wouldn't have to worry about forgetting the appointment, not with those constant reminders.

They were past Clarkdale now and just about

to head into Old Town Cottonwood. Part of her thought it might be a good idea to stop there and hang out for a while, if only to shake off her worries about what had just happened up on Paradise Lane, but then she told herself that wasn't such a good idea. Much better to go straight home and, with any luck, convince Marc to hang around for dinner. They could get some takeout and eat at the house, since going to a restaurant didn't seem like a very good idea, either, not when pretty much everything they needed to talk about was something they wouldn't want overheard by civilians.

"Hear anything from Devynn?" Marc asked, and Bellamy shook her head.

"Not yet. I suppose I shouldn't have been expecting too much—the store seemed pretty busy today, and even if Jeremy got back to her quickly, she'd still have to wait for the right time to text me when she wouldn't get interrupted by a customer."

Marc nodded but didn't reply, which seemed to tell her he was okay to wait on any in-depth conversations until they were safely back at the house.

They'd get there a little past six, which was earlier than she usually ate dinner. Still, it seemed smarter to pick something up while they were still out, rather than going all the way to the ranch and then having to head back into Sedona once they decided what they wanted to eat.

"Did you want to grab some dinner?" she asked, hoping she didn't sound too diffident. "There are some places in West Sedona where we can get takeout."

Something about his grip on the steering wheel seemed to ease slightly.

Had he been worried that she would expect him to drop her off at the house and call it a day?

"That sounds good," he said, and again, she thought he sounded just a little too casual.

So, like her, he'd been hoping this drive back to Sedona wouldn't be the end of their day together. Once more, that familiar warmth filled her, but she told herself she needed to stay casual.

"There's a Thai place," she told him. "Or we can get pizza from either Pisa Lisa or Moondog."

"'Moondog'?" he repeated with a lift of his eyebrows.

"It's really good," she told him. "And a little less fancy than Pisa Lisa."

"I'm good with not fancy," he replied, and now a smile played around his lips. "As long as it's okay with you."

"After all this running around, I'm just fine with not fancy," she said, grinning in return. "What's your favorite kind of pizza?"

Now he looked almost shame-faced. "You're going to laugh."

"I won't," she promised. "Well, as long as it's not anchovies, because yuck."

Marc chuckled. "No anchovies. I really like Canadian bacon and pineapple, even though my parents have told me on more than one occasion that liking Hawaiian pizza is a crime against the pizza gods."

How in the world had this guy turned out to be absolutely perfect in every possible way?

"Well, if it's a crime, then I'm a criminal, too," she said with a grin. "Because that also happens to be my favorite. So let's head over to Moondog and order the biggest Hawaiian pizza they have."

"Do they have cheesy bread?"

Boy, did they. And while Bellamy never ordered it unless she was sharing, she knew she'd have Marc there to do some of the heavy lifting and make sure it didn't go to waste.

"Yes," she said cheerfully. "And I've got a bottle of chianti at the house, so I think we're good to go."

"Sounds like a plan. Just tell me how to get to Moondog."

"I can do that."

She settled against the back of her seat, doing her best not to grin like an idiot. Sure, someone had tried to steal the amulet, but they hadn't succeeded, and Angela and Connor would be in Jerome to keep an eye on things from here on out.

Better yet, Marc hadn't uttered a peep about heading back to Tucson now that the problem had been handled, which meant it sure sounded as if he planned to hang around for a while longer.

Now she'd just have to figure out the best way to make sure his time here in the Verde Valley lasted for as long as possible.

8

Since the courtyard was in shadow when they got to the house, pizza and cheesy bread in hand, Marc and Bellamy decided to eat outside. Whoever had designed the outdoor living spaces, they'd done a very good job, since everything was laid out with an eye for an understated, natural beauty, whether that was the grouping of sandstone boulders and wind sculptures off to one side, or the fountain—an unusual feature made of sheets of sandstone and brass that had been treated to show interesting shades of deep umber and metallic green, the sort of thing Marc would like to offer his clients in Tucson—that dominated the center of the courtyard.

Its splashing added some soft background noise as they sat down at the table under the overhang. Now that the sun wasn't beating down on them—although it still had probably an hour before it would completely disappear behind Mingus Mountain, some twenty miles to the west —the air felt friendly and warm rather than oppressively hot.

Bellamy had scooped up a bottle of chianti from the wine fridge in the kitchen along with a pair of glasses, so now all they needed to do was sit there and eat the wonderfully cheesy bread and pizza and wash it down with wine. Despite everything that had happened today, Marc could feel himself relaxing with every passing moment, as if all the worry and speculation had taken place in an utterly different world, one that seemed to have very little connection to the friendly, warm space where they now sat.

"This is some good pizza," he said as he lowered his half-eaten slice to his plate.

"Told you," Bellamy replied with a smile. "I mean, Pisa Lisa is really good, too, but I wanted something homier tonight."

Especially since he wasn't sure whether a higher-end pizza place would have even deigned to make them a Hawaiian pizza. No judgment at Moondog's as Marc had handed over a couple of twenties to the guy behind the counter. Bellamy had made a few noises about paying, but he'd pointed out that she was already providing the wine and the venue, so it was only fair that he should cover the food.

"It's nice that you can be in a place that feels so far away from everything but is still close enough to town that your takeout isn't cold by the time you get it home," he commented.

She nodded, but because she'd just taken a bite of cheesy bread, she had to wait until she was done chewing before she could respond.

"Yes, I was kind of surprised by that. But even though the ranch is technically outside Sedona's city limits, it only takes about ten minutes to get to all the restaurants and other businesses on the west end of town."

Maybe that was part of the reason why she'd felt okay with staying here. Splitting hairs, Marc supposed, since you could see the town's famous red rocks in pretty much every direction from the property, but still, it wasn't part of the city despite sharing the same zip code.

"Nice work if you can get it," he remarked, and she grinned at him, then sipped some chianti.

"Yeah, I kind of fell in clover," she said. "The homeowner is a regular at Sedona Vines, and one night during happy hour we were chatting about how I was commuting from Jerome and wasn't sure whether I should try to find a house someplace a little closer, like maybe in Page Springs or Cornville.

And he said he had his house up for sale but didn't like the idea of it sitting empty while it was on the market, and offered to pay me to watch the place for him. Obviously, I jumped at the chance."

Marc thought he would have, too, if he'd been given a similar offer. Sure, he liked his vintage house in the Sam Hughes neighborhood down in Tucson, liked how it was close to so many restaurants and so much nightlife, thanks to its proximity to the university, but it couldn't really compare to a house like this one, with its multi-million-dollar views.

Not that he would have been able to afford a place like this, even with the combination of the stipend from his clan and the money he earned running his landscape business. The house he'd bought hadn't been too much of a stretch, just because the home was being sold by the former owner's heirs and they'd wanted to get it off their hands as quickly as possible, but this place? It had to be worth seven figures…and not the low range, either.

"Why's he selling?" Marc asked then. If he'd owned a place like this, he would never have wanted to move.

Bellamy shrugged and reached for another slice of pizza. "He said his portfolio was too big and that he didn't come here enough to justify owning the house. I get the feeling he's not much of a desert guy. At least, he said he also has houses in Telluride and Vancouver and condos in New York and L.A., and they were enough to keep him busy."

Not for the first time, Marc wondered what it would be like to have the freedom of movement that the civilian population seemed to take for granted. True, most people weren't rolling in the kind of cash that allowed this Ike guy to own so many premium properties, but even so, regular civilians could still pick up and live anywhere they liked, rather than being stuck in the clan territory where they'd been born.

And sure, that wasn't completely true anymore, because with the way things had changed over the past twenty-five years or so, members of the McAllister clan had gone to live among the de la Pazes and the Wilcoxes and even the Castillos in New Mexico, but still, they didn't move around nearly as much as nonmagical people did.

"Must be nice," he said, and Bellamy gave an understanding nod.

"I know. I suppose I could let myself be jealous, but I decided to just be happy to stay here for as long as it all lasts." She paused there to sip some chianti before she set the glass down again. "And after it's sold, then I guess I'll fall back on my original plan of trying to find a place somewhere between Jerome and Sedona."

Since her tone was almost philosophical rather than resigned, Marc could tell she'd already made her peace with the way this couldn't be a permanent solution to her housing situation.

"Or maybe in Sedona itself?" he suggested before adding, "I mean, it seems as if everyone is okay with you living here, so…."

"Define 'okay,'" she said with a grin. "My dad still isn't too thrilled with me, although I think in his case it's just as much empty nest syndrome as anything else. But yeah, since everything's been hunky-dory between the McAllisters and the Wilcoxes for longer than I've been alive, it seems kind of silly to keep treating Sedona as if it's supposed to be this mysterious, off-limits kind of place."

While Marc was inclined to agree with her on that point, he couldn't help asking, "So, you don't think there's anything to the Sedona vortexes and that stuff?"

Still smiling, she settled against the back of her chair. "Well, I wouldn't say it's 'nothing.' There are places here where, if you go there alone and settle into your thoughts, you really can feel the energy and how it's different from anyplace else you've ever been. At the same time, I'm not sure it has much to do with our witch powers.

Regular people can feel those energies, too—sometimes their skin tingles, or they experience a sensation of calm and grounding with the earth. Other people just feel energized. Anyway, back in the day, maybe it was a good thing for the two witch clans to avoid the place, if only to give more of a buffer zone between our two territories. Right now, though, I think we're shooting ourselves in the foot by avoiding such prime real estate."

Marc couldn't help chuckling at that comment. "Expensive real estate, I'm guessing."

"Oh, yeah." She reached for a slice of pizza and took a bite, her expression now almost contemplative. "Housing prices are way higher in Sedona than they are in Cottonwood or Clarkdale, or even in Jerome itself, although things there tend to be more expensive because there are so few houses to go around. But honestly, even though it's nice to have a short commute right now, I'm not going to worry about it too much. It's not like I'm having to drive around Phoenix."

Or even Tucson, although he had to admit the worst thing about his hometown was how there weren't any real freeways and you had to drive overland everywhere. If you were used to it, then the setup wasn't such a big deal, but still, people who were accustomed to being able to jump on the highway to get where they were going always suffered a rude awakening when they dealt with having to drive across town for the first time.

Bellamy's phone, which had been sitting on the tabletop, gave a soft *bing* then, and she sent Marc an apologetic look.

"I should probably check that," she said. "It might be Devynn getting back to me about the Olsen clan."

"It's fine," he replied. "I was just about to grab another slice anyway."

Her gray eyes danced at him, even as she reached for her phone and unlocked it. For a few seconds, she was silent as she scanned the text she'd just received, but then she shook her head and set the cell phone back down on the table.

"Jeremy couldn't find anything at all," she said, now sounding disgusted. "Or at least, as far as he can tell, the Olsens have been a nice, polite, law-abiding clan for generations. No sign that any of them have ever left their territory in Minnesota, nothing to show there's been any kind of drama with them at all."

Unlike the Arizona clans, Marc thought ruefully, although he realized that most of the turmoil they'd been involved in really hadn't been of their own making. Still, someone looking in from the outside probably would have thought they were a big old hot mess.

"But," Bellamy went on, her tone a little more

cheerful, "Devynn says that's just from a quick inspection, and that Jeremy's going to keep digging just in case one of them maybe went rogue and they did their best to sweep it under the rug."

"Any mention of the amulet?" Marc said. Probably not, but he figured it couldn't hurt to ask.

"Nope," she replied. "I suppose it's the sort of thing they would try to keep on the down-low—even if that Lawrence Pratt guy might have talked about losing the amulet to a couple of witches in the Arizona territories. I kind of doubt he did, though. From the way Devynn described the situation to me, he didn't want anyone to know about the artifact or what he was using it for. So I have a feeling when he went home with his tail between his legs, he wouldn't have said anything about it."

That story made the most sense. After all, the warlock had been using the amulet so he could play magician to an unsuspecting public. That wasn't the sort of thing you'd want to confess to your clan's *prima,* even though Marc had a feeling the truth must have come out eventually. It was kind of hard to hide that sort of thing from someone whose magical powers were so much stronger than yours.

"Well, I guess we'll just have to see if Jeremy's able to dig up anything," he said, doing his best to sound cheerful. "In the meantime, it seems as if the elders and Connor and Angela have everything managed, so I suppose we don't have to worry about it too much."

"No, I suppose we don't," Bellamy responded, although she didn't seem too pleased by the prospect, judging by the way one corner of her mouth turned down and she avoided his gaze as she reached for her glass of wine again.

Was she worried he'd pack it in and go home now that he'd delivered his warning and the McAllisters were properly on guard?

Maybe he shouldn't flatter himself.

On the other hand, he couldn't ignore the way they got along so well, how it felt as if they'd known each other forever rather than only a couple of days. And it was also refreshing to be around someone who didn't seem to care too much that he had prophetic dreams. Even among his own clan, there were people who would give him the side-eye when they thought he wasn't looking, as if they believed he'd have a sudden vision of them standing in front of him wearing only their underwear or something.

It didn't work that way, of course, but he was kind of tired of having to explain the minutiae of his seer's gift. Maybe that was part of the reason why he'd mostly dated civilian girls, telling himself that he much preferred women who took him at face value. And sure, there had been a huge part of his life he hadn't told them about, but wasn't it that way most of the time when you started dating someone?

None of those relationships had been very serious, and he could tell his parents were starting to get impatient with him. Not to the point where they'd started leaving bridal magazines around the house for him to find whenever he visited, but enough that he could see they weren't planning to humor him indefinitely.

Why was it such a big deal for witches and warlocks to get married early, anyway? This wasn't the bad old days when you needed a bunch of kids to work your farm, or when infant mortality —if your clan was unlucky enough to not have a healer—was sky-high. What difference did it make if he waited until he was thirty, or whenever he felt ready?

Because most witches and warlocks…even if they weren't searching for a consort, like his cousin Rosa would soon be…still were able to recognize the person who was their soul mate, their perfect match in every way. That was part of the reason why divorce rates were very low among witch-kind, even though it did happen from time to time.

He wouldn't allow himself to stare at Bellamy —that would have been way too obvious—but all the same, he couldn't help wondering if she might be the one. Gorgeous and smart, the sort of woman who didn't seem to be fazed by much and was also easy to be around?

Sign him up.

"But I also don't think we can let our guard down," he continued, and something about the way she sat in her chair appeared to shift subtly as she sat up a little straighter, her gaze moving back toward him. "That's why I think I'm going to check with my hotel tomorrow morning and see if I can extend my stay by a few days, just to be safe."

Bellamy's lips pursed. Rather than tell him that wasn't necessary, though, she only said, "Or you could try getting an Airbnb. It might be more comfortable than a hotel room."

He hadn't even thought of that, but she was right. After all, he had a couple of weeks to play with before he absolutely had to be back in Tucson, and if he was going to hang around the Verde Valley, he might as well give himself a place where he'd have a little extra room to spread out.

For one wild moment, he wondered if Bellamy might offer to have him stay here, and then he shot down that notion pretty quickly. Not only would it be awkward, but for all he knew, there was some sort of clause in her contract with the homeowner to ensure she wouldn't invite any guests to stay at the property.

That didn't mean he wouldn't try to focus on getting a vacation rental here in Sedona, where he could be closer to her. Logic might suggest it made more sense for him to stay in Jerome, closer to the *prima's* house and any future attempts at seizing the amulet, but Marc reassured himself that if he did have any more prophetic dreams while he was here, he was only a text or a phone call away. After all, he didn't have the sort of power that would be much help in a situation like this once he'd given his initial warning.

Even as the thought passed through his mind, however, he had a feeling he was probably being a little disingenuous. Although he'd never been called upon to use the shielding talent he'd inherited from his father for very much, he knew it might come in useful if he needed to protect the amulet from some sort of magical interloper.

On the other hand, the only way that would work was if he just happened to be in the exact right place at the exact right time, and with Connor and Angela coming back to Jerome to keep watch over the thing, Marc guessed his own magical ability might be superfluous.

"An Airbnb is a good idea," he told Bellamy. "I'll check into that tomorrow."

"There's probably plenty of availability," she

said. "August is usually the slow season around here, although we get lots of day-trippers from the Phoenix area because even though it's hot, it's still about ten degrees cooler in the Verde Valley than it is down there. But those aren't the kind of people who'd be renting Airbnbs."

Off in the distance, thunder rumbled, and Marc looked up at the sky. To his surprise, clouds had moved in while they were eating, and now both the moon and the stars had been obscured.

"I was wondering if those thunderheads were ever going to do something," Bellamy remarked, not looking too concerned by the shift in the sky.

"Can you sense what's going on with the weather?" Marc asked then. He figured it was probably safe to broach the question, since she'd already told him that her gift was working with the wind.

For a few seconds, she looked thoughtful. Before replying, she broke off a piece of cheesy bread and ate it in an almost contemplative sort of way, as though doing so would allow her the time she needed to formulate her reply.

Then she said, "Sort of? I mean, I'm not a true weather witch like Addie Grant up in Flagstaff, but since weather tends to move with the wind, I can kind of feel what it's planning to do. During monsoon season, it's a little harder, just because the winds are so unpredictable and it's often really tough to say where a thunderstorm wants to move. This one"—she paused to tilt her head toward the sky, even as another boom of thunder echoed across the landscape—"was taking its sweet time figuring out what it was going to do. But I guess it finally decided we'd gone long enough without rain."

As if in answer to those words, a few fat drops began to fall, almost evaporating before they hit the ground because the air was so dry. But then more and more began to patter against the flag-stone pavers that covered the courtyard, the blessed moisture beginning to soak into the planters where the wind sculptures—now spin-ning wildly as the breeze picked up—were installed.

"I love that smell," she added, and closed her eyes as she inhaled the scent of wet stone and earth.

"Petrichor," he said, and she smiled, still with her eyes shut.

"Right. I remember the first time I smelled rain falling on the red rocks here in Sedona. There's something magical about it, don't you think?"

Marc supposed there was. Or at least, he knew there was definitely something magical about the woman who sat at the patio table with him, her lovely chin tilting upward as she drank in the suddenly damp air.

In fact, she got up from her seat and walked out into the rain, arms spread wide to embrace the storm and the miracle of the moisture falling all around her. Maybe some people would have thought that foolhardy at best, considering the way thunder continued to rumble overhead, but he guessed that she could sense the movements of the weather better than he and wouldn't have gone out into it if she hadn't known it was safe.

And he remembered how he used to play in the rain when he was a little kid, entranced by the rare storms that moved across his desert hometown.

It was definitely something to be celebrated… as was Bellamy McAllister herself.

Without really thinking, he got up from his chair and stepped out into the rain as well. The heavy drops were colder than he'd anticipated, and he could already tell how the temperature had dropped a good ten degrees or even more, falling from the mid-eighties where it had been when they sat down to dinner to somewhere closer to the upper sixties.

"You're crazy," Bellamy said with a grin. Her coppery hair was already plastered to her head, but she was still the most beautiful thing he'd ever seen.

"So are you," he replied, returning her smile.

For just a moment, they both stood there in silence, gazing at each other.

And then he took a step forward…and so did she.

Another step, and they were standing so close that he could almost sense the heat of her body under the rain-soaked clothes, hear the thudding of her heart.

Were they going to do this?

He thought they probably were.

Her face lifted to his, and it seemed the most natural thing in the world for him to bend down and press his mouth against hers, to taste the tang of pineapple and the darker fruit of chianti on her sweet lips, to pull her toward him so they were pressed body to body as the rain continued to fall.

Thunder crashed, and he could practically feel the zing of electricity and taste the sharpness of ozone on the air as the lightning bolt hit the earth, at most a few hundred yards from where they stood.

Bellamy pulled away slightly and said, "We should probably go inside."

Yes, as much as he'd loved kissing her as the rain poured down around them, getting hit by lightning didn't seem like a very good way to end their evening.

Not when he knew he wanted to stick around

a good long time so he could continue to be entranced by her.

"Good idea."

They hurried under the cover of the patio roof, pausing to gather up the remains of their dinner so they could take it inside. Once they were back in the house, the chill of the refrigerated air hit his rain-soaked clothing, and he had to hold back a shiver.

"Would it be absolutely crazy if I turned on the fireplace?" Bellamy asked, and he shook his head.

"Not any crazier than standing out in the middle of a thunderstorm."

She shot him another grin, and then she went over to the fireplace and flicked the switch to turn on the gas. Immediately afterward, she headed to the thermostat, presumably to shut off the A/C until they'd gotten warmed up.

"Want a towel?"

Marc looked down at his rain-spattered clothing. He wasn't quite as soaked through as Bellamy, but a good toweling-off seemed to be just what he needed.

"Yes, thanks."

"Back in a sec."

She went down the hallway and then came back a moment later holding a pair of cheerful towels in southwest shades of turquoise and rust and cream. "Here you go."

He sent her a grateful smile and then did what he could to blot his wet hair and his damp T-shirt. There wasn't too much he could do about his jeans, but they hadn't gotten as wet as his shirt, so he hoped they would dry quickly enough.

"We should stand in front of the fire," Bellamy suggested. "That'll help speed things up."

Another very good idea. He headed over to the fireplace, and she followed a pace or two behind. Once there, she worked at getting the worst of the wet out of her hair and her clothes, although really, he thought the only sensible solution for her was to change into something dry.

A conclusion she seemed to have arrived at as well, because after a moment, she shook her head and looked up at him, her expression now rueful.

"So much for my *Singing in the Rain* moment," she said. "Do you mind if I get out of these wet clothes? Yours don't seem to have suffered as badly, but—"

"It's fine," he told her. "I can already tell the fire is helping, so I don't mind waiting here for you."

"Be just a sec," she replied, then went on her tiptoes so she could press a kiss against his cheek. "Don't go anywhere."

Go anywhere? As far as he was concerned, he

was just fine with standing here for as long as it took.

In that moment, he knew he would never willingly leave her.

She'd kissed Marc Trujillo. Kissed him in the rain like she was trying to re-create a scene from *The Notebook* or something.

And it had been wonderful. More than wonderful.

Sublime. Yes, that was it. Sublime…heavenly…any other adjective she could think of to describe something that hadn't seemed to be quite of this earth. Sure, she'd kissed more than a couple of guys along the way, but she knew none of those kisses would remain with her until the day she died.

But that one with Marc….

Honestly, she hadn't planned for any of this to happen. Sure, she knew she was attracted to him, but he'd mostly just seemed friendly despite a couple of glances that she might or might not have thought showed some interest. Nothing smoldering, though, that was for sure, and she figured he either didn't feel about her the same way that she felt about him, or at least had decided they couldn't have much of a future, not when they lived hundreds of miles apart and had very separate lives.

Well, the kiss they'd shared seemed to have blown that idea out of the water.

Acutely conscious that he was waiting for her back in the living room, she peeled herself out of her damp jeans and wet blouse, then realized her bra was soaked as well. As much as she would have liked to just put on a tank top and yoga pants and said the hell with it, she wasn't sure what kind of message that would send.

Other than she'd be all too happy to bring him back to the bedroom and make sure he was properly warmed up.

But no, she wasn't going to do something that crazy. Exactly once in her life, she'd had a one night stand, and even though it had been fun enough, she'd found herself wishing afterward that she hadn't jumped straight into bed with the guy like that.

Especially since he'd pretty much ghosted her afterward. Not that she'd been expecting some kind of long-term relationship with him, but still, she thought that was kind of rude.

And sure, this wouldn't be a one-night stand, not when she'd been hanging out with Marc for the past couple of days, but still, she thought it better to play it at least a little safe until she knew for sure where they stood.

So she put on a clean bra and a Sedona Jeep Adventures T-shirt and a baggy pair of cargo pants, and headed back to the living room. He might as well see her at her sloppiest and then decide whether he was really that attracted to her or not.

He smiled as she approached, which seemed to signal he didn't much care what she wore.

"Getting dried out?" she asked, and he nodded.

"The fire is helping a lot. Still, I think the next time we want to stand in the rain, I should probably switch into some swim trunks or shorts or something first. Jeans like to stay wet."

That they did. But because she really didn't have anything he could change into—even the loose-fitting cargo pants she wore now probably wouldn't get past his well-muscled thighs—she only said, "I can get you my blow dryer, if you think that'll help."

He chuckled. "Thanks for the offer, but I'm okay."

Just as soon as he finished speaking, though, his expression abruptly sobered, and those deep, dark eyes met hers, steady and yet as hot as the flames dancing in the fireplace behind him.

It wasn't the sort of look you'd get from someone who only wanted to be casual.

"And…are *we* okay?" Bellamy asked, figuring

she might as well get it out in the open. She knew she'd never responded to a kiss the way she had to the one she'd shared with Marc a few minutes earlier, but even though his expression seemed to indicate otherwise, she still wanted to be sure this wasn't some sort of off-hand encounter for him.

At once, he moved away from the fire and took her hands in his. It didn't seem as if getting soaked in the rain had chilled him too badly, since his fingers were warm.

Reassuring.

"We're okay," he said quietly. "Or maybe… more than okay. From the first instant I saw you, I felt some kind of connection, but since I was here on what some people might have called official business, I wasn't sure whether I should act on it."

"But you did anyway," she replied, and he let go of one of her hands so he could reach over and push a damp strand of hair away from her face.

"I did," he echoed, and then smiled. "I suppose I could take the easy way out and say I was just caught up in the moment, but honestly, I would've been happy to kiss you in the parking lot of a gas station if that's how things ended up."

The image was so silly, she couldn't help but let out a small laugh. "Well, I guess it's a good thing that we decided to eat in. The courtyard is much more romantic."

"True." His gaze strayed to the patio, where

the flashes of lightning had already begun to lessen, a signal that the storm was moving away. To the north and west, she thought, so he probably wouldn't have to contend with it on his way back to Cottonwood. When he looked back at her, though, his expression seemed almost diffident. "So…you have tomorrow off, right?"

"I do," she said, a nervous little tingle going through her body. It sure looked to her as though Marc Trujillo didn't plan on going anywhere. "What did you have in mind?"

His fingers found hers, and tightened slightly. "I was kind of hoping you might want to give me a tour of the local wineries."

Oh, she could do that.

Most definitely.

"It's a date," she said.

9

Marc had been worried that he might have to fight his way through the thunderstorm while driving back to his hotel, but it looked as if it had veered north rather than heading due west, so it turned out to be a non-issue. All the same, he couldn't help thanking the storm.

If it hadn't poured down on them at Bellamy's place, would they have even kissed?

He honestly couldn't say for sure. Oh, the attraction had been there…getting stronger by the moment, as far as he'd been able to tell…but without that outer impetus, they might have waited a day or two more.

Maybe.

And when he got inside his room, he found he was far too keyed up to go to sleep right away, so instead he got out his laptop, connected to the hotel's wifi, and poked around on the Airbnb website, hoping he could find something in West Sedona so he wouldn't be too far away from Bellamy.

Sure enough, there was a fun little house in a neighborhood only about five minutes from Sedona Vines. He'd known there probably wouldn't be anything in the area where the house she was caretaking was located, just because they were all big multimillion-dollar homes in that neighborhood and not the sort of thing people would generally offer on a vacation rental site.

But the place he'd found was definitely close enough, so he went ahead and booked it for the next two weeks. Maybe that was being ambitious, but his next commission didn't start until the twenty-seventh, so he figured he had plenty of time.

Plenty of time to spend with Bellamy.

And when those two weeks were up?

Well, he supposed he'd figure that out when the time came.

For now, though, he thought he'd just play it by ear and hope for the best.

With the rain gone, Bellamy went back out to the courtyard and looked up at the sky. The moon sailed overhead, a little plumper than it had been the day before, and she let out a breath, allowing herself to relax into the afterglow of her goodnight kiss with Marc. She'd walked him to the door, and they'd stood in the foyer for a long moment, each of them understanding that this night needed to end…even as neither of them had wanted to say goodbye.

But they'd already made plans to have brunch at Enchantment Resort in Boynton Canyon before they headed over to Page Springs to visit the wineries there. Luckily, they would all be open, so she wouldn't have to worry about that.

No, the harder part would be deciding which ones they'd have to skip. If they went and did a wine tasting at all six of them, they'd be positively blotto by the time the afternoon was over.

Well, definitely Angel Hill Cellars, the winery that Connor and Angela owned, and D.A. Ranch, and Page Springs Cellars as well. Their wine was fabulous, and with the way the property backed up to Oak Creek, you really couldn't pick a prettier spot to hang out and drink a glass of wine and forget about the rest of the world.

She glanced back toward the house and thought of the dream Marc had told her about, of seeing the safe with its precious cargo blocking his way as he tried to go inside.

Had the dream been trying to tell him that

protecting the magical artifact might get in the way of their budding romance?

She sure hoped not.

Even though the storm had moved on, the air still felt alive, almost electric. A wild breeze caught her damp hair, and she breathed it in, glad of this chance to let herself absorb what had happened between her and Marc this evening…to let herself think about what it all might mean.

Except….

Were those voices she heard on the wind?

No, she had to be imagining things.

Or maybe someone in one of the properties bordering hers was having a blow-out party.

But what she heard didn't sound like music or people laughing and talking. No, it was a sort of odd whisper, something that felt as if it was at the very edge of her hearing, a subvocalization that seemed to slide away into nothing the more she tried to focus on it.

Clearly, she was going crazy.

But even as that half-humorous thought slipped through her mind, Bellamy knew she wasn't nuts. She'd heard something out there, even if she had no idea what it could have been.

Frowning, she went into the house and locked the bifold glass door behind her. Once that was done, she headed over to the panel for the alarm system and turned it on. Maybe it wouldn't do much to protect her from the strange whispering she'd heard on the wind, but she still felt better after she'd put even that small security measure in place.

No doubt Connor and Angela had done the same thing in their big house up on the hill in Jerome, although she guessed they would also employ subtler ways to make sure their home was protected against whoever had tried to steal the amulet. If that person made a second attempt, Bellamy doubted they'd even be able to set foot on the front walk before the *prima* and *primus* knew someone had tried to invade their sanctuary once again.

She wanted to pick up her phone and text Marc, and let him know about those strange whispery voices she thought she'd heard outside, but she told herself she would see him tomorrow anyway. Besides, how much could he even do, other than offer a comforting presence to reassure her she wasn't as alone as she felt right now?

Not a whole hell of a lot, probably. No, it would be much better to go to bed and lie there and think of how it had felt to have his arms around her, and how wonderful it had been to have his mouth pressed against hers.

Besides, she couldn't help wondering if he would dream again tonight, a true dream that might help guide them to the person who'd broken into Angela and Connor's house. If Marc was already in bed, Bellamy knew she would feel guilty about waking him up.

Barring that, if he also reported odd, whispery voices in his dreams, then she'd know for sure she hadn't been imagining the whole thing.

That seemed to settle the matter. She went down the hallway to the master suite, resolved to get a good night's sleep no matter what.

However, that didn't stop her from turning on all the lights as she went.

Marc knew his sleep had been restless, although once he awoke, he couldn't say exactly why. He didn't remember any of his dreams, which he hoped was a good thing.

If danger still lurked out there, his gift should have tried to warn him about it.

He hoped.

But even though he didn't feel quite as ready to face the day as he would have liked, that didn't stop him from showering early and getting dressed, then packing up his things. The Airbnb he'd rented the night before was empty, and the host had told him he could check in early for a small fee.

He'd paid it gladly, knowing it would be much

better to be settled in Sedona before he went to pick up Bellamy for brunch. That was why—after running across the street to the Red Rooster Café to grab a cup of coffee—he was checked out of the hotel and leaving Cottonwood just a little after nine-thirty, which he figured should give him plenty of time.

The nav in his truck guided him right to the address of his new digs, which were located in a quiet neighborhood that backed up to the red rocks and some hiking trails. As he unpacked his clothes and put his toiletries away in the master bath, he wondered if Bellamy was into hiking at all. It sure looked as though there would be plenty of places to explore around here.

She didn't strike him as the overly pampered type, so maybe he'd broach the subject at brunch. Yes, she'd be back at work after today, but she'd made it sound as if she generally didn't start her shift until at least noon, which meant they'd still have time to hit the trails early in the morning before the sun got too hot.

Or maybe he shouldn't get his hopes up. At home in Tucson, he'd gone hiking a lot, also in the early morning before the heat got too brutal. He loved wandering back to the Tanque Verde falls or driving up to Mount Lemmon to get away from the hot weather to a place where he could happily wander in ponderosa pine forests that felt as if they were very far away from the desert city.

Whether Bellamy shared that love?

He supposed he'd find out soon enough.

It was less than a mile from his Airbnb to the ranch where Bellamy was staying; he had to stop at the gate and use the intercom to get her to buzz him in, but soon enough he was rolling down the gravel lane that led to the house, obscurely comforted by all the security measures in place to protect the property. Sure, he supposed someone could jump the split-rail fence that surrounded all five acres, but he'd noticed cameras placed at strategic intervals along the perimeter and guessed that anyone who did such a thing would get captured on the security footage.

Unless, of course, they were a witch or warlock with the power of invisibility, in which case they'd be a lot more difficult to track.

Maybe that wasn't so implausible a scenario. After all, someone had broken into Angela and Connor's house in broad daylight, and it didn't seem as if any of the neighbors had noticed anything strange. His grandmother lived two doors down from the *prima* and *primus,* and she hadn't mentioned seeing any intruders or any people who looked out of place on the quiet street.

Or possibly the would-be thief had the power

of teleportation. It was a fairly rare gift, nothing that anyone in the de la Paz clan currently had in their arsenal, but that didn't mean the person who'd tried to steal the amulet might not possess that talent. After all, it would be a pretty useful type of power to have if you were a magical thief with sticky fingers.

His thoughts chased themselves around and around, and he did his best to tell his brain to shut up as he got out of his truck and walked over to the front entrance. Almost as soon as he rang the doorbell, Bellamy opened the door and smiled at him. Today she wore a pretty embroidered blouse and jeans and sandals that showed off toes glimmering with metallic pink polish.

"Right on time," she said, and he grinned back at her.

"Well, my Airbnb is pretty close, so I would've had to work hard to be late."

She stepped out of the way and he came inside, feeling cold air swirl around him. The day was sunny and bright, with absolutely no sign of the thunderstorm that had passed through the night before, and he could tell it was going to be another scorcher.

"You're sure we don't need reservations for brunch?"

"On a Monday morning? Nope," she replied, answering her own question. "Besides, it's not a full-on brunch like we'd get on the weekend, just their normal menu. But I think you'll like it. Just let me grab my purse."

He waited in the foyer while she went to fetch her bag, and soon enough, they were climbing into his truck.

"You can just keep going down Dry Creek," she told him after he'd turned the vehicle around and pointed it back down the lane that led to the main road. "After that, follow the signs—they'll take us straight to Enchantment."

Which proved to be the case, since everything was so well marked that Marc knew he could have gotten to their destination without once having to check the nav. They had to slow to a crawl once they were on the resort grounds, thanks to all the "golf cart crossing" signs and the pedestrians making their way to the putting greens that bordered the access road, but still, it was only a quarter after eleven when he pulled into the parking lot for the resort's main building, which housed its various restaurants.

When he got out of the truck, however, he wasn't looking at their brunch venue, but instead at the red rock walls that soared up on all sides, so close, it almost felt as if he could reach out and touch them.

"This is...pretty spectacular," he said, and Bellamy smiled.

"Isn't it? And the views are even better from the restaurant, since we'll be up a few levels. Let's go."

She slid her hand into his, and he found himself thrilling at her touch. When he'd met her at the house, he'd wondered if he should kiss her, but the moment hadn't felt quite right.

Now, though, she was holding hands with him as if it was the most natural thing in the world, and once again he found himself marveling a little at how easy things were between them. He hadn't been this comfortable with people he'd known his entire life, but only a few days around Bellamy McAllister made him feel as if she'd always been a part of his world.

He could only hope that feeling would continue.

As she'd predicted, the restaurant wasn't hugely busy, so they were shown to a table over by one of the windows without having to wait longer than a couple of minutes. And she'd also been right about the views—the restaurant had been built on an incline, so they were probably a good fifty feet higher here than they'd been in the parking lot, with those stunning red rocks feeling even more immediate now, close enough that he could see all the little divots and hollows and outcroppings that millennia of erosion had left behind.

"No wonder they call it 'Enchantment,'" he remarked after the hostess had handed them a couple of menus and told them their server would be over in a few minutes.

"It's one of my favorite spots in Sedona," Bellamy replied. "If we weren't going wine tasting after this, I'd say we should sit outside on the patio after brunch and have a drink. But I suppose it's better if we pace ourselves."

By which he guessed that she didn't plan to drink any alcohol with their meal.

And that was fine. To be honest, he was half drunk on the surroundings…and the company…already.

"Good idea," he agreed, and looked down at the menu.

Bellamy only gave it a cursory glance, seeming to signal she'd eaten here enough in the past that she already knew what she wanted. Everything looked amazing, but since they were going to be hitting the wine tasting rooms after this, Marc thought he should go with the breakfast burrito rather than something lighter so he could lay down a solid base.

"Everything's great here," she said, then paused to send a brief glance around the room. Although the hostess had said their waitress would be over shortly, there wasn't any sign of her yet.

Lowering her voice, Bellamy added, "Any dreams last night?"

No wonder she'd made sure they couldn't be overheard. There were other diners in the restaurant, of course, but no one was seated close enough to them to be able to hear what they were saying.

"Not really," Marc replied, feeling like something of a failure even though he knew he couldn't really control when the dreams appeared…or what they might decide to show him. "Why?"

Another hesitation, one that appeared to have been prescient, since a pretty Navajo woman who looked as if she might be in her middle thirties approached their table and asked if they'd like anything to drink. Because he'd already had his coffee that morning, he asked for iced tea, and Bellamy followed suit.

Once their server had departed to fetch their drinks, he sent Bellamy a direct look.

"Did something happen after I left last night?"

Her fingers played with the handle of the fork at her place setting, and then she let out a breath and settled her napkin on her lap.

"I'm not sure."

He raised an eyebrow, and she spread her hands, looking helpless.

"No, really. It was…."

She stopped again, since the waitress had

returned with their iced teas. Then it was time to place their orders, something Marc was glad they'd gotten out of the way, since at least now they probably would have at least ten or fifteen uninterrupted minutes before the food arrived.

A sip of iced tea, and then Bellamy said, "I went outside after you left. Doing that always helps to ground me."

He couldn't help smiling. "You needed grounding after our evening together?"

Gray eyes met his, level, unblinking. "What do you think?"

Well, considering he'd felt as if he was on Cloud Nine during the whole drive over to Cottonwood, he supposed he could see why Bellamy had seen the need to come back down to earth.

He helped himself to some iced tea as well. "I don't want to flatter myself."

Now she grinned, the tense moment broken. "Maybe you should."

He chuckled, but since her expression abruptly sobered, he knew she wanted to get back to business.

"Anyway, when I was standing out in the courtyard, I thought I heard something on the wind. It almost sounded like voices."

That seemed a little odd, but sound could

travel in weird ways at night, carried on the desert breeze. "Your neighbors?"

She shook her head. In the bright light from the floor-to-ceiling windows that dominated the space, her loose hair was almost the same ruddy hue as the red rocks surrounding them on all sides.

"That's what I thought at first, too. But there wasn't any music, and it sure didn't sound like people partying. More like whispers, or words spoken so quickly I couldn't really understand any of them."

Well, that didn't sound creepy at all. Even though they were sitting in a restaurant with other people, brightly lit and certainly not sinister in the slightest, he couldn't quite prevent a chill from running down his spine.

"Has that ever happened before?"

"No," she said at once. "I'm not a psychic. I'm not supposed to hear words on the wind, or whatever was going on last night."

She paused there so she could reach for her glass of iced tea and take a sip. Gray eyes met his again, more bleak than ever.

A breath, and then she said, "I'm worried that maybe there was a real reason why all those Wilcox and McAllister witches in the past said we needed to stay away from Sedona."

10

HE HADN'T LAUGHED AT HER, WHICH HAD been Bellamy's greatest fear when she'd decided she needed to confide in Marc, to tell him the troubling ideas that had been floating around in her brain while she was getting ready that morning.

What if there really was something about Sedona that had been playing with her witchy powers?

No, he only looked thoughtful, and glanced past her to the red rocks outside the restaurant's windows before he returned his attention to her once again.

"But…don't plenty of McAllister witches come and roam around Sedona all the time?"

"To shop and eat and go to the movies, sure." Bellamy swirled her straw around in her iced tea, doing her best to collect her scattered thoughts. "But they don't sleep here, or spend twenty-four/seven around the red rocks and vortexes. Maybe that's what it takes for Sedona's energies to start working on their witchy powers."

For a moment, Marc didn't say anything. He hadn't looked away, though, which she believed must be a hopeful sign. If he thought she'd completely gone off the deep end, then she doubted he would have maintained their current eye contact.

"Maybe it is," he said at length. "Is it something you could talk to Angela and Connor about?"

Bellamy honestly didn't know. Sure, both the *prima* and *primus* had gained crazy powers when they inherited their positions—powers that expanded even further when they became consorts—but still, it wasn't as if they'd also had all sorts of esoteric knowledge beamed directly into their brains. They had to figure things out for themselves, the same as anyone else.

"I suppose we can start there," she replied, then shook her head. "Or maybe talk to the elders first. I don't want to be bugging Connor and Angela with every little thing."

"I'm not sure this is a 'little thing,'" Marc said, words that reassured her even more. He was taking her concerns seriously, not dismissing them as the result of too much chianti and those amazing kisses they'd shared. "Not when you haven't experienced anything like this before."

No, she hadn't. Sure, when she was a kid and her powers had first awakened, she used to stand on the overlook near McAllister Mercantile and let the wind ruffle her hair, and she'd pretended that those winds had all sorts of secrets they could tell her, if only she could figure out how to make her magical gift do what she wanted.

Now it seemed as if those winds were actually trying to communicate with her at last, and she wasn't sure she liked the sensation very much.

If, in fact, anything really was happening, and her overactive brain hadn't made up the whole thing.

She wished it was that easy. But whatever it was that she'd heard the night before, it had been real.

"Well, it still makes sense to contact the elders first," she said, even as she hoped Marc wouldn't find it awkward to be talking to his grandmother about this stuff. To Bellamy, Tricia was just one of the elders, someone she hadn't had much need to communicate with, except at communal events like the big McAllister Thanksgiving and Christmas potlucks.

But she was Marc's grandmother, and maybe he didn't want her to know that things were starting to get serious with one of the McAllister witches.

If they even were serious. Yes, she and Marc had kissed the night before, and merely sitting across the table from him like this was enough to send a happy little thrill through her every time their eyes met, but it was still early days for the two of them.

However, he showed no sign of hesitation when he said, "You're right. Maybe it would be better to talk to your clan elders before we go over their heads and speak with Angela and Connor. Besides, it seems as if Allegra Moss has been an elder for a long time, right? If anyone might know something about this, she should."

Bellamy supposed he had a point there. Allegra had been an elder since before even Angela was born, which meant she'd been overseeing the McAllister clans' doings for more than fifty years.

And it wouldn't be smart to dismiss Levi, either. Although his soul inhabited a human body, he was still something just slightly other, so he might have some unique insights into the problem as well.

"We can call your grandmother after we eat," Bellamy said. "And then go from there."

She hoped she didn't sound too disappointed as she spoke. Sure, this was much more impor- tant, but she'd really been looking forward to an afternoon tasting wine with Marc and pretending that the rest of the world didn't exist.

"Sounds good," he agreed.

The waitress came back with their food then, so the next few minutes were spent digging into their meals...and trying to pretend that their plans for the day hadn't just been upended. Instead, they talked about other points of interest around Sedona that Marc might want to visit while he was staying here.

"What about hiking?" he asked, his tone a little too deliberately casual.

Judging by the way he'd posed the question, he was probably hoping she'd tell him she was an enthusiastic hiker...and was also steeling himself for disappointment if it turned out she was a much bigger fan of the great indoors.

"How can anyone live around here and *not* want to go hiking?" she replied, and then did her best to hold back a smile when he practically sagged with relief.

"That's what I was hoping you would say."

"You hike a lot in Tucson?" she asked, genuinely curious. "Isn't it really hot?"

In between bites of breakfast burrito, he assured her that, while Tucson was pretty much a furnace in the summer, you could still squeeze in an hour or so of hiking if you started early enough —and also that you could go up to Mount

Lemmon, part of the Catalina range, where temperatures were usually about twenty degrees cooler than the valley floor.

It sounded like fun…even as she privately admitted to herself that she still thought the hiking around Sedona must be a lot better.

"And even though I have to work tomorrow through Saturday," she said. "The earliest I start is noon, which would give us plenty of time to go for a hike. Want to try the Devil's Bridge tomorrow?"

"Sounds ominous," Marc said with a grin.

"Well, I wouldn't advise falling off, but the view is amazing. And with school starting up now and more people staying closer to home base, it probably won't be too crowded."

"Then I'd love to try it."

There. They'd made plans for tomorrow with not a hint of awkwardness. Marc sure didn't give the impression of anyone who planned to disappear any time soon, and Bellamy could visualize the two of them going for a hike every morning—and maybe having breakfast afterward—before she had to head into work. Since she had to be on shift until nine on Tuesday through Thursday and then until midnight on Friday and Saturday, that didn't leave a lot of time for socializing.

When she'd been handed her schedule, she hadn't thought much about it, knowing she didn't have what anyone could call a social life, so it hadn't mattered that she'd be working late every night.

Now, though, she found herself chafing at all the current restrictions on her time, which was stupid, right? Hadn't getting hired as the assistant manager at Sedona Vines been her dream job?

Well, it had when she didn't have anyone in her life. Now, though....

Now she would just have to suck it up. Yes, she was having fun with Marc—despite all the witchy complications that seemed to have cropped up over the past couple of days—but she couldn't allow a good time to get in the way of her career. Soon enough, he'd be back down in Tucson, and it would be stupid for her to do anything that would jeopardize her position at the wine tasting room.

They talked about the various trails they could try, and then, once they were done with their food, Marc got out his phone so he could text Tricia and see if there was a time when they could meet with the elders.

It appeared fate had stepped in to give them a reprieve, though, because he set his cell phone down on the tabletop and frowned slightly.

"My grandmother says Allegra's down in Phoenix for the day. I guess she has some kind of eye condition that none of the healers have been able to fix, so she has to go see a specialist once a month. But they can talk to us tomorrow."

"It'll have to be in the morning," Bellamy reminded him. "I have to be at work at noon."

His expression fell. "So…no hiking?"

Well, at least she could reassure him on that point. "Oh, we'll still have time to go up to the Devil's Bridge, since I doubt your grandmother and the other elders will want us on their doorstep at the crack of dawn. If we can meet them at ten, I think the timing will work out okay."

Instant relief shone in his dark eyes, and he picked up his phone and sent another text. The reply came back immediately, and he nodded as he read it before returning the phone to his pocket.

"My grandmother says ten o'clock is fine." He paused there, sensual lips curving in a smile. "Exactly how early were you planning on hiking?"

"Six-thirty?" she suggested.

He didn't even blink, which seemed to tell her that he was used to getting up at o'dark thirty so he could hit the trails before the sun got too warm. "That works. I'll pick you up then."

She almost replied that she should do the driving, since she knew where they were going and he didn't. However, she decided to let it go, mostly because his truck was much better suited for the rough roads heading out to the trails than her little Fiat. Oh, sure, her car did okay as long as you didn't try to make it go places designed for four-wheel drive, but she'd gotten a flat tire several times from a particularly sharp rock and knew the route wasn't without its hazards.

"Sounds like a plan," she said.

With everything set, they finished the rest of their meal and then headed out to his truck. By that point, it was well past noon, and she knew all the tasting rooms they were planning to visit would be open.

"Where first?" Marc asked as he backed the truck out of its parking space and headed down to the little feeder lane that would lead them to the main road.

"Angel Hill Cellars," she said promptly. "That's Angela and Connor's vineyard, although it's their friend Tony Rocha who runs the place. It's a gorgeous piece of property, and I figure it's better to start there rather than leave it to the end and maybe run out of time."

Or just decide that they'd drunk enough and needed to quit before they were too impaired. That was probably why the local wine tours were so popular—with someone else driving, you didn't have to worry so much about that sort of thing—but Bellamy hadn't wanted their day to be dictated by someone else's schedule. They could share tastings and be judicious about when they ordered a glass, and if they spaced their visits out enough, they should be fine.

Angel Hill Cellars was located about halfway along Page Springs Road as it wound its way through the canyon. Although Connor and Angela had bought the place some twenty-five years earlier, it had already been a functioning winery when they purchased it, so the vines were well-established and the big barn they used as the tasting room had the mellow feel of a place that had been around for decades and planned to be there for at least that many more.

A few cars were parked in the lot, but not many, telling Bellamy that, while a few people had ventured out to go wine tasting this Monday afternoon, the vast majority of the tourists were now safely back in Phoenix or wherever it was they'd come from.

And there was Sabrina Rocha working behind the counter. She lifted her hand in a wave as Bellamy and Marc came in.

"A friend of yours?" he asked in an undertone.

"That's Tony and Sydney Rocha's daughter, Sabrina. She graduated from ASU a couple of years ago, and now she works in the tasting room."

As she spoke, she couldn't help sending Marc a surreptitious look to gauge his reaction to the other woman. By any standard, Sabrina was a stunner, with her honey-colored hair and warm-toned skin and green eyes, but it didn't seem as if he'd noticed. And while Bellamy had never thought of herself as the jealous type, she was still very glad to see the way Marc had barely registered that the other woman was even female.

"I suppose at some point I'll get used to the way you know everyone around here," he said as they approached the counter.

Now she couldn't help smiling. "Hazards of living in a small town, I guess." She paused there, then asked, "I suppose Tucson isn't at all like that?"

"Nope," he said, expression amused. "I mean, there are a lot of de la Pazes and we've been there a long time, but still, there are more than a million people who live in Tucson. There's no way in the world you could ever know all of them."

That was for sure. Did he like the anonymity that living in a big city provided him, or would he be happier someplace smaller, more intimate?

Bellamy reminded herself that it was far too early to even be thinking such things, and then tried to put it all out of her mind, since they were now at the counter and Sabrina was sliding a couple of tasting menus toward them.

"First time here?" she asked Marc.

Luckily, her expression only showed polite interest and nothing else.

"Yes, I've never been to Page Springs before," he replied.

"Marc's visiting from Tucson," Bellamy supplied. "Marc, this is Sabrina Rocha, an old friend of the McAllisters. Sabrina, this is Marc Trujillo."

Maybe just a flicker in Sabrina's green eyes, probably noting the way Bellamy had pointed out that she'd known the McAllisters for a long time...and therefore was privy to their secrets.

"You're from the de la Paz clan?" Sabrina asked.

Marc hesitated for a second, then nodded. "Yes, but my mother's a McAllister."

Sabrina smiled. "Well, that's fun. Then it's probably high time you visited Angel Hill Cellars. We're kind of famous around here. Do you want a white flight, a red, or a combo?"

On the drive over, Bellamy and Marc had already agreed to share tastings so they wouldn't get utterly wasted, and that was why they decided to start with a combo flight. Sabrina was definitely knowledgeable about the wines, even though she'd gone to Arizona State to get a degree in marketing rather than sticking around here and earning her certification in enology the way Bellamy had done.

They ran through all of the wine samples and

then decided to get a couple of glasses of chardonnay to finish up.

"You should have those out by the pond," Sabrina told them as she handed over their drinks. "We finally replaced the pergola out there, so there's lots of nice shade."

Marc and Bellamy agreed that sounded like a good idea and headed outside. As promised, a large pergola covered a concrete pad furnished with several tables and a little conversation area with two love seats facing one another, and a few yards away, ducks and geese floated on the surface of the water, doing their best to beat the heat.

"If the pergola is new, where did all the vines come from?" he asked as he settled himself in a chair at the table nearest the pond, then cast a curious look up at the lush grapevines that offered shelter from the midday sun.

"Oh, that was a big undertaking," Bellamy said as she sat down in the seat next to him. For just a second, her knee brushed against his, and another of those happy little thrills went down her back.

The guy definitely had an effect on her, that was for sure.

"How so?" he asked, then lifted his glass of chardonnay so she could clink hers against it.

Tradition satisfied, they both drank, and then

she said, "There was an older pergola here that had all the grapevines growing on it, but the wood was starting to rot and Connor and Tony knew they needed to do something about it. So they got a bunch of people to carefully unwrap the vines from the pergola and laid them on the ground, and then they came back in and rebuilt the thing in one day so the grapevines wouldn't suffer too much."

"They look happy now," he said, craning his head to look up at the lush leaves and the clusters of pale grapes that hung from them. Bellamy wasn't sure if they would be included in the harvest, but they were pretty.

"Oh, everyone did a great job of preserving them," she replied. "I think Connor was prepared to plant all new ones if he had to, but luckily, it turned out that the original vines survived just fine."

Marc was silent for a moment as he sipped his chardonnay and watched a pair of ducks squawk at each other before retreating to opposite sides of the pond. Dappled shadows moved across his handsome features, and he appeared unusually contemplative.

"This is a gorgeous place," he said at length. "I like how you can have such different biospheres so close to one another. You don't have to drive very far to be someplace completely different."

Well, that was true. Jerome felt very different

from Cottonwood and Clarkdale, just as those towns were utterly different from Sedona. And Page Springs, lush and green thanks to the creek that ran through the narrow canyon, was its own space as well.

"It was a fun place to grow up," she said, then added, only halfway teasing, "even if it turns out that Sedona is messing with my head somehow."

His brows drew together, and she could tell he didn't want to view the situation quite so lightly. "I'm not sure if 'messing' is the right word. Maybe it's nothing…or maybe there really is something about the vortex energy that affects witchy powers."

Because they were the only ones out here, they didn't have to worry about anyone overhearing what they were saying. Otherwise, Bellamy doubted he would have been quite so casual with the W-word.

"Hopefully, we'll find out when we talk to the elders tomorrow," she said, and sipped some of her chardonnay. It was cool and crisp, with just the slightest buttery taste and absolutely no oaki-ness at all.

Tony Rocha wouldn't be caught dead putting his chard in oak barrels. No, it was stainless steel all the way for his whites.

Marc nodded. "Yes, it would be good to know what's going on."

If it was anything at all. The experience had been just surreal enough that Bellamy still wasn't sure what to make of it. She still might have imagined the whole thing.

Because how powerful was Sedona if it had already begun to exert its influence on her when she'd only been sleeping at the ranch for a couple of days?

She didn't know if she wanted to contemplate that slightly alarming prospect, so she did what she could to push it out of her head. No, much better to concentrate on the cool taste of chardonnay on her tongue, and the way the bright August sun danced on the waters of the pond.

Odd how no one else was out here, considering how comfortable the air felt under the pergola. But maybe the two other people in the tasting room—an older couple who looked as if they might be in their late fifties or early sixties—had decided they didn't want to leave the comfort of the air-conditioned space just in case it turned out to be too warm outside.

And Marc seemed to understand that she preferred to be quiet for a while, to just sit there and drink in the day and not allow too many troubling thoughts to crowd her mind. More than ever, she thought how lucky she was to have met him, how he could have stayed safely in Tucson and only called or texted his grandmother to let her know about his dreams rather than driving all the way up here.

Something had told him he needed to be here in person, though. Was that simple dumb luck, or had some sixth sense decided to exert itself even outside his dreams, subtly compelling him to make the trip north?

They might never know, and she realized she needed to be okay with that.

After they finished their wine, they went inside and handed the empty glasses off to Sabrina, who told them she hoped they'd have a nice rest of their day.

Which of course they did, going next to D.A. Ranch and doing a tasting there before sharing a glass of zinfandel on the big farmhouse's wraparound porch, and then at last ending up at Page Springs Cellars, where they decided to go straight to having a glass each so they could head outside and stand on the large balcony that overlooked Oak Creek.

Enough people were occupying the space that Bellamy knew she and Marc couldn't share any confidences regarding his visions or the strange voices she'd heard on the wind the night before. That was all right, though; she liked simply standing there and sipping at her glass of Mule's Mistake and listening to the murmur of the creek as it wound its way through the canyon and down to the spot where it joined the Verde River several miles to the south. Cottonwoods and oaks and sycamores clustered on the creek's bank, making the place feel like a green oasis in northern Arizona's high desert.

"What's it like in the winter?" Marc asked out of seemingly nowhere, and she smiled.

"Colder."

He shook his head. "Do you get much snow?"

"Not really. Sure, we'll get a storm every once in a while that drops a few inches, but most of the time, it's melted within a few hours. We don't usually have the kind of storm that leaves you stuck in the house or anything, although it does happen sometimes." She paused there, remembering a few choice occasions when Main Street had gotten plowed but all the little side streets in Jerome were left buried under six inches or more of snow. People broke out their sleds and skis to get around—and were extremely grateful once all the white stuff finally melted.

That didn't happen very often, though, and much less here in Page Springs, which was about a thousand feet lower in elevation than Jerome.

"But the trees will be bare until late March or early April, and we definitely have four seasons here." She paused and looked up at him, at the fine outline of his nose and jaw and brow as he gazed at the creek. "Why? You thinking of relocating or something?"

His dark eyes glinted. "It's tempting."

Because of the natural beauty of the area, which clearly had enchanted him…or maybe another reason, one she wasn't sure either of them should voice aloud?

"I suppose you could make a case for that," she replied, doing her best to sound nonchalant. "I mean, your mother is from Jerome, so that makes you half a Verde Valley guy, right?"

Now he turned toward her, and something about the way his eyes met hers made her wish they were all alone out here so he could take her in his arms and kiss her the way he had last night.

But then he grinned, saying, "I'm not sure it works that way."

No, it didn't. Or at least, while witches and warlocks moved into different territories from time to time, it was only because they'd fallen in love and made a commitment to someone from another clan. It wasn't as if they picked up and moved whenever the mood struck them.

"Maybe not exactly," she allowed. "But…."

She let the word trail off because she honestly wasn't sure what she wanted to say. That she was pretty sure she was already falling for him…falling hard…and that she'd be more than happy to have him living in the Verde Valley permanently?

Of course she wouldn't blurt out something so crazy, not when she'd only known Marc Trujillo for a couple of days.

On the other hand, nothing was stopping her from thinking it.

Thinking it hard.

His free hand stole toward hers where it rested on the balcony's railing, his fingers folding around hers, warm and reassuring. Even that gentle touch was enough to send a rush of heat through her, and she lifted her glass of wine to her lips so she could take a sip to hide the tumult of her thoughts.

"I like it here," he said quietly. Then, "I like you."

The words came out before she could stop them. "Just 'like'?"

A corner of his mouth quirked. "Okay, maybe a little more than that."

Well, there it was. No, they hadn't come out and declared their undying love for each other, but on the other hand, Bellamy thought they'd just taken an enormous step forward.

She swallowed the last of the wine in her glass, then said, "You want to get out of here?"

"Absolutely."

Although they didn't do anything so undignified as run straight back to the tasting room, their steps were much more hurried than they would have been under other circumstances. And once they were back out on 89A, Marc spoke again.

"Did you want to go to your place, or would you rather see the Airbnb I'm renting?"

"The Airbnb," she said promptly. No, of course Ike hadn't done anything so Victorian as to forbid her from having gentleman callers or anything like that, but at the same time, she wasn't sure how she felt about spending the inevitable end to their afternoon at the ranch. For whatever reason, Marc's vacation rental felt much more like neutral ground.

So he drove to a quiet neighborhood just north of the main drag and maybe ten minutes at most from the place where she was currently living. The Airbnb was a small two-bedroom house with whimsical Southwest decor, maybe not something she would have chosen for herself but which she thought fit the location perfectly.

She didn't have much time to examine the interior after that, because Marc pulled her into his arms and kissed her, kisses redolent of rich red wine and something else, a warm flavor that she thought was his and his alone. Now a heat that rivaled the upper nineties outside surged through her body, telling her that she didn't care whether she'd only met him the day before yesterday, that she didn't care about anything at all except getting into the bedroom as quickly as possible.

But then he pulled away for a moment, gazing down at her with an almost worried look on his face.

"We're not—we're not going too fast, are we?"

While Bellamy appreciated his concern, she knew there was nothing to worry about. This was exactly where they needed to be…and she had a feeling they would have ended up here even if they hadn't spent the afternoon drinking wine.

"No," she replied, taking his hands and holding them tight so he'd know she meant every word. "It's definitely not too fast. I want this, Marc…I want you."

That seemed to be the only encouragement he needed, because he bent to kiss her again, kiss her so fiercely that she wasn't sure whether her knees were about to give way then and there.

And then he took her down the hall to the main bedroom, which had a wonderful king-size bed piled high with pillows. Those pillows were soon scattered across the floor as Marc pushed them out of the way and then yanked back the covers.

They fell onto the bed, still caught up in their embrace, as if neither of them wanted to be the first to let go. But then Bellamy grabbed the hem of his T-shirt and pulled it up and over his head, and he chuckled and did the same with the embroidered blouse she wore, although she noticed he was careful to toss it onto the chair in the corner and not the floor the way she'd done with his shirt.

Her hands moved over his smoothly muscled chest, marveling at how strong he was—from all that hiking, or the yard work she assumed must go along with his landscape business?—and how his naturally warm-toned skin was tanned a few shades deeper thanks to the hot summer sun. He bent to kiss her throat and she let out a gasp…a gasp that turned into a satisfied moan as he worked his way down to her breast, pausing to unhook the front clasp of her bra so he could close his lips around her nipple.

Oh, dear Goddess, that was good. She buried her hands in his heavy hair, losing herself as he licked and suckled…felt the heat as his fingers found the button of her jeans and undid it, then tugged on the zipper.

Those clothes were only a barrier to what she wanted. She kicked off her jeans, and then worked on Marc's as well, adding them to the pile on the floor. Once they were both only clad in their underwear, they kissed again, bare skin to bare skin, needing the contact, needing to make this moment as tactile as possible.

And then even their underwear was too much in the way, so she grabbed hold of the waistband of his boxer briefs and pulled them down, letting him spring free.

Oh, he was definitely ready…and big.

That was all right, though. She knew she was ready, too.

He slipped his fingers under her panties, caressing her for a moment before he also slid them down her legs and tossed them out of the way. Now she was bare to him, and he continued to stroke her even as his mouth closed on her nipple once more.

Had anything ever felt this good before? Bellamy didn't think so…even as she realized they were just getting started.

His mouth moved away from her breast, kissing her all down her stomach, pausing for just the barest second before his tongue touched the sensitive nub.

She cried out, arching her back, fingers clutching the sheets as he made love to her with his mouth, taking his time, teasing her nearly to a climax then slowing, doing whatever he could to draw this out.

It was exquisite agony, and she loved every second of it.

The orgasm hit just a few moments later, and she let herself cry out, body practically convulsing as the waves of pleasure flooded through her.

Sweet Goddess, she knew she'd never experienced anything like that before.

She was still panting when Marc moved against her, his rigid cock pressing against her opening.

"Is it okay?" he whispered.

"More than okay," she said, knowing that those of witch-kind didn't need to worry about protection. Or at least, the women of the Arizona clans had no need to be concerned, not when the witches from the McAllister family had made sure everyone knew about the charm of Brigid, the one that ensured every single pregnancy was a wanted one.

Marc pressed his lips against her neck, then slid into her. At once, Bellamy wrapped her legs around him, feeling the heavy muscles of his thighs, moaning as he filled her, finding the empty places and making them whole.

They seemed to float in a liminal space, one of light and heat and utter bliss. She knew another climax was approaching, her entire body thrumming with pleasure, and then as he released, she let out a breath and allowed the ecstasy to thrill through every limb, every cell and nerve, her entire being telling her this was what she'd been waiting for all her life…even if she hadn't known it.

Afterward, they clung to one another for a

long moment, their heavy breaths mingling, becoming one. And even when they were two people again, he continued to hold onto her hand, as if he couldn't bear to lose that point of contact.

"Is it too soon to say that I love you?" he asked, and her eyes warmed with happy tears.

"It's never too soon," she whispered. "Never."

Those dark eyes, so depthless she thought she could get lost in them forever, met hers for a long moment.

"Then I love you, Bellamy McAllister."

Her fingers tightened on his.

"And I love you, Marc Trujillo."

11

Afterward, they did their best to act normal—although Marc was glad that Bellamy was just fine with stepping into the shower together and indulging in some playful intimacies there—and then got dressed. He wasn't quite sure how she managed it, but she was able to repair the damage to her admittedly minimal makeup with whatever she carried in her purse.

By the time they returned to the living room, it was almost seven o'clock.

"We should probably think about getting something to eat," he said.

She sent him a look that managed to be amused and lascivious at the same time. "I would have thought you'd just had plenty to eat."

Who knew she had such a dirty mind? He grinned at her and said, "Yes, and it was delicious.

But I think I could go for something a little more solid."

"Do you want to do takeout again?"

That would probably be for the best. Not that he was worried about being seen in public with Bellamy McAllister—just the opposite, in fact—but if they were alone together at the house, they wouldn't have to worry so much about anyone overhearing what they were saying.

"If you don't mind."

Her gray eyes twinkled. "Well, I could complain about having to stay in when I just went to all that work to put my face back together, but it's definitely better when I don't have to worry about every single word I'm saying."

Exactly what he'd just thought, so at least they were on the same page there. "Then I guess we just have to decide what we'd like to eat—and who around here does takeout."

"Just about everyone unless it's someplace really fancy," she said. "So it's more what we're in the mood for."

They decided on Thai, and Bellamy got out her phone and called in the order, since she knew the restaurant and he didn't. Not for the first time, Marc thought about how much easier it made things when you were with someone who had plenty of local area knowledge.

Not that he would have cared if she'd been as

new to the Verde Valley as he was. They could have discovered everything together.

As it stood, though, her familiarity with Sedona helped a lot, since it only took about fifteen minutes from deciding what to eat to getting back to the Airbnb with their bags of food in hand. Before they'd left, they'd set the table, so everything was waiting for them—including one of the bottles of wine they'd picked up during their winery excursion that afternoon.

He'd even found a box of candles and some candlesticks in the sideboard in the dining room, and he thought they added a nice touch. The owner of the vacation rental had told him anything in the house was fair game, so at least he didn't have to worry about using something that might turn out to be off-limits.

"I like it," she said as she sat down at the candlelit table and Marc followed suit. "I had no idea you were into the romantic stuff."

"Well, I'm not sure I'm ready to strew rose petals everywhere you walk, but my mom always had candles at dinner, so I suppose I'm just used to it."

A grin, and Bellamy lifted her glass of wine. "Then let's drink to always dining by candlelight."

He thought he could get behind that idea, so he raised his glass as well and touched it to hers. "To candlelight."

They both drank—a gorgeous red blend they'd bought at Page Springs Cellars right before they left—and then they got down to the serious business of divvying up the wontons and spring rolls, the hot and sour soup and pad thai and cashew chicken. Everything smelled great, and was about as different from the pizza they'd had the night before as you could get.

A comfortable silence fell as they took their first few bites. Usually, these sorts of moments right after being intimate for the first time had always felt awkward to him as he and his partner did their best to settle into a transformed version of their relationship. With Bellamy, though, Marc could only think again of how right this felt, as if it was all new and shiny and old and cozy at the same time.

Was this what it felt like to find your soul mate?

Maybe so. He just knew he never wanted this to end...and that he had absolutely no regrets about telling Bellamy he loved her, because he did.

And she'd said she loved him, too, the ring of truth in her voice so clear that it might as well have been the tolling of a temple bell.

"So, any strategies for tomorrow?" she asked as she dunked a wonton in the bowl of sweet and sour sauce they'd set out, and he blinked at her.

"'Tomorrow'?" he repeated, wondering if she was asking about the hike they had planned.

Her smile bordered on indulgent but wasn't quite there. "When we meet with the elders."

Oh, right. All he could do was lift his shoulders. "I suppose we just tell them everything that's happened and see what they think."

A flicker of a dimple appeared next to her mouth. "Everything?"

Several of the activities they'd just indulged in flashed through his head, and he found himself very glad that his olive complexion wouldn't allow him to blush in a highly visible way. "All right, not *everything*," he replied, and raised an eyebrow at her.

He could only imagine what his grandmother would think if she learned that he'd jumped into bed with Bellamy McAllister only a few days after meeting her. True, he was a grown man and no one in his family had any real say in his personal life, but still….

"But most of it," he said. "The voices you heard, the way you're not sure whether being here in Sedona is affecting your powers somehow."

Her expression abruptly sobered, and she reached for her glass so she could help herself to another swallow of wine. "Maybe we should try an experiment," she said, and he found his eyebrow lifting again.

"'Experiment'?"

"Well, we're both planning to go hiking tomorrow morning, right?"

He nodded.

"Then how about we swing by my place after dinner, and I can pack my hiking gear and a few other things so I can stay over here tonight? That way, I might be able to tell whether what I experienced at the ranch was a Sedona thing in general or something that's only connected to that particular property."

Marc had been hoping they'd spend the night together, so he wasn't put off at all by this suggestion. Since he hadn't slept at the Airbnb yet, he had no idea whether the Sedona energies would affect him as well, or whether this was something that seemed to be focused solely on Bellamy, for whatever reason.

"That sounds like a good idea," he said. "Because you're right—it'll help to know whether the ranch has its own powers, or whether this is all about Sedona in general."

"Or whether I imagined the whole thing."

"I don't think you did," he said, knowing how serious he sounded now. "You're not the sort of person to make up that kind of thing."

Their gazes held for a moment. Her expression was thoughtful, and he got the feeling she was glad that he hadn't discounted her concerns, hadn't tried to tell her it was all in her head the way a lot of other guys might have done.

"Okay," she said. "It's a plan."

They returned to their food, and after they were done eating and had cleaned up, they got in his truck and drove over to her place. She had a small overnight bag packed in a very short amount of time, and once again he found himself thinking how easy she was to be with—no drama, no fuss, just doing what needed to be done.

And, it seemed, more than happy to spend the night with him.

The alarm went off way too early the next morning. Bellamy opened her eyes and blinked, staring at the ceiling overhead. It was plain white drywall, not the tongue-and-groove that covered the ceiling in the main suite at the ranch, and for a second, she couldn't quite recall where she was.

But then Marc rolled over and slapped his hand on the alarm clock and she remembered everything—the way they'd come home from wine tasting yesterday and made love in this very bed, how they'd decided it would be better if she slept over…how they'd stayed up far too late, exploring one another's bodies until they passed out from sheer exhaustion.

No wonder that alarm clock going off had sounded like a fiend from hell. They'd probably gotten six hours of sleep at the most.

Marc leaned down and pressed a kiss against her temple. "How'd you sleep?"

"Just fine," she said. No strange whispers in her mind, nothing to make her think there was anything particularly different about the night that had just passed.

Well, except she and Marc Trujillo had made love. More than that, they'd declared their love for each other as well. No plans for the future yet—it felt too early for that—and still, Bellamy knew everything about her world had changed.

"Good to hear. How about some coffee, and then we can get ready to hit the trails?"

Right then, she was questioning their decision to go hiking so early. It seemed like it would have been much more fun to stay in bed and have an encore of last night's activities.

But she knew Marc really wanted to go hiking, and it wasn't as if they wouldn't have tonight to snuggle in this bed and get acquainted with each other all over again.

"Okay," she said, and pushed back the covers so she could find her panties and put them on. "Time to explore the great outdoors."

∾

Marc could see why Bellamy had chosen this hike. It cut through the Secret Mountain wilderness, traversing rocky trails that eventually led them to the aptly named Devil's Bridge, a span of natural rock that led from one side of a canyon to the other, with a dizzying drop beneath.

Good thing he wasn't afraid of heights.

Neither was Bellamy, it seemed, because she went out in front of him, sure-footed as a mountain goat. It was something of a marvel to watch her walk across the slender rock bridge, stray strands of hair bright as a new penny in the morning sun, her lightly tanned legs slim and yet sturdy at the same time as she took one step after another.

Clearly, she hadn't been lying about being an experienced hiker. Not that he'd any reason to believe she hadn't been telling him the truth when she'd said she was familiar with this trail, but he supposed he'd been wary because he'd had a couple of rough experiences in the past when a girl he'd been dating had sworn up and down that she loved to hike, only to find her practically freezing in fear the first time she had to make her way across some even slightly rocky ground.

No worries about that kind of paralysis with Bellamy, that was for sure. And she'd appeared cheerful and upbeat this morning despite the lack of sleep, which seemed to tell him that either the

Sedona vortexes had taken the night off or there had been a completely different reason why the Wilcoxes and the McAllisters had agreed all those years ago not to make the red rock city their home.

Maybe there wasn't any need to talk to the elders after all. He didn't like the idea of canceling at the last minute, but if it turned out nothing was going on here —

Bellamy froze a few feet in front of him, body stiff, hands dangling at her sides. He hurried over to her, wondering if she'd had a sudden agoraphobic episode or something. It happened sometimes, even to experienced hikers.

But when he stopped next to her and took her hand in his, he could feel how cold and clammy her skin was, how oddly nerveless her fingers appeared to be.

"Bellamy," he said, his tone urgent, "are you okay?"

She didn't even look at him. Instead, her gaze was fixed on something deeper in the canyon, although he couldn't see anything except scrub juniper and patches of cholla cactus and a few spindly cottonwood trees, their leaves fluttering languidly in the soft morning breeze.

"He's out there," she said, her voice oddly emotionless, like videos he'd seen of people speaking while hypnotized.

"Who's out there?" he asked. Her blank tone and expression were jarring, considering how animated she usually was, but he did his best to sound reassuring, calm.

Behind her sunglasses, her eyes closed, then slowly opened again. "The voices are trying to tell me."

"What voices?" he said. It occurred to him that he should have encouraged her to keep moving, that trying to hold a conversation while standing in the center of a narrow, rocky bridge wasn't the smartest thing to do.

Unfortunately, she seemed rooted in place, and he wasn't sure how she would react if he tried to gently urge her along.

If they lost their balance, it would be a *very* long drop to the ground below.

"The voices you heard at the ranch the other night?" he asked, and at least she nodded.

"Yes. The voices on the wind are trying to tell me he's out there."

The sun beating down on them was already hot, even though the hour had barely inched past seven-thirty, but right then, Marc thought he might as well have been dunked in a tub of ice water.

"Who's out there?" he asked again, trying not to sound overly urgent so he wouldn't upset her. She seemed to be in thrall to the voices she heard on the wind—well, more like a breeze, just enough to play with the ends of her hair as she stood there on the stone bridge—and he didn't want to do anything that might make her react violently.

"The Collector," she replied, then pulled in an odd, hitching breath, almost as if she had something caught in her throat.

The Collector? Who the hell was that?

But then she blinked, and gave him a curious glance. "Marc, what the hell are we doing standing in the middle of the Devil's Bridge? We should keep going—this really isn't kind of place where we want to be hanging out and having a chat."

No kidding. "You don't remember what just happened?"

Her russet brows drew together. "No…what are you talking about?"

"We can discuss it once we're off this bridge."

She seemed to realize that was the only sensible thing to do, because she nodded, even as she still looked confused.

"Okay. Let's get going."

Tricia McAllister sent Bellamy a worried look.

"You really don't remember anything that happened?"

They were all sitting in the living room at Tricia's house—Levi and Allegra and Tricia, the three elders, with Marc and Bellamy close to each other on the couch as he held her hand. She was glad of the contact, glad how he felt so real, so reassuring, because that whole episode on the Devil's Bridge had scared the living shit out of her.

Never in her life had she had anything like that happen. When she'd heard the voices the other night while standing on the patio at the ranch house, the experience had been somewhat unsettling, but she'd still remembered who she was and what she was doing.

Today, though…today it was as if the voices had put her in some kind of a goddamn trance.

"Nothing," she replied. "I mean, I remember going hiking with Marc, and I remember starting to walk across the bridge, but after that, everything just went…dark…for a few minutes."

"It was frightening," he put in. "It felt like she'd completely checked out."

"But she spoke to you."

Marc nodded, and his fingers tightened on Bellamy's. "Yes, she answered me when I asked her a question. She said the voices on the wind were trying to tell her that the Collector was out there."

The three elders exchanged worried glances.

"Have you ever heard of someone like that, Levi?" Tricia asked, and he shook his blond head, which now showed a few strands of silver.

Odd to think that he was aging like a regular person, even though he'd always said his body was just as human as anyone else's. Still, this was the first time Bellamy truly understood that Levi's claims of mortality had been the simple truth.

"Not that I can recall," he said. "Not in this world…or the one I came from."

Allegra's sparse brows drew together. Her pupils looked oddly dilated, and Bellamy wondered if that was an after-effect from her visit to the ophthalmologist the day before.

"I've never heard of such a person, either," she said. "This is…concerning."

That was one word for it. Bellamy thought the "Collector" must be someone pretty scary, or she didn't think the voices on the wind would have been trying so hard to warn her about him.

"But you say nothing happened at Marc's Airbnb the night before?" Tricia asked then.

Color flushed Bellamy's cheeks, even as she thought, *Well, I wouldn't exactly call it 'nothing.'*

However, she knew that wasn't what Marc's grandmother had meant. She guessed this must be pretty embarrassing for him, to all but come right out and say they were sleeping together, but she supposed he was a big boy and could handle whatever he needed to. Besides, he was obviously single, and so was she, and if two consenting witch-kind decided to get together, then it was nobody's business but their own.

"No," she said. "Everything was quiet. I didn't hear any voices, or have any bad dreams, or anything like that."

For a moment, the three elders didn't say anything. Levi looked particularly thoughtful, though, so Bellamy wasn't too surprised to hear him speak first.

"Are there any maps of the vortexes in Sedona?"

"There must be," Tricia replied. "They're a big draw for the tourists. Why?"

"Because if Sedona energy is involved in all this—I'm not saying it is for sure, but that's the only theory we have to work with right now—then it's possible Bellamy heard the voices out on the Devil's Bridge because there's a strong vortex in that area," Levi replied. "Likewise, it could be that the property where the Airbnb is located is relatively quiescent. We'll need to do more research to be sure."

In a way, those words felt oddly comforting to Bellamy. If something outside her was trying to reach out and communicate, to use her magical power of harmony with the winds to send an important message, then she sort of liked the idea that she'd gotten hit so hard out on the Devil's Bridge because the vortex energy in that area was insanely strong. True, she'd never heard of the vortexes sending people into a trance, but their effects did tend to vary from person to person.

"Let me get my laptop," Tricia said, rising from her chair. "I should be able to find something online."

"How did you feel after you got back to the house?" Allegra asked then, probably thinking she should do something to fill the awkward silence that had fallen after Tricia left the room.

"Fine," Bellamy replied at once. "I mean, I was a little tired from the hike, but after I took a shower and had something to eat, I was ready to get going."

Marc gently released her hand, saying, "I asked her the same thing. Once we were away from the Devil's Bridge area, she seemed fine."

"I *am* fine," Bellamy told him, then returned her gaze to the two elders. "I'm not going to lie—the whole thing was a little creepy. But it's not as if I've had weird voices in my head ever since or anything like that."

That wasn't to say she hadn't been on edge the whole time, wondering if those strange whispers were going to start up again. If, as Levi had postulated, the Airbnb sat on neutral ground, they wouldn't have been able to reach her there, and once she and Marc had left Sedona to drive over to Cottonwood, she would have been well out of range of the vortexes and any influence they might have on her.

Small blessings, she supposed.

"Here we go," Tricia said as she came back into the living room. She set her laptop down on the coffee table and then opened it, showing that she'd already found an online map of the various vortexes in the Sedona area. "There's a huge one in Boynton Canyon—"

"But we had lunch at Enchantment yesterday morning and nothing happened," Bellamy protested.

"True," Levi said. "You were in a public place, though, and often, the mere presence of others can be enough to protect you from those sorts of forces."

Maybe that was something of an explanation. Still....

"Boynton Canyon is more than a mile from the Devil's Bridge," she pointed out. "How much area does one vortex cover?"

The three elders looked at one another. Tricia inclined her head toward Levi, as if to let him know he should be the one to answer.

Maybe he'd studied the vortexes. Although Bellamy had spent plenty of time at their house when she was hanging out with Bree, it wasn't as if she'd ever felt the need to sit down and have a scholarly talk with her friend's father about the Sedona vortex situation, so she had no idea how much he actually knew.

"It depends on the vortex," he said. "Some are quite large, while others are smaller." He paused there to study the map on the laptop's screen. "This only shows the largest vortexes, the ones that attract tourists and hikers. That doesn't mean the area isn't dotted with more."

"Which means we should maybe find an expert on them?" Marc suggested. "Someone who's really studied them and knows a lot more than the publicly available information shows?"

This sounded like a great idea to Bellamy. Surely there must be someone who'd made the vortexes their life's work and would be able to offer a lot more in-depth details about their exact locations.

However, none of the elders looked too thrilled by that prospect.

"Reaching out to a civilian could open a whole new can of worms," Tricia said, both her tone and her expression doubtful. "They'd certainly want to know why you were asking for such detailed information."

"Then I'll lie," Bellamy responded, crossing her arms.

Did they think she was some stupid kid who

didn't know how to be circumspect around a civilian? She was twenty-two years old, not twelve.

Come to think of it, even her twelve-year-old self would have known not to let any information like that slip out around a nonmagical person.

"Bellamy's right," Marc said, his voice warm, reassuring. It felt so good to have him sitting there next to her, to know that he didn't think she was crazy…and that he'd help her do whatever was needed so they could get to the bottom of all this. "We don't have to be entirely honest about why we want this information. Heck, we could just tell the guy we wanted to find someplace that was super-energetic for us to have our wedding ceremony or something."

Had he really just said that? Sure, he'd told her he loved her but….

It's just a story we can use to tell the vortex expert, Bellamy reminded herself. *It's not as if he actually asked me to marry him or anything.*

Her inner voice didn't sound very convinced, though. In the witch clans, once you realized you had this sort of connection to a person, you generally made it formal sooner rather than later.

Well, she could worry about that after they'd dealt with their more immediately pressing matters.

Surprisingly, none of the elders looked too put out by Marc's suggestion.

"It's true that lots of people go to Sedona to get married," Allegra said.

"And it's also true there are plenty of woo-woo types who want to make sure their vows are in harmony with the universe, or whatever," Tricia put in. "So I don't think anyone will ask too many questions. No, the hardest part will be finding someone who knows what they're doing and isn't a complete crackpot."

Levi smiled. "I can manage that part. Let me do a little research, and then we can see how to proceed from there."

"And this 'Collector' person?" Marc asked then.

"I'll talk to Connor and Angela and see if they've ever heard of anyone like that," Tricia replied. "As *prima* and *primus,* they have access to information that even we elders don't."

"And possibly the de la Paz *prima* as well," Allegra suggested. "She has a huge library of magical books her clan has collected over the years. There might be something in one of those volumes that could provide some information."

Right. Bellamy slipped a sideways glance at Marc, but he only nodded, as if he thought reaching out to his clan's *prima* seemed a logical thing to do, considering she was sitting on a repository of knowledge unmatched among the witch clans of the Southwest.

A ringing sound came from Tricia's laptop, and she pulled it toward her, frowning slightly.

"I'm getting a FaceTime call."

"Well, go ahead and answer," Levi told her. "It could be important."

Brows still pulled together, she touched a button to accept the call. From where she was sitting, Bellamy couldn't see much of the screen, but she caught a glimpse of a dark-haired Hispanic woman in her middle forties, heavy dark hair pulled away from her face into a thick pony-tail that fell over one shoulder.

"Hi, Tricia," the woman said, and even though the words were casual enough, her strained tone was anything but. "This is Zoe Sandoval. I thought I should reach out and let you know that someone just tried to break into my library."

12

Marc's first reaction to his *prima's* words was utter shock…but then he did his best to reassure himself by recalling that Zoe had said "tried to."

So…all those magical books and grimoires were still safe?

"But you're all right?" Tricia asked, even as Levi and Allegra scooched closer to her so they could also see the de la Paz *prima.*

"I'm fine," Zoe replied, and now she sounded more irritated than anything else. "They didn't get in. The books are safe. But I thought I should give you a head's up that there's a rogue witch or warlock out there who's decided it's a good idea to help themselves to some magical goodies."

Next to him on the couch, Bellamy shifted positions, her expression almost nervous. Marc thought he could see why—he highly doubted that Connor and Angela had told Zoe about the amulet, figuring it was safe and McAllister clan business, nothing that the de la Pazes needed to worry about.

Clearly, though, it was. Or rather, he had a feeling the attempted thefts must be connected.

The work of the Collector?

Why else would the wind have been whispering at Bellamy, warning her about that very person?

"Did you see who it was?" Levi inquired.

At once, Zoe shook her head. "No. This was more a magical attack on the wards we have set up, someone trying to brute-force their way past them. Luckily, they held—I and the other witches and warlocks who set them up worked really hard to make them as strong as possible, and I have a feeling this person, whoever they are, wasn't expecting them to be that tough."

Had the Collector…if that was who they were really dealing with…somehow learned about the way the books had been pilfered from the de la Paz clan before and thought the grimoires must be an easy target?

Well, they'd just learned the hard way that his clan wasn't about to get caught with their pants down again.

"We also had someone try to steal an artifact

from us," Levi said, his tone precise, controlled, as if he hoped by speaking carefully that he might be able to defuse some of the tension in the situation.

"'Artifact'?" Zoe repeated, voice sharpening. "What kind of artifact?"

The elders looked at each other, and once again, Marc got the impression they would have preferred to keep this information within their clan.

However, if someone was going around trying to steal any magically charged objects that weren't nailed down, then it sure felt as if it was time for the Arizona clans to close ranks and protect everyone against the interloper.

"An amulet," Tricia said. "Something that was brought to us out of the past by one of our clan members. It strengthens the magical gift of anyone who holds it, so you can see why it might be a target."

"Like Hayley's talent?" Zoe asked, voice still far too sharp. Most of the time, Marc thought her the most laid-back *prima* he'd ever heard of, even more casual than Angela, but clearly, she was disturbed by this information.

And he wondered, not for the first time, exactly how Zoe felt about Hayley McAllister. Sure, all that had happened more than twenty-five years ago, and yet, once upon a time, Zoe had summoned Levi to this plane when she was desperate and sure her consort search had gone completely sideways. She'd been happily married to her husband Evan ever since then, but did she ever feel a twinge when she thought about Levi, about what might have happened if Evan hadn't turned out to be her soul mate?

Well, whatever Zoe's feelings on the subject might be, Marc doubted he had the guts to come right out and ask her. Some topics were better left alone.

"More or less," Levi said. "I'll admit we haven't done many tests with the amulet to determine the exact scope of its powers. Angela and Connor both thought it safer to keep it locked up."

"But someone tried to steal it."

"They did," he replied, his voice still calm, soothing. "They didn't succeed, however."

He stopped there, and Marc wondered if he was going to confess that the thief had managed to break into the *prima's* house. Sure, the wards had prevented him—or her—from removing the safe and its precious contents from the premises, but the incident had still proved that their magical defenses weren't quite as impregnable as they thought.

"I suppose that's something," Zoe said. She paused there for a moment, expression more troubled than ever. "We'll all need to be on high alert until we find the person responsible. Any other valuable artifacts lying around that I should know about?"

Her dry tone seemed to suggest she wasn't too thrilled with the McAllisters for keeping such an important matter from her. Although Marc was sympathetic, he also knew that whatever information the Arizona clans shared amongst themselves —or with the Castillos in New Mexico, since their *prima* was Angela's younger daughter—was done purely out of mutual understanding and not because there was some sort of formal treaty or other agreement in place that might compel them to do so.

"No, only the amulet," Tricia said. Her tone was very businesslike, and Marc had the feeling she was doing what she could to defuse the situation. "Or at least, that's the only one we know of. But I have to believe if any McAllister had stumbled across something powerful, they would have let us or Angela know about it."

Wishful thinking? Marc didn't want to think so, mainly because everything he'd seen or heard from the McAllister clan seemed to suggest they were forthright people, not the kind who would keep secrets from others.

Especially if those secrets might turn out to be dangerous.

Zoe seemed to take Tricia's words at face

value, because something about the tense set of her shoulders appeared to relax a little, and although she didn't allow herself to lean against the back of her office chair, she also didn't seem to be sitting so rigidly upright.

"I suppose that's something," she said. "None of my security cameras caught the person who tried to break in, so either they have the power of invisibility in their bag of tricks, or they have some kind of other talent that can interfere with technology. You'll need to be really on your guard."

Next to him, Bellamy pressed her lips together, looking even more troubled. Marc, on the other hand, wasn't too surprised by his *prima's* revelation. After all, it seemed as if Connor and Angela had a pretty sophisticated security system in place at their house, and yet the thief appeared to have bypassed it without any trouble.

"We're definitely on our guard," Levi said. "And we'll pass this information along to Marie Begonie and Lucas Wilcox as well, since they're the ones who keep an eye on things in the Wilcox clan when Connor's here in Jerome."

Right—the Wilcoxes didn't have elders the way the McAllisters did, or even like the de la Paz clan had had in place for generations. True, Marc's clan wasn't quite as formal about it, but every de la Paz *prima* had a group of experienced witches and warlocks from within the family whom she could consult when her own experience and intuition failed her.

"I suppose that's all any of us can do," Zoe replied. She hesitated for a moment, then said, "I'll keep you posted if anything else happens. Have a good one."

The FaceTime call ended there, and the elders looked over at Bellamy, who once again shifted uncomfortably on the sofa.

"I think you had better call in to work," Tricia said gently, and at once Bellamy's brows drew together.

"I started less than a month ago," she protested. "Do you want my manager to think I'm a total flake?"

Levi suddenly looked very stern, an abrupt change from the pleasant expression he usually wore. "Clan business supersedes any outside work," he told her. "You know that."

Everyone in all the witch clans knew that—it was part of the reason why so many of them owned their own businesses or worked as independent contractors. While they did their best to function in the modern world, if something major was going down with their family, they knew they had to put all other considerations aside and focus on that.

And even though Bellamy's chin was stubbornly set, Marc could tell she'd realized she was on the losing side of the argument here. If your clan elders told you to do something—well, as long as it wasn't illegal—then you did as they said.

Even if it meant pissing off your manager.

"Fine," she said, although her tone indicated it was anything but fine. "I really don't see the point, though. It's not as if this Collector person is going to come barging into Sedona Vines or something."

"No," Levi replied, his mouth twitching just the slightest bit. "But I need you available if I do manage to find someone who can help guide you to Sedona's more powerful, hidden vortexes. If you're able to hear the voices better when you're standing in one, it just makes sense that you should be there to see if you can find out more about the witch or warlock who seems so bent on taking our valuable artifacts away from us."

For a second or two, Bellamy didn't respond. Marc could almost see her turning the various arguments over in her head, trying to decide if any of them would have any effect on Levi or the rest of the elders.

"I'll call him," she said. "But only once we're done here."

"Oh, we're done," Tricia said. "We have Zoe's warning to keep in mind, and Levi has some research to do. At this point, we're in sort of a holding pattern."

The mutinous set to Bellamy's jaw signaled she thought there shouldn't be any reason why she couldn't go into work if all they were doing was sitting around and waiting. But Marc thought he saw his grandmother's point—maybe they didn't have anything concrete to go on right now, and yet if Levi found the vortex expert they needed, it would have looked even worse for her to have to drop everything in the middle of her shift and disappear.

"Then I suppose we'll head back to Sedona and wait," she said, and got up abruptly from the couch, slipping her purse over one shoulder as she rose. "Marc, let's go."

He wasn't about to argue, not when she sounded like that. Most of the time, she seemed like the most easygoing person in the world, but everyone had their limit and he supposed she'd just hit hers.

"We'll wait for your call," he told Levi, and the elder inclined his head.

"Hopefully soon."

Tricia and Allegra both murmured goodbyes, clearly wanting to be polite without setting Bellamy off any further. Once they were safely inside the cab of his truck and pulling away from the curb—in general, Marc liked to drive manually when he could, but this time he thought it was probably a better idea to let the vehicle take over—Bellamy let out a huff of a breath.

"It's like they don't even realize that I just started this job a month ago," she said as she fished around in her oversized bag to locate her phone. "I mean, sure, if I fell and broke my leg or came down with bubonic plague, I probably wouldn't get too much grief for calling in. But some vague 'family business' kind of bullshit?"

"Is your manager really that much of a hard-ass?" Marc asked, and she sighed again.

"Not really. Or at least, I've never run into a situation where I've seen him come down on someone at work. Then again, it's not like any of us has given him a reason, either."

She stopped there, phone in her hand, and stared down at it for a long moment.

Then she said, "Okay, let's get this over with."

The phone rang twice, three times, and Bellamy found herself hoping it would roll over to voice-mail. Sure, that was a chickenshit way of getting out of her shift at the last minute, but at least then she wouldn't have to find out right away whether Jack Hardy, her supervisor, had a short fuse or not.

But then he picked up, saying, "Hey, Bellamy. What's up?"

He didn't sound upset or suspicious, which she supposed was a good thing. Still, there wasn't any easy way to do what she needed to do.

"Hi, Jack. I hate to do this, but I've had some urgent family business come up and I won't be able to come in to work today."

A surprised pause on the other end. Then he said, "Is everything okay?"

Probably not. She said, "Um…I'm fine. But my family really needs me. Hopefully, it won't be too busy today."

As soon as those words were out of her mouth, she wanted to wince. True, Tuesdays and Wednesdays tended to be pretty slow at Sedona Vines, but it was never a good idea to suggest that you might be wishing for a quiet day when those were the times when the wine shop barely broke even.

However, Jack didn't seem to notice, or maybe he'd just decided it was better not to call her out on the comment. "It'll be fine. Marcy was saying she wanted some more hours, so I'll get in touch and see if she can come in today."

Marcy Phillips only worked part-time because she was getting her enology certification at Yavapai Community College, just as Bellamy had. However, she probably had enough wiggle room in her schedule that she could take Bellamy's shift today.

"Oh, that's good," she replied.

"Should I see if she can come in tomorrow, too?"

As much as Bellamy wanted to say no, that everything should be handled today, she had no way of knowing if that was even the truth. It might take Levi longer to find the vortex expert than he'd expected, or it was possible that even if she was directed to the exact right spot to communicate with her voices, they might send her down a rabbit hole that would consume a huge amount of her time.

Either way, it seemed as if she should be cautious here.

"That's probably a good idea," Bellamy replied. "But if this is going to take any longer than that, I'll let you know."

"Okay. Keep in touch."

He ended the call there—presumably so he could reach out to Marcy—and Bellamy returned her phone to her purse. By that point, they were down the hill and driving through Cottonwood, and she had to admit she felt a little better now that she had the dreaded call over with.

"That sounded like it went okay," Marc ventured, and she nodded.

"Yes, Jack seemed cool with it. And I'm taking

tomorrow off, too, so with any luck, we'll have all this handled by then."

"Good." He was silent for a moment. "It's almost noon—do you want to grab some lunch somewhere?"

Her stomach had been so knotted during the conversation with the elders that food was about the last thing on her mind, but she realized now that she was hungry. They'd each had a breakfast bar while they were hiking out to the Devil's Bridge, and she knew that wasn't enough to hold her until dinner.

Not even close.

"Maybe we should have stopped in Cotton-wood," she said.

That ship had sailed, though, since they were well past Old Town and heading toward 89A. Yes, she supposed they could have turned around, but then another idea occurred to her.

"We can go to Cornville."

Marc hadn't been driving, but he'd still had his eyes on the road, keeping watch in case anything cropped up that might require him to take over from the truck and steer manually. Now, though, he looked over at her, expression one of faint surprise.

"Where's that?" he asked.

She couldn't help smiling. Yes, his mom's side of the family might have come from Jerome, but she got the feeling they hadn't done a whole lot of exploring in the Verde Valley when they'd traveled here to visit the grandparents and instead had gone straight to the place where his mother had grown up.

"It's a little town sort of on the other end of Page Springs Road," she said. "When we get to the intersection with 89-A, just keep going straight instead of turning left to go back to Sedona."

"And what's in Cornville?"

"Some of the best burgers you've ever eaten," Bellamy replied. "I don't know about you, but after that hike this morning, I'm starving."

"So am I," Marc admitted. He looked pleased at the prospect of some solid food, and who could blame him?

This had been a rough morning no matter how you looked at it.

They passed the highway and drove past the planned community of Verde Santa Fe, and then wound down into the river bottom where Cornville was located. It was a small town of only a few thousand residents, but it did have a couple of hidden treasures.

Including G Burgers, their current destination.

Because it wasn't quite noon yet, the parking lot wasn't too crowded. They headed inside and walked up to the counter to place their orders, then went off to one side to wait for their food to be ready.

"We can sit outside," she suggested.

"It's still pretty hot today," he pointed out.

Only the truth, although she thought it was probably going to be a few degrees cooler than yesterday.

"Yes," she said, "but most people are going to stay inside and enjoy the air conditioning, which means we'll have more privacy on the patio."

An eyebrow lifted, but he seemed to see the wisdom of her suggestion, because he replied, "That makes sense."

The cooks at G Burgers were fast, so they only had to wait a couple of minutes for their food to be ready before they headed outside. Calling the outdoor dining area a patio was probably a stretch, since it was just a slab of concrete with some shade overhead and a few metal tables with matching chairs, but since no one else was out there, she thought it was the best place to eat their lunch.

She waited until they'd both had a few bites of their burgers and washed them down with iced tea before she said, "Do you really think some vortex guy is going to help with all this?"

"The mythical vortex expert?" Marc returned with a lopsided grin.

Since she'd thought about the same thing, she

couldn't help smiling in return. "Well, Levi seems to think he can find someone like that, so I suppose we have to trust his intuition. Still, even if that kind of expert does exist, I'm not sure whether he'll really be able to help with our particular problem."

Marc dunked a fry in the little paper cup of ketchup that sat on the tray in front of him, his expression now thoughtful. "I don't know. I mean, Levi does have a point. If you can find a vortex that's powerful but also isn't overrun with tourists, that might give you a chance to let the voices speak to you."

"If I should even be listening to them," she said sourly. "For all I know, they're some kind of weird magic this Collector person is using to put me off my stride."

Judging by the way Marc's brows pulled together, Bellamy could tell he hadn't considered that particular angle to the problem.

"Maybe," he allowed. "On the other hand, you'd think the last thing the Collector would want you to know is any particular details about him. It's pretty obvious that he's trying to operate in stealth, to slip in and take what he wants without anyone knowing who he is or what he's up to."

Marc had a point there. Bellamy supposed she might have been thinking precisely the opposite because she wanted a reason to avoid exploring this any further, to take a step back and say she didn't think it was such a good idea after all to listen to the voices.

Ever since her gift had manifested when she was eleven, it had been reliable and simple and, she thought, kind of boring. It wasn't as if she could call a tornado into being or make it rain or do any of the stuff a real weather witch could do. No, she could summon some serious straight-line winds when necessary—like she'd done when a brush fire was threatening some homes on one of Jerome's lower levels and she'd made the winds reverse direction and have the fire double back on itself, effectively putting it out—but it had never done anything terribly out of the ordinary.

Until now.

And if she could blame the vortexes for this sudden shift in her abilities, well, then, that had an easy enough solution.

She'd just get the hell out and go back some-place neutral and safe, like Jerome or Cottonwood.

Except that she had an agreement with Ike to watch the ranch until it was sold, which could take months. The money wasn't a huge amount, just two grand a month, but when you added that to the free housing and the stipend she got from the McAllister clan, well, it would definitely be enough to keep her going if it turned out she had to take too much time off and annoyed her boss enough that he had no choice but to let her go.

Marc reached over and laid a hand on her knee. "It's going to be okay."

"Was I being that obvious?"

He smiled. "Let's just say that I could tell you were thinking deep thoughts."

She supposed she was. While she wasn't the sort of person who tended to fall into a doom spiral, she also had to admit that she'd never encountered this sort of situation before. Witchy talents were supposed to be what they were, not start morphing into something very different.

Something frightening…something she wasn't sure she could control.

"I guess it feels like I don't know myself anymore," she said. "Have you ever heard of someone's witchy gifts suddenly turning into something else?"

"No," he replied at once. "But then, it's not like I've made a study of those sorts of things, either. There's one thing I've noticed, though… and my *prima* has, too."

"What's that?" Bellamy inquired, glad to focus on something outside herself for a bit. No one else had come to join them on the patio, probably because it was pretty toasty today and she could already feel sweat beginning to drip down her back.

And because they were alone, that meant she and Marc wouldn't have to watch what they were saying.

"My main talent is the dreams," he said. "I inherited that gift from my mother. But I also got some of my father's magic as well."

"Which is…?"

"I can do this," he said.

For the briefest second, an odd little bubble of light surrounded him before it winked out of existence once more.

"Pretty," Bellamy commented. "But what does it do?"

"It protects me from magic and physical objects," he said. "Me, and anyone who's inside the bubble with me. The field my father can generate is larger, but still, my gifts doubled up because I got them from both sides of my family. And we've seen some of the same things in other people whose parents are from two different witch clans."

"Like my friend Devynn," Bellamy said softly. "Her father's gift is being able to hide his witch nature, and her mother can give herself an extra five minutes whenever she wants it. Devynn's time-travel talent is a little different, but still, she got it double barrels."

Marc nodded, then took a bite of his mushroom swiss burger. Once he was done chewing, he said, "It's not always consistent—there are people in my clan whose parents came from two different witch families and they still only got a talent that doesn't have any relation to their mother and father's gifts—but it does seem to happen at least half the time. That's why I think the way our clans have started to commingle is changing us somehow."

Something about that statement felt vaguely ominous to Bellamy, although she had to admit that having two witchy gifts had to be beneficial from an evolutionary standpoint if nothing else.

Not that she would know. She had only the one because the egg that had helped create her had come from a regular woman, not a witch.

And honestly, right now her one and only talent was causing enough problems. Bellamy wasn't sure what she would do if she had to deal with more than that.

"Is this something Zoe has talked to Angela and Connor about?" she asked, and Marc shrugged.

"I don't know. I suppose it's more of an interesting side effect than anything else." A pause as his gaze met hers, and the corners of his mouth lifted slightly. "It's not like I think it's going to stop anyone in the Arizona witch families from looking for a partner outside their clan if they haven't found the right one yet."

His tone was casual enough, and yet Bellamy couldn't hold back a small thrill of anticipation nonetheless. They were from two different clans and yet had declared their love for each other anyway. Thirty years ago, this would all have been unthinkable, but now it was just part of the way things were.

She supposed the real question was what they planned to do about it.

"No, I guess not," she said with an answering smile.

He opened his mouth, as though he intended to reply, but then a couple of guys in T-shirts printed with the logo of a local construction company came outside and took the other empty table, and that seemed to be that, at least as far as any confidential witchy conversations went.

Without missing a beat, Marc made a comment about which trail they should hike tomorrow morning, and they went on to a discussion about whether they should head back to the Secret Canyon wilderness, or whether they might want to drive down to the Village of Oak Creek and explore Bell Rock. All totally innocuous, the sort of conversation anyone in the area might have, and it was clear the newcomers had absolutely no interest in it, since they launched into a discussion about whether the countertops that had been ordered for their current job would actually show up today or whether the supplier down in Phoenix would find some way to stall again.

Since she and Marc had already paid for their meal up front, all they had to do was drop their trays back inside after they'd disposed of their trash in the bin helpfully placed near the door.

"My place, or back to the ranch?" he asked as they climbed into his truck.

Maybe it would have been smarter to go to the ranch, just to see if she picked up on any vibes there. But because they might be doing some experimenting along those lines very soon, Bellamy thought she'd be happy to put that off for as long as possible.

"Your place," she said promptly, and sent him a smile. "I can think of a few things we can do while we're waiting to hear from Levi."

"Say no more," Marc replied with a grin.

With any luck, she'd be able to forget all about this for a few hours.

13

THEY'D JUST EMERGED FROM THE SHOWER IN the Airbnb's main suite—all that activity in the bedroom had made them sweaty despite the air conditioning—when Bellamy's cell phone rang from inside her purse.

"I'd better get that," she said, pulling her towel more tightly around her as she hurried over to grab the phone.

Marc watched as she picked it up and said, "Hello?" A pause, and then she replied, "Oh, hi, Levi. What've you got for us?" Another pause, longer this time. "Let me get a pen," she said, and then gestured frantically at Marc.

Was there even a pen in the bedroom? He didn't know for sure, but a moment's rummaging in the nightstands didn't turn up anything. A shake of his head to let her know that a pen didn't seem to be handy, and she spoke again.

"Let me go into the kitchen to find something to write with. The hazards of being in a house that isn't yours."

She chuckled slightly, and Marc had to admit she was playing it pretty cool. Based on what she'd just said, it would be impossible to know for sure whether she was at the ranch…or over at his vacation rental.

Then she headed into the kitchen, where he knew for a fact there were a couple of pens in the "everything" drawer near the fridge. He followed a pace or two behind, then hurried over to the drawer so he could extract one of the pens in question, along with a small notepad.

Bellamy shot him a grateful smile as he set them down on the countertop for her, then picked up the pen.

"Okay, I'm ready." Another of those pauses while Levi spoke, and she responded, "Clint Greaves. Got it."

Mr. Greaves, Marc assumed, was the vortex specialist. What else could he be with a name like that?

"And he's expecting my call?" Bellamy asked next. A few seconds of silence as she listened to Levi's answer, and then she said, "Okay, we'll call him right away. Thanks." She touched her finger to the screen to end the call and looked over at Marc. "Well, he found our guy. Or at least, he found someone he thinks can help us."

"Then I guess we should get in contact," he replied, even though he figured that was what she already planned to do next.

"On it," she said, then opened the keypad on her phone so she could type in the number she'd written down a moment earlier. "Mr. Greaves? Hi, I'm Bellamy McAllister and—"

She stopped there as though she'd been cut off. Her mouth pursed, but it seemed she was making herself listen to the person on the other end even though she didn't appear to be too happy about being interrupted.

"Okay," she said at length. "We'll meet you there in fifteen minutes."

And she ended the call and looked over at Marc.

"He wants to meet us at Crescent Moon Ranch," she told him, and he found himself frowning.

"Where's that?"

"Down by Red Rock Crossing," she replied. "It's a park owned by the Forest Service. Kind of popular, so I'm surprised Mr. Greaves wants to meet there. I would have assumed he'd have something more private in mind."

"And there's a vortex at this Crescent Moon Ranch?"

She shrugged. "I think I might have seen one on the map your grandmother showed us at her house, but I can't remember for sure—I was looking more in the Secret Mountain wilderness area. Anyway, we need to get going, because it's going to take us at least ten minutes to drive over there."

That seemed to decide things. Bellamy hurried into the bedroom and grabbed her purse so she could stow her phone inside, and then they both went into the garage and climbed into his truck before heading over to their meeting place. Since Marc didn't know exactly where he was going, he just told the nav, "Crescent Moon Ranch, Sedona," and the vehicle headed out of the neighborhood where his Airbnb was located and down to the main drag without any hesitation.

As Bellamy had warned him, their drive took most of the fifteen minutes she'd promised on the phone, mainly because the second half of the trip wound through an area with houses on large parcels of land where the speed limit dropped to only twenty miles an hour. Eventually, though, he saw the signs directing them to Crescent Moon Ranch and Red Rock Crossing, so he took control of the truck and guided it the rest of the way.

Or rather, most of the way, since they had to

stop at a ranger shack on the way in and pay fifteen bucks for the privilege of going into the park.

"Did Mr. Greaves warn you about the fee?" Marc asked with a grin as they pulled away from the shack and into the parking lot proper.

"No," Bellamy replied, looking somewhat annoyed. "He sort of left out that part. But I'll pay you back."

"It's not a big deal."

She lifted an eyebrow, and he chuckled.

"Okay, you can buy me a drink after we're done messing around with the vortexes."

Now she cracked a little bit of a smile, telling him she probably wasn't quite as irritated as she was pretending to be.

Or maybe she was just really looking forward to that drink.

"It's a deal."

A few cars were parked here and there, not too many, which wasn't that much of a surprise, considering it was a Tuesday afternoon and late enough in the day that it was too hot to go hiking unless you planned to walk in the creek for a good part of your journey and stay cool that way. At the far end of the lot was a Jeep Wrangler probably older than Marc, with a tall, thin man standing near the driver-side door.

"You think that's him?" Bellamy murmured.

"Probably," Marc replied. "At least, he looks like he's waiting for someone, so it makes sense."

He pulled into the space next to the Wrangler and then turned off the engine. The two of them unfastened their seatbelts and got out, even as the man standing by the Jeep sent them an expectant look.

"Bellamy McAllister?" he asked her, and she nodded.

"Yes, I'm Bellamy, and this is Marc Trujillo."

Clint Greaves extended a hand. His skin was tanned and lined, his nose beaky, and he looked like someone who'd spent most of his life outside.

"I'm Clint. I hear you want to know more about vortexes."

For some reason, Marc hadn't expected the older man to put it that baldly. Then again, there wasn't anyone around to overhear what they were saying, and it was probably better to get right down to business.

He shook the man's hand, and Bellamy did the same.

"Yes," she said in reply to Clint's comment. "We were wondering if there are more vortexes here in Sedona than the ones you see on the maps online."

The other man's eyes glinted. They were bright blue, startling against his deeply tanned skin.

"Oh, there are plenty," he replied. "The stuff

you find online—that's for the tourists. But those who really know Sedona, know her well, understand that's only scratching the surface."

"And there's a vortex here?" Marc asked.

Clint nodded and swept an arm toward the creek, barely visible from the parking lot. "Pretty much all of Oak Creek is a vortex, but it's stronger in some places than others. I've got something to show you."

After delivering that remark, he opened the door of his Wrangler and pulled out what looked like one of those old-fashioned little folders schoolkids might use to hand in a report. He pulled back the cover to reveal a detailed map of Sedona with a clear plastic overlay.

That overlay was covered with bright blue starbursts, some larger, some smaller.

"Are those all vortexes?" Bellamy asked as she peered over the man's shoulder.

"Yes," Clint said. "We've been mapping them for a long time. This is the latest version—it was just updated last month." He handed the folder to her and she took it from him, eyes scanning the map and all those blue starbursts. "You can study it later, though. For now, I want to take you to the beach."

"'The beach'?" Marc echoed, a little startled. Weren't they at least three hundred miles from the nearest ocean?

Bellamy smiled. "It's a place along the Red Rock Crossing trail called Buddha Beach." She paused and looked over at Clint. "The vortex is stronger there?"

"A lot of people think so. Come on."

And he began walking toward the edge of the parking lot, where a trail wandered away into some cottonwood trees. He didn't look over his shoulder, indicating that he was going to go where he wanted and it was up to them whether they wanted to follow along.

Marc shrugged, and the two of them hurried to catch up to their guide. It was a good thing they'd dressed casually and put their hiking boots back on before they left the house, because even though the trail was relatively flat and easy enough to traverse, it was just rocky and uneven enough that it wasn't the sort of place you'd want to be wandering around in while wearing flip-flops or something similarly flimsy.

The landscape was beautiful, though, and even if it turned out that this little hike was a wild goose chase and nothing more, he wasn't sorry they'd come. In fact, he thought he'd like to return with Bellamy at some point so they could explore it on their own.

Funny how his mind was already imagining a future with her here, as if his stay at the Airbnb didn't have a fixed endpoint...and even though they hadn't made any concrete promises to one another beyond that single exchange of "I love you."

Maybe that was all they needed.

Clint didn't seem too disposed toward conversation, and definitely wasn't playing tour guide, possibly because he was waiting until they reached their destination to prove more explanations about the vortexes. Bellamy also remained silent, as if she'd decided it would be better to get to their destination and see what happened next. As beautiful as their surroundings were, they'd come here for one reason and shouldn't allow themselves to get distracted.

The trail eventually emerged into an open area where they had to traverse a span of smooth red rock, pocked here and there with little hollows that still held some rainwater from the storm two nights earlier. And beyond the red rock was the quiet murmur of the creek as they came down onto a rocky beach dotted with little cairns made of river stone.

Now Clint looked almost disapproving as he paused on the beach. "The tourists like to make those," he said as he nodded toward the stone constructions, some of them only a few inches high, some of them almost as tall as his knees. "We try to discourage it, since the whole point is not to disturb the landscape, but they keep building the damn things anyway." He paused there, his back toward a large red rock formation in the distance that Marc recognized as Cathedral Rock, even though he'd only seen it in pictures before now. "But the vortex energy is strong here, so I wanted to see how you reacted to it. No right or wrong, of course—different people experience different things."

Which was also what Bellamy had told him, that one person might feel a tingling along their skin, while someone else might experience a surge of energy and yet another would have nothing more than a deep feeling of calm, of belonging.

Marc looked around at the creek and the brilliantly green cottonwood trees and the red outlines of Cathedral Rock off in the distance, but he had to admit he didn't feel any different. Then again, this was more about Bellamy than it was about him. As far as he could tell, the vortexes hadn't affected him at all. Was that because the magic he carried inside was very different from hers, or simply because she'd spent more time in Sedona than he had?

"What is it, exactly?" Bellamy asked, gray eyes also scanning the landscape from behind her sunglasses. "The vortex energy, I mean."

"Magic," Clint said simply, and then cracked a smile that deepened the laugh lines around his eyes. "Although maybe you don't believe in magic."

Marc looked over at Bellamy, and her lips twitched in amusement.

Boy, was their vortex guide off base about that.

But since they certainly weren't free to tell him that they were both from witch families and knew all about magic, Marc stayed silent.

"I believe in a lot of things," she said, which he supposed was a good enough answer. "I guess I was just wondering if there was any kind of scientific basis for the energies people believe exist here."

Clint nodded. "That's one of the theories. Something about the composition of the red rocks and all the iron they contain creating energy fields that don't exist anywhere else in the world. I suppose that's as good an explanation as any."

Right—the distinctive reddish hues of the rock formations in Sedona came from an abundance of iron oxide, and even though other places in the world also had reddish rocks, none of them were the exact shade you found here. Marc could see why people might think the concentration of those minerals could create vortexes of unusual energy.

"Got it," Bellamy replied. She looked up at Cathedral Rock, probably still a good half mile away, and then down at the creek. "I think I should walk in the water."

"Go ahead," Clint told her. "A lot of people think that's where the energy is the strongest."

Was that such a great idea? What if she got caught up in the vortex energy like she had on the Devil's Bridge and started speaking in tongues or something?

Marc tried to tell himself it would still be fine. After all, it sure looked as if Clint had plenty of experience shepherding people through vortex areas, so it probably wouldn't be the first time he saw someone act a little crazy while caught up in the moment, thinking the vortex energy was acting on them.

And even though he knew Bellamy wasn't psychic—at least, not in the way people generally thought of such things—she seemed to guess what was passing through his mind, because she flashed him a peace sign and said, "It's cool, Marc. I'll be fine."

Smiling, she wandered down to the water's edge, then paused to pull off her hiking boots and socks. Because it was another hot day, she'd put on a pair of cargo shorts, so she didn't have to worry about rolling up her pants and getting them out of harm's way.

She walked a few feet out into the water, then stood there with her eyes closed, hands loose at her sides, as if she was doing her best to relax and let the vortex speak to her.

"Is that water very cold?" he said to Clint in an undertone.

"Oh, yeah," Clint replied. "Even at the peak of summer like we are now, it never gets much warmer than fifty-five, maybe sixty degrees. Oak Creek is fed by snow melt from up in Flagstaff."

Marc supposed he should have already known that. To be fair, he hadn't done a huge amount of research on Sedona since it was just enough of a drive from Tucson that he couldn't really count it as a day trip.

If the water really was that cold, Bellamy didn't seem to be too worried about it. She stood there silently, eyes still shut, and didn't appear to have moved at all in the last minute or so.

He wondered what she was thinking.

Damn, the water was freezing. Sure, she'd known it would be—her dads had brought her here on outings plenty of times when she was a kid, and she'd splashed and played in the creek as if it wasn't any big deal. After all, if you came here in the summer, you'd dry off plenty fast once you stood in the sun for a couple of minutes.

But she wasn't supposed to be thinking about how chilly the water was.

No, she was supposed to be trying to see if the vortex energy here was even stronger than it had been out on Devil's Bridge.

She thought she could sense it pulsing under the thin layer of reality that most people saw, almost like a slow, strong heartbeat, or maybe the rhythm of the world's biggest bass drum. It felt calm, unhurried, and in that moment, Bellamy let herself be buoyed up by its strength, by its utter belief that all was as it should be, and no one here should have any reason to give in to worry or fear.

Yes, this felt very different from the energy at the Devil's Bridge, which had been wild, almost jangly, like the winds that sometimes came from the east and brought with them warm, dry air that put everyone on edge. Even as that thought passed through her mind, though, she heard them again.

Out there….

Watching….

Waiting….

The Collector? she thought, feeling a little foolish. After all, she had no way of knowing if those voices belonged to anything that could be considered an intelligence, or whether the vortex energies were dredging them up from some hidden place in her brain.

The Collector…and others, the voices whispered, and at once, Bellamy frowned.

You mean there's more than one of them?

One Collector, the voice said, *many servants.*

Well, that didn't sound good at all.

So was it the Collector who'd tried to steal the amulet and break into the magical library at Zoe de la Paz's house, or one of his minions?

How can we know who they are? Bellamy asked.

You will know, the voices said. *You will know.*

And then they faded away. She stood there for a moment longer, but somehow she could tell that they wouldn't come back even if she called out to them.

As far as they were concerned, they'd delivered the message they needed to.

Annoyed, she opened her eyes. Marc and Clint Greaves were still standing on the bank of the creek, having some sort of low-voiced conversation, although she couldn't hear what they were saying. She could tell they'd been trying to stay quiet so they wouldn't disturb her while she was communing with the vortex energies.

Well, the voices had been clearer here, that was for sure. It seemed Clint had been right when he'd said some vortexes were stronger than others.

But even though the voices had provided

some useful information, she wasn't sure what she was supposed to do about it. So the Collector had an army of minions he summoned to do his bidding? How in the world were they supposed to fight something like that? It felt as if the people in charge in the Arizona clans were hanging on by a thread as it was.

She supposed that was something they'd need to figure out. Right now, she was a conduit for this information, nothing more. It wasn't as if she had much to offer when it came to finding the Collector's servants.

You will know, the voices had said.

Right now, she felt as if she didn't know much of anything.

But she made her way to the bank where her boots and socks waited, and picked them up so she could go over to the spot where Marc and Clint were standing. No point in putting her footwear back on until she'd given the sun a chance to dry her feet and legs.

"What did you think?" Clint asked as she approached.

"Yes, it's very strong," she said, then gave Marc a sideways glance, just enough to let him know she'd experienced something important but couldn't discuss it in front of a civilian. "I'm not sure why I haven't noticed before—I've been to this spot plenty of times."

"It could be you weren't ready until now," Clint replied calmly. "I've seen that happen before. People spend years in Sedona, and then out of nowhere, they have an awakening, a deeper understanding of themselves and the world around them. This was probably the right time."

Bellamy supposed that was one way of looking at the situation. Right now, though, she needed to think of a good excuse to get back to the truck so she could talk to Marc in private.

"Thanks for guiding us here," she said. "But we're meeting a friend in a half hour, so we should probably head back to town."

Maybe Marc's eyebrow lifted ever so slightly. However, Clint only said, "Fair enough. It's usually a good idea to step back a little after you've had your first real vortex experience. Wouldn't want you to overdose."

His tone was dry enough that Bellamy couldn't be sure whether he was joking or not. However, he hadn't tried to tell her she needed to stay out here a while longer, and that was the important thing.

"Right," she said with a smile. "But this has been…enlightening."

He tilted his head at her, a knowing glint in his clear blue eyes, as if he'd somehow guessed she'd experienced a lot more than she wanted to let on. After that, though, he led them back to the parking lot, and then paused next to his Jeep.

"That map I gave you," he said, and Bellamy nodded.

"We appreciate having it."

He made a sound that was almost but not quite a chuckle. "Sure. We always want to make them available to the true seekers." A pause, and then he added, "But if I find it online, we'll need to have a few words."

Again, she wasn't sure whether he was joking. However, since it seemed as if she needed to reassure him, just to be safe, so she quickly said, "Oh, no worries about that. We'll keep it hidden."

"See that you do."

Then he hoisted himself into his Wrangler, which seemed to be the signal that it was time for them to get in Marc's truck. Once again, Marc gave her one of those expectant glances, but he waited until they were away from the parking lot and driving on Lower Red Rock Loop as they headed back to town.

"You heard something," he said at length, and Bellamy nodded.

"I did. The voices were pretty clear this time, but I also felt clearer, too. On Devil's Bridge, it felt almost as if I went into a trance or something. Today, though, I remember every bit of what happened."

"Which was?"

Briefly, she explained how the voices had told her about the Collector's servants, how there seemed to be a whole lot of them.

"So I'm pretty sure the person who broke into Connor and Angela's house isn't the same one who tried to get into your *prima's* library," she concluded. "Which means those bastards could be all over the place."

Marc frowned, and she could tell he was less than thrilled by that piece of information. "But the voices said we should be able to tell who these servants are?"

"Well, that's what they told me," Bellamy replied. "But they didn't give me any hints as to exactly how we're supposed to manage that."

"Especially when it seems as if they're pretty damn good at evading security cameras," Marc said, brows still pulled together. He was letting the truck drive itself, which she thought was probably a good idea. Right then, he looked way too distracted to be piloting the thing on unfamiliar and curvy roads.

"Yes," she said, and didn't quite sigh. While they had a bit more information than they'd had before, the voices' message had still been pretty cryptic. "But I suppose all we can do is pass along what the voices told me and see if the elders and Connor and Angela can figure it out."

Even as she spoke, she wished she could do more. Sure, it was the responsibility of the *prima* and *primus*—and the elders—to really delve into problems like this, but at the same time, the voices had reached out to her, not them.

Which meant she should probably be doing more than just sitting back and twiddling her thumbs.

Marc reached over and took her hand, fingers warm and reassuring as they wrapped around hers. He still had his left hand ready to reach out and touch the steering wheel in case something happened with the self-driving system—even though incidents like that were few and far between these days—but it still felt good to have him make that contact, to let her know she didn't have to go through this alone.

"We'll go back to the Airbnb and look at that map Clint gave us," he said, and his voice was also comforting, calm and sounding as if not much was going to ruffle him.

And boy, did Bellamy need that, considering how rattled she felt at the moment.

Looking at the map would be a good place to start. If nothing else, they'd be able to tell if the ranch had its own vortex energy, something that had awakened a part of her powers she hadn't even known existed.

Leaning over, she pressed a kiss against Marc's cheek.

"Sounds good. And after that"—she paused and finally allowed herself the sigh she'd held back a few moments earlier—"after that, maybe we'll have a better idea of what we should do next."

14

"THERE'S DEFINITELY A VORTEX AT THE ranch," Bellamy said, one fingertip touching a small blue sunburst off Dry Creek Road. "It's not huge like the one at Red Rock Crossing or some of the others around town, but…."

"But maybe it was still enough to awaken something in you," Marc finished for her.

They'd made it back to the Airbnb without incident and now sat at the small round table in the dining area, poring over the map Clint Greaves had given them. A couple of tumblers of water sat nearby, although neither of them had been touched yet.

Bellamy's mouth pursed, and Marc got the feeling she wasn't a huge fan of that interpretation of the situation. As far as any of them were concerned, your witchy powers were supposed to be the same your entire life after they manifested when you were around ten or eleven, sometimes as late as twelve. They weren't supposed to take on new and strange dimensions over time.

But no one had really known what being exposed to the vortexes over an extended period could do to a witch or warlock. Once again, Marc wondered why those long-ago Wilcoxes and McAllisters had concluded that the area shouldn't be settled by witch-kind. From what he'd been able to tell, the two clans hadn't exactly been best friends back then, and arriving at any sort of an agreement should have been extremely difficult… if not downright impossible.

Maybe something about the energies in Sedona had frightened them, had made them realize they'd encountered a force they really couldn't control. That might have been enough to keep them away.

"I suppose so," Bellamy allowed in response to his comment, although she continued to focus on the map, nodding to herself as if what she saw confirmed suspicions she'd been harboring for a while. "And here's another vortex at the Devil's Bridge, so I suppose that explains that incident."

"It's interesting," Marc said as he stared down at the street grid of Sedona with its overlay of little blue starbursts. "There really aren't any in the main part of town, except for one at the very end of Uptown just before you head up into Oak Creek Canyon. I wonder why."

"Maybe the civilians who settled here instinctively knew they shouldn't be living right on top of a vortex," Bellamy replied. "Or maybe it's just that vortex energy concentrates in the wilder areas." She paused there, lips pursing. "I think we need to go back to the ranch."

He'd somehow known she would make that suggestion, so her comment didn't throw him off too much. "To see how the vortex there works on you?"

"Yes," she said. "And on you. It might be sort of against my agreement with Ike to have you staying there, but I know the vortex didn't work on me until I'd slept there for a night, so we need to see if it does the same thing to you."

Very scientific. Maybe he wasn't super thrilled about being a lab rat, but on the other hand, Bellamy had survived sleeping at the ranch just fine. Yes, she'd come out of it with her gifts strangely enhanced, and yet possibly that was a good thing. His prophetic gift seemed to have taken a hike the past couple of days, and if staying at the ranch might kick it into high gear so it could show him a vision of the Collector's minions, whoever they were, then that would put him and Bellamy in a much better position than they were now.

"Okay," he said easily. "Just let me pack a few things."

Was this a stupid idea? Maybe it would have been smarter to put together some camping gear and sleep under the stars by one of the other vortexes they'd seen on the map.

Problem was, none of them were located in designated camping areas. True, people camped where they weren't supposed to all the time, but Bellamy wasn't sure she wanted to get evicted by a Forest Service ranger while they were trying to see if the vortex energies worked on Marc as well.

Besides, she'd had her "awakening"—even though she kind of hated to think of it that way— at the ranch, so it just made sense to have him stay there with her.

It would sure be a hell of a lot more comfortable.

And since Ike had texted her overnight some-time, telling her he was going on a business trip to Singapore and might be kind of hard to reach for the next few days, it wasn't as if she had to worry about him showing up out of nowhere and conducting a pop inspection of the property.

"All set," Marc told her as he closed the dresser drawer where he'd stowed the clothes he'd brought along. His toiletries were already stored in the bathroom, so that part was taken care of. "Now what?"

"Well," she said with a grin, "I did tell you I owed you a drink."

His expression turned amused, although he sounded serious enough as he replied, "You don't think it'll mess with our little experiment here?"

"Of course not," she said. "I had wine that first night I heard the voices on the wind, and we drank the night before we had our hike on the Devil's Bridge. I don't think that has anything to do with it. I think we're just supposed to…sort of live our lives, I guess."

"Don't you think we should at least call my grandmother and let her know what happened at Red Rock Crossing?"

That probably made the most sense. They could tell Tricia about Bellamy's experience, and then she and Marc could go off and enjoy the rest of their afternoon.

Unfortunately, they couldn't have that drink at Sedona Vines, since she was supposed to be out dealing with a family emergency, but they'd think of something.

"Okay," she said. "Let's give her a call."

His grandmother sounded startled by what Bellamy had to relay, but she didn't ask too many questions, and only said she'd pass along what she'd heard to Angela and Connor and the other elders.

"So that's handled," Marc said as he returned the phone to his pocket. "Where should we go have a drink?"

"Here, probably," Bellamy replied, now looking a little shamefaced. "I mean, I called in to work because I'm supposedly in the middle of a family emergency. I'm not saying my boss has spies everywhere or anything like that, but a lot of people in this town know me from the wine tasting rooms and might say something if they saw me off partying hearty at the bar at Enchant-ment or whatever."

He had to admit she had a point there. And really, this was a beautiful spot...with a beautiful wine fridge.

If that drink turned into another, and they decided to have a little fun afterward, it would be a lot easier if all they had to do was walk down the hall to the bedroom.

"Sounds good," he said. "Let's go see what you've got."

Most of the stuff in the wine fridge was bottles she'd obviously bought at the local grocery stores or maybe Trader Joe's, although the closest TJ's was all the way over the mountain in Prescott. There were also a few bottles he could tell had come from local wineries, but the pinot grigio she pulled out clearly had come from Safeway.

"Is this all right?" she asked, brandishing the bottle. "I don't have too many whites from the wineries around here, but this stuff is actually pretty good."

"It'll be fine," he said.

And it was, cool and crisp and just what they needed as they sat on the patio and watched the fountain splash away in the sun. Striped lizards sat on top of the wall, clearly soaking up the rays, and the whole place felt so relaxed that it was hard for him to remember they were apparently sitting on top of a vortex here.

He didn't feel any different. But then, Bellamy also hadn't noticed any changes...well, until she heard voices whispering on the wind.

They sipped wine in silence for a moment. Then she said, "I think I could get used to this."

Was she talking about being at the ranch with him, or not having to worry about being at work?

Probably a bit of both.

"I like the idea of cocooning here," he told her. "I don't mind not going out. And we'll order in tonight, just to be safe."

"DoorDash doesn't come all the way out here," she said, but she didn't look too worried.

"Then we'll call it in and I'll go pick it up," he replied. "That way, no one will get a single glimpse of you. Sound like a plan?"

"Sounds perfect." She sipped some wine, expression almost contemplative as she watched the fountain's waters dance in the sunlight, sparkling like little diamonds as they fell from tier to tier. A hummingbird approached, wings a blur as it sipped delicately from the water before it flew off again. Without looking at him, Bellamy added, "I'm kind of annoyed the voices didn't give me any details as to what we're supposed to be looking for. Yeah, go ahead and tell me we have enemies everywhere, but then leave me to figure it out on my own."

"You're not on your own," Marc said. For a second, their gazes met, and her lips curved into a partial smile, one of acknowledgment. "I'm here, and the elders know what's going on, so we'll all work on this together. And everyone knows they need to stay vigilant, so I don't think there'll be any repeats of what happened at Connor and Angela's house…or at my *prima's*."

Or at least, he assumed everyone in their various clans knew to be careful. He'd had a text show up on his phone not long after Zoe's phone call to the McAllister elders, telling everyone in the de la Paz clan that there had been an attempted break-in at her house and that they needed to be watchful in case something like that occurred again. And although Bellamy hadn't mentioned it, he had to assume Angela had probably done the same thing for her own clan.

An assumption Bellamy confirmed a moment later, since she said, "Yes, Angela posted in the group chat that there'd been some shenanigans and people should be extra vigilant. And then my dads messaged me a little bit after that, wanting to make sure I was okay. I told them I was, but…." The words trailed off, and she helped herself to a swallow of pinot grigio. "They're worried, and I get it. They don't like that this is happening right after their baby girl left the nest. Problem is, I don't think there's anything they can do to help. My dad Jordan is a civilian, and my dad Kirby is a pretty strong warlock, but his gift is finding things, which I don't think is going to help much in this particular situation."

Probably not. If the amulet—or the grimoires in Zoe's library in Scottsdale—had actually been stolen, then maybe Kirby could have helped track them down.

Determining the identities of the thieves involved?

Not so much.

"Well, I understand why they'd be concerned," Marc said. "A lot of this would be frightening enough on its own without also worrying that their only daughter is out of the house for the first time."

Once again, Bellamy's clear gray eyes caught his, and held. A secretive little smile played around her mouth as she replied, "Except that I'm not *exactly* living on my own right now, am I?"

Officially, she was supposed to be. But he would be staying here tonight, and he guessed she'd want him to stay the next night as well. After that?

He supposed he'd have to see what happened next, but with the ranch's owner out of the country and no one checking on what she was up to, Marc thought it didn't make much sense for him to keep paying for the Airbnb if he wasn't even using it.

Well, they could figure that out later. It wasn't as if he was hurting for cash or anything close to it.

"I guess not," he said. "And I think I like playing house with you."

Her eyes glinted, or maybe that was just a reflection from the dancing waters of the pond. "You do?"

"Very much."

He set down his glass of wine and went over to her, taking her by the hands so she was standing as well and it would be easier to pull her into his arms and kiss her, tasting the tartness of the pinot grigio on her tongue…feeling how his body responded as she pressed against him.

No words, but she took him by the hand and led him inside, moving quickly through the living room and down a hall that passed an office and a media room, and terminated in what he guessed was the master suite. It was a big space, maybe twenty by twenty, with a plaster kiva-style fireplace in one corner and a huge square canvas of what he thought might be Cathedral Rock hanging above the equally enormous bed.

After that, he didn't have much opportunity to pay attention to the decor, because Bellamy was tugging at his belt so she could pull it loose, her fingers flying down the buttons of his 501s. At the same time, he unfastened the button and zipper of her cargo shorts, and soon enough, they were on the floor, along with the sleeveless cotton blouse she wore and his T-shirt with the "Ski Mt. Lemmon" legend on it.

They fell onto the bed, which was big and billowy, much more luxurious than the mattress at his Airbnb…or his bed at home, to be honest. She kissed him on his throat, and then her kisses were moving down his chest, lower and lower, until she came to his boxer briefs, which she pulled down with little ceremony so she could take him into her mouth.

She'd done this to him before, but it felt even

better this time. Maybe it was the wine, or maybe it was the simple realization that he loved his woman more than he'd ever thought he could love anyone, that it didn't matter if they were chasing vortexes or eating Thai or simply being— every moment with Bellamy McAllister was perfect.

Just as she was utterly perfect now, bringing him close to a climax and then drawing back so she could remove her underwear and sink down onto him.

God, that was amazing. He reached up to her caress her breasts, which were high and rounded but not overly large, each of them just the perfect size to fit into his cupped palms. She moaned, back arching as he touched her and she rode him, and he knew this was exactly what he'd needed… what they'd both needed.

He could feel the orgasm on its way, his body pulsing with heat and need and sensation. Their fingers knotted together, and they held on when they both climaxed, with her coming maybe a second or two before he did. But they rode it out together, hands still clasped, until at last she let out a sigh and climbed off him so she could fall onto the bed, body pressed against his.

"How'd you know that was exactly what I needed?" she asked, and he bent to kiss her.

"Because it was just what I needed, too."

They got burgers to go from Nick's because it was close and they both wanted something hearty and fun after that afternoon's activities. Or rather, Bellamy called in the order and Marc went to go pick it up, since they were still doing their best to maintain the fiction that she was off handling some mythical family emergency.

Actually, she supposed it wasn't that mythical when you got right down to it, but the situation wasn't exactly something she could discuss with her civilian boss.

It was fun to sit at the big dining table and watch as the twilight faded into night, though, and to share another of the bottles they'd gotten during their visit to the various tasting rooms in Page Springs. If she'd been alone here, she might have been a lot more hinky about the gathering darkness outside, or how the nearest neighbor wasn't close enough to hear her if she screamed for help, but now that she knew Marc would be staying the night, the place felt downright cozy.

"And I suppose we'll see tomorrow morning if this place has worked its magic on you," she said, then took a bite of her Guinness burger, messy with sautéed onions and gorgeously gooey cheese.

He nodded, expression thoughtful. "It'll be interesting to find out. If it kicks my visions into overdrive, that can only be a good thing. They've been pretty quiet ever since those dreams I had down in Tucson."

Come to think of it, he was right. Bellamy had to believe that if Marc had had any prophetic dreams since coming to the Verde Valley, he would have told her about them, but that didn't seem to have happened.

Too bad, because a dream that showed what the Collector looked like and exactly where they could find him would have been pretty helpful.

True, she knew visions didn't always work that way, but a girl could hope.

"I suppose we'll just have to wait and see," she said.

"I suppose so," he echoed, then reached over to pick up his glass of zinfandel. It worked great with the burgers, and even though they were drinking the only bottle they'd bought, it wasn't as if they'd have to drive too far to go back to Javelina Leap and buy another one.

Or two…or three….

After dinner, they headed into the living room to watch a movie on the enormous TV mounted on one wall, bigger than anything she'd ever seen before. With a television like that, who needed to go to the movies?

So they snuggled on the couch and watched some silly action film, the sort of thing she wouldn't have chosen for herself but was entertaining enough. And afterward, they went to bed, falling into each other's arms and making slow, languorous love until they both basically passed out while still clinging together.

The next morning, Bellamy didn't think she felt any different—well, except for enjoying the afterglow of being spectacularly laid several times the day before—but this experiment wasn't really about her, not when she already knew the vortex here at the ranch had woken up corners of her magical gift she hadn't even known existed.

No, this was all about Marc.

He roused next to her, eyes opening as he stared up at the tongue-and-groove detailing on the ceiling.

"Well?" she said.

A blink, and then he gave a lift of his shoulders, just heavy enough with muscle to make him appear damn good either in or out of a shirt, but not so much that he looked like one of those guys who spent every spare moment in the gym.

"No dreams," he replied, and a wave of disappointment went through her, even though she'd tried to prepare herself, knowing that everything they were doing right now was pretty much a shot in the dark.

"Nothing at all?"

He pushed himself up to a sitting position and

pulled in a breath, almost as if he was centering himself to assess his current physical and mental condition.

"Nothing that I remember," he said. "I mean, I slept great, but I know that's not the outcome we were hoping for."

At once, she leaned over and pressed a kiss against his cheek. "It's okay. We're all flying blind here. And a decent night's sleep is always a good thing, especially since we don't know what we'll be facing today."

If it was even anything at all. Neither of them had heard through their various clan networks that any other incursions had occurred, so maybe the Collector's would-be thieves had already exhausted their bag of tricks.

Or maybe they'd only retreated so they could regroup and figure out a new plan of attack.

Marc still looked troubled. "I was really hoping being here at the vortex would get my visions going again. But so far...*nada.*"

"Well," Bellamy said, doing her best to sound much more upbeat than she felt, "it's not as if we knew for sure what was going to happen. I think the best thing we can do now is get some coffee in us and have breakfast."

"You've got supplies for that?" he asked, looking a little surprised.

Not that she could blame him. They'd been

going out or bringing home takeout this whole time, with not a single mention of putting something together here at the house. He probably thought there wasn't a single speck of real food at the ranch, except maybe those Kind bars they'd taken with them to Devil's Bridge the other day.

"A few things," she said. "I mean, don't expect pancakes or waffles or anything. But I can make eggs and toast and bacon, if you're cool with that."

She figured he probably would be—so far, she hadn't seen a single hint of dietary restrictions about him—so when he nodded, she wasn't surprised.

"Okay, then," she went on. "Let's have breakfast, and then we can figure out what our day is supposed to look like."

And hope it would be as blissfully quiet as their morning had been so far.

15

THEY SHOWERED SEPARATELY THAT MORNING, with Bellamy going first because she had to wash her hair. And although Marc had more than enjoyed their shower activities the day before, he could understand why she'd want to be alone to take care of her hair rather than have him all over her.

Anyway, he was feeling plenty satisfied right now, so he was okay with this morning being relaxed.

Or as relaxed as it could be, considering how he couldn't figure out why the small vortex here at the ranch had activated more of Bellamy's powers while it didn't seem to have done a damn thing for him.

But after he'd showered as well, he came out

to the main part of the house to find her sitting at the dining room table, laptop in front of her as she frowned at the screen.

"Everything okay?" he asked, going over so he could place a gentle kiss on the top of her hair. Her hair smelled sweet and was still slightly damp, although it looked as bright copper as ever.

"Sure," she said, although her voice was almost absent, as if she was still more focused on what she was reading on her laptop than on him.

"Did you find something?" he asked, and she nodded.

"I thought I'd try to do a little more research on vortexes while you were in the shower. One thing I didn't know is that there are different kinds. There are inflow vortexes, which are located in valleys and canyons, and upflow vortexes, which are on hillsides or mesas. I guess the inflow vortexes are more associated with feminine energy —Red Rock Crossing is one of those."

None of this made a whole hell of a lot of sense to Marc, but since he'd barely known anything about Sedona's vortexes before this except that they existed, he supposed he should cut himself some slack.

"So…what kind of vortex are we sitting on right now?"

"Everything I've found says that canyons and valleys are inflow, so I suppose that's what we're dealing with here." She closed her laptop, her expression now almost speculative. "And I wonder if that's why it didn't have any effect on you."

"Because inflow vortexes are all about female energy," he responded, and she looked pleased.

"That's what I was thinking. And I had another idea."

"Which is?" He didn't like to sound so wary, but since they still didn't know exactly what they were dealing with, it just seemed smarter to be cautious.

Her mouth quirked, signaling that she'd correctly interpreted his tone and was more amused by it than anything else.

"How would you feel about having my cousin Bree stay over tonight to see if the energies here affect her powers?"

Bree McAllister, Marc recalled vaguely, was the blonde woman, maybe a year older than Bellamy…if even that…who'd been singing at the Tantrum tasting room in Cottonwood a few days ago. She was strikingly pretty and had a gorgeous voice to match, although even then he'd only had eyes for Bellamy and no one else.

"Is singing her talent?" he asked. "Because she's already pretty good. Unless you want to see whether the vortex energies will turn her into an opera singer or something."

Now Bellamy just grinned. She had a glass of

ice water sitting on a coaster nearby, and she picked it up so she could take a sip.

"No, she comes by that voice without any magic," she replied. "Bree's talent is sort of hard to pin down because it's kind of…everything at once."

"You mean she controls all the various witch powers?" Marc had a hard time even conceiving of such a thing. Then again, Bree's father was Levi McAllister. If anyone in the clan was going to have an unusual set of talents, you'd think it would be one of his children.

A pause as Bellamy considered the question, and then she said, "It's not exactly like that. It's more like…she can sort of call on the power she needs in any particular situation."

"Like a Swiss Army knife kind of witch?" he responded, and she sent him another of those brilliant smiles, bright enough to outshine the hot summer sun outside.

God, she was beautiful.

"I suppose that's one way you can put it," she replied. "Except…none of those talents are very strong. Sure, she can help your tomatoes grow bigger, but she can't coax a plant right out of the ground the way I've seen some people with green witch powers do. Or, she can fix a sprained ankle and maybe even a broken arm, but she can't tackle any of the big healing stuff, like cancer or heart disease." Bellamy set her glass of water back down before continuing. "She told me one time that she thinks none of her talents are super strong because they're all spread so thin."

That didn't sound like quite so much fun. Even though his own gift had been a little too quiescent lately, when it decided to kick in, it was fairly strong. And the protection bubble was always there when he needed it. Sure, it didn't cover quite as large an area as the ones his father could cast, but considering the only occasion he'd really needed it was one time when he was hiking and had blundered into a swarm of bees, he thought he was okay with that. It had done the job, and that was the important thing.

"So anyway," Bellamy went on, "that's why I thought it might be a good idea to see if the vortex here would work on Bree's talent…or talents, depending on how you look at it. They're not very strong to begin with, so she should be able to notice a change right away."

Although Marc wasn't sure he was overly thrilled about the lack of privacy that having Bree McAllister stay here for a night or two entailed, he had to admit Bellamy's plan sounded pretty solid to him.

"You think she'll go for it?" he asked then, and her shoulders lifted just a little.

"I'm hoping she will. Luckily, it's the middle

of the week, so it's not as if she should have any gigs tonight. Mostly she works Friday through Sunday, although every once in a while she's asked to play on a weeknight. Anyway, all I can do is ask."

"Then I suppose you should text her," Marc replied. It would be good to get to the bottom of this vortex thing, and if it turned out Bree's powers really were enhanced by spending some time here, then at least it would prove that the ranch's vortex did seem to affect only women.

So, did that mean he should try going to one of the outflow vortexes, the ones on the hilltops and mesas, to see if they did the same thing for him?

Maybe, although he wasn't sure how he was going to manage sleeping there. As Bellamy had already pointed out, most of Sedona's most powerful vortexes were located on Forest Service land, which meant you couldn't just pitch a tent wherever you wanted.

When he mentioned that small complication to her, however, she only shook her head, still looking a bit amused.

"It's actually not as big a deal as you think. Airport Mesa is one of the most powerful vortexes here, if this map Clint Greaves gave us is at all accurate, and there's a hotel built right on top of it

—Sky Ranch Lodge. We can stay there for a night or two and see what happens."

He had to admit that sounded like a pretty decent plan as well. Sure, it meant he'd be paying for yet another place to stay, but he was okay with spending a couple of hundred extra bucks to find out if he was vortex-impervious or whether he just needed to experience the right kind to really supercharge his powers, so to speak.

Bellamy got out her phone, saying, "I'm going to text Bree now. Why don't you see if Sky Ranch Lodge has any rooms available for tomorrow night?"

"Sure," he replied, and also plucked his phone from his pocket. He figured he'd try one of the discount hotel apps first, and if they didn't have anything, then he'd just call the place directly and hope for the best.

But it turned out Expedia had two rooms left for August thirteenth, so he went ahead and made the booking, securing a king room for two nights just in case it turned out that he needed a little more time to really determine whether the outflow energies of the Airport Mesa vortex had affected him at all.

Just as he was finishing with the reservations, Bellamy's phone binged. She picked it up, looked down at the screen, and then settled against the back of her chair, looking relieved.

"That was Bree. She said she doesn't have anything going on until Friday night, so she's cool with participating in our little experiment. What time do you want her to come over?"

As late as possible, flashed through Marc's mind, but he knew that wasn't a very friendly response. Bree McAllister was helping them out, after all, so as much as he would have liked an intimate dinner with Bellamy tonight, he knew he should do what he could to make her cousin feel included.

"I don't know…five-thirty or six? We can try some pizza from Pisa Lisa tonight."

"No pineapple, I assume," Bellamy replied, mouth quirking a little. "You wouldn't want my whole clan to know your dirty little secret."

He chuckled, thinking that if loving Hawaiian pizza was the biggest secret he needed to conceal, then he was probably doing okay. "I think I can live with pepperoni for one night."

Smiling, she typed out a quick reply to her cousin, presumably letting Bree know the timing of her arrival. Another response came back lightning fast, telling Marc that she'd probably been camped on her phone, waiting to hear back regarding their plans.

"Well, that's done," Bellamy announced as she set down her phone, then pushed back her chair so she could stand up. She put her arms around him, squeezing just the smallest bit, and then murmured in his ear, "I know we won't be able to do anything while Bree is staying here, but that doesn't mean we can't have some fun before she arrives."

A woman after his own heart. Not for the first time, Marc wondered what he'd done to deserve a woman like Bellamy McAllister. It wasn't as if he was a bad person or anything like that, but he also didn't think he'd been the sort of outstanding warlock that would attract a woman who was so amazing in every way.

However, he wasn't going to argue. If the universe had decided to put them in each other's paths, then he was more than happy to go along for the ride.

"That's a great idea," he said, and took her by the hand and led her down the hall to the bedroom.

Bellamy was pretty sure she'd gotten rid of all evidence of hers and Marc's activities that afternoon—the bed in the master bedroom was neatly made, and she'd gone into the bathroom and carefully applied mascara and lip gloss…along with some concealer to cover the marks he'd left on her neck. They were still kind of there if you looked close enough, but her loose hair should serve to hide most of them.

At exactly five-thirty, her phone pinged again.

I'm at the gate. Can you buzz me in?

Sure. Just give me a sec.

She went over to the security panel on the wall in the kitchen and pressed the button that operated the gate. Marc had been sitting in the living room, half-heartedly watching a Diamondbacks game, and she called out,

"Bree should be here in a couple of minutes. I just got the gate for her."

At once, Marc picked up the remote so he could turn off the TV. As he stood, he said, "Have you thought about what you're going to do about work?"

Oh, she'd thought a lot…well, when he hadn't been sending her to another plane of existence as another orgasm shuddered its way through her.

"I guess I'll just have to take the rest of the week off," she told him. "I mean, all this is so up in the air that I just can't see my way clear to spending all day at work."

She tried to sound blithe about the whole thing, but she supposed her concern must have been mirrored in her face, because he immediately came over and took her hands in his.

"Is that going to cause a problem?"

"I don't know," she said honestly. "It's asking a

lot, especially since I only started there a month ago. But as Levi said, clan business comes first. So if I get fired, I get fired. I'll find something else."

Even though she didn't want to find something else. Getting hired as assistant manager at Sedona Vines had been a big step for her, and even though there were plenty of jobs available at the various tasting rooms around the area, positions that put you on an actual career track were a lot fewer and farther between.

Well, she supposed there was always her old bedroom at her fathers' apartment above the candy shop if everything fell apart, although going back home would feel like utter defeat.

Marc pressed his lips against her forehead, his touch very gentle, as if he knew he couldn't initiate anything when Bree was about to ring the doorbell at any second. "Let's hope that doesn't happen." He stepped away so he could meet her gaze, his dark eyes full of understanding. "But if it does, we'll figure it out together."

Together. Crazy to think they actually had a "together" when she'd been so relentlessly single only a few days earlier.

But she was very glad she wasn't having to navigate all these complications on her own.

The doorbell rang then, so the two of them went over to answer it. When Bellamy opened the door, Bree was standing outside, an overnight bag slung over one shoulder and a slightly mystified expression on her face.

"If this is a vortex, I can't really feel anything," she said as she stepped inside.

"I didn't, either," Bellamy replied. "It was only after I slept here that I noticed some…changes."

Bree's eyebrows lifted ever so slightly, but then she glanced over at Marc. "Hi," she said. "I'm Bree McAllister. You were at Tantrum Wines the other day, right?"

"I was," he said as he extended a hand. "I'm Marc Trujillo. Thanks for participating in our experiment."

"Wouldn't miss it," Bree said with a grin, even as the three of them left the foyer and went farther into the house. She set her overnight bag down on the floor behind the couch and looked around, expression clearly impressed. "I figured this place would be pretty awesome, but this is amazing. What a great gig!"

"Yes, I sort of lucked into the whole thing," Bellamy replied. "But let me show you where you're going to be sleeping. Marc and I think you probably won't need to stay here for more than one or two nights, depending on what happens."

She hoped it wouldn't take anything more than that, not when Marc had booked a two-night stay at Sky Ranch Lodge starting tomorrow. True, she could always have him head over there while she remained here with Bree, but she had to admit that didn't seem like a great solution.

They might not have been together for very long, and yet she hated the idea of having to sleep apart from him.

He waited in the living room while she took Bree to the other side of the house where the secondary bedrooms and bathrooms were located. Each room had its own *en suite* bath, which Bellamy had to admit was pretty convenient, and they were so big that in most houses, they would have been more than sufficient for the main suite.

This wasn't most houses, though.

Bree looked approving, especially when she saw that the room where she'd be staying also opened onto a patio a little smaller than the main courtyard off the living spaces. "It's definitely bigger than my bedroom at the apartment," she remarked.

Since Bellamy had been there plenty of times, she knew her cousin was only telling the truth. About six months earlier, the apartment over the art gallery on Main Street had become available, and Bree had been able to snap it up. Part of her lease required that she had to keep an eye on the gallery if the owner needed to step away, but it didn't sound as if her responsibilities were too onerous or interfered with her various singing gigs.

"The house is almost seven thousand square feet," Bellamy said. "So there's a lot of room to spread out."

Her cousin Bree headed into the bathroom, which was also where the walk-in closet was located. After storing her overnight bag in there, she came back out and closed the door.

"So…is this thing with you and Marc serious?"

"We've only known each other a couple of days," Bellamy protested, although she knew the words sounded weak even to her.

Bree pursed her mouth. She'd pulled her long blonde hair into a ponytail and was wearing a tank top and jeans and only a little bit of lip gloss, but she still looked like a princess who'd decided to go slumming.

"We're witches, Bellamy," she said. "The normal rules about relationships don't apply to us. You know that."

She supposed she did. Or rather, while she'd understood on an intellectual level that witches and warlocks often had attractions that developed quickly, that they generally had a unique ability to find their soul mate, she had begun to think it would never happen to her, that she'd settle for some decent guy—probably a civilian, since before Marc, she hadn't met any warlocks who really got her motor running—and figure out what to do with the rest of her life going from there.

Clearly, that hadn't happened.

"I like him a lot," she replied. "And I know he likes me. We're good together. But right now, I think we're both just focusing on getting to the bottom of everything that's been going on during the past few days. This vortex stuff. The Collector, whoever that is."

Bree's expression turned much more serious. "My father told me about that. I still find it hard to believe that anyone has the kind of magic that could get past the wards the elders and Connor and Angela placed on their house."

"But they did," Bellamy said, doing what she could to sound level and matter-of-fact, even though she knew deep down that she was worried about the way the would-be thief had been able to succeed at such an incursion. "And Zoe de la Paz's house, too, which means we're not dealing with some sort of one-off situation here. It's kind of scary."

That was one word for it. However, even though Bellamy had found herself sort of creeped out here and there by what was going on, she was much more interested in unknotting the various mysteries she and Marc had encountered than letting herself get sucked into emotional reactions.

Except for the reaction she'd had to him, of

course. She wasn't about to step away from those emotions.

"But I also think they're on top of it," she continued briskly. "No one was expecting that kind of incursion. Now, though, we've all been tipped off and know to keep our guard up. It's going to be okay."

Bree didn't respond for a moment, but then her mouth curved into a half-smile. "Especially if sleeping here for a night or two kicks my gifts into high gear. It would be nice to have something that wasn't so…wimpy."

It had been tough for her cousin to realize that her powers weren't terribly strong despite having a father who was some sort of otherworldly being and who possessed magic that was stronger than that of anyone else in the clan except for Connor and Angela. Bree had soldiered along pretty well, but still, she continued to look at herself as a disappointment even if no one else thought of her that way.

Her brother Shane, who was almost two years older, had inherited a gift that Marc's McAllister uncle also possessed, being an absolute whiz in the kitchen who could whip up just about anything and have it be Cordon Bleu level of quality. No, that sort of talent wasn't going to change the world or anything, but it was very strong, powerful enough that Shane was already working as the head chef at The Asylum, the fancy restaurant in the Grand Hotel at the top of the hill in Jerome.

Because there wasn't much point in saying that Bree's grab bag of talents was still useful even if individually they weren't all that powerful, Bellamy decided to let it go.

"Well, we should go out to the living room and talk about our plan of attack," she said.

"'Attack'?" Bree echoed. "I thought this was all about me just staying here and seeing if the vortex energy does anything to me."

"It is," Bellamy replied. "But we also need to know how best to test your gifts tomorrow to see if there's been any changes. When it happened to me, I didn't have any idea what was going on. Now I know it was the vortex, making it so I can't just control the winds, but also hear the messages they have for me."

"That seems like a pretty cool enhancement," Bree said. "So I'll cross my fingers that I get something similar."

Bellamy didn't know about "cool"—hearing voices was the sort of thing that could get you shipped off to the funny farm—but she let it go. Those whispers on the wind had been helpful in their own way, had provided information that she otherwise would have never been able to obtain.

Just because they were disconcerting didn't mean she could ignore them.

They went back out to the living room, where Marc was sitting on the couch. He was watching the game again, but with the sound muted, so it wasn't too intrusive.

"All settled?" he asked, and Bree smiled.

"I am. This is an incredible house, so I don't think I'm going to mind hanging out here for a bit."

Hopefully, just for one night. Bellamy knew she couldn't control that outcome, though, so instead they chatted a bit about Bree's powers—they all agreed that testing her skill with growing things was probably the safest, and thought she could work with it tomorrow by making one of the cacti planted out in front of the house bloom again. That time had already come and gone, but if she could get that barrel cactus to burst forth with bright yellow flowers when it was completely out of season, then it would prove that even a single night's exposure to the inflow vortex here had made a difference. And since they went outside just to make sure she couldn't perform that feat right now—she concentrated with all her might on the cactus, but nothing happened—it seemed pretty clear that any changes in her powers would be due to the vortex located here and nothing else.

After that, they pulled up Pisa Lisa's menu online and decided on dinner, going for a large pepperoni pizza and a side salad and some of the restaurant's famous tiramisu for dessert. They all seemed pretty relaxed with each other, and Bellamy found some of her worries receding.

This was all going to work out just fine.

16

IT WAS A MUCH MORE RELAXED EVENING THAN Marc had been expecting. Bree was friendly and low-key, and she didn't seem to have any trouble accepting his status as Bellamy's new boyfriend.

True, the two of them hadn't said anything so definitive about their relationship, but he somehow knew that was where they stood…even though they hadn't come right out and announced that they now considered themselves boyfriend and girlfriend.

He also liked listening to the banter between the two women as they talked about the times they'd shared growing up in Jerome, which he had to admit sounded kind of magical…no pun intended. Although witches and warlocks didn't tend to be helicopter parents in general, thanks to the way they knew a grown-up in the clan was almost always around and ready to step in if someone needed a ride home or a Band-aid or something, it sure seemed to him as if the adults in Bellamy's hometown were even more relaxed. Apparently, no one appeared to have a problem with the clan's children roaming around unsupervised—usually with some civilian kids from the neighborhood tagging along as well—whether they were hanging out in some of the abandoned mine shafts that still peppered the hill or finding secret little ravines to build forts or play hide-and-seek.

Thinking about it now, he thought that sounded like a great way to grow up…a great way to raise your children.

And his gaze had strayed to Bellamy, who clearly didn't seem nearly as interested in watching the horror movie they'd chosen for that night's viewing as she did in catching up on old times with Bree.

Fine by him, since he wasn't into the movie and would rather have listened to the two women talk anyway.

They'd gone to their separate wings of the house and gotten ready for bed. Bellamy kissed him goodnight, and even that sweet brush of her lips against his was enough to make his body stir, to wish he could pull her against him and make love to her all over again.

Even with Bree way on the other side of the house, though, he didn't feel quite comfortable doing that, so he'd made himself kiss Bellamy back and wish her a good night, and then closed his eyes and hoped sleep would come soon.

It was a sleep without any dreams, unfortunately, which seemed to be the signal that however powerful the vortex might be here, it wasn't the kind that would have any influence on his powers.

"Anything?" Bellamy asked when she rolled over to face him the next morning, and he shook his head.

"Nope. So it looks like I'm headed up to Sky Ranch tonight to see if I have any better luck there."

She didn't look too thrilled by that prospect, probably because she knew she'd have to stay behind here if it turned out that her cousin's powers hadn't suffered a sea change after one night at the ranch house. But she only nodded, saying, "Well, we were prepared for that possibly happening. So let's get some coffee going and see if Bree had any better luck."

The other woman wasn't anywhere in evidence when they emerged from the main suite and headed into the kitchen to start brewing that morning's pot of coffee. Maybe Bree tended to sleep late; he could see why she might do that if she spent a lot of her evenings performing at the local resorts and bars. Wine tasting rooms didn't stay open nearly so late, but it was possible she double-booked on those days, playing at a winery in the afternoon and then a hotel bar in the evening.

After he and Bellamy had poured themselves some coffee and were discussing whether the remaining breakfast supplies would be enough to feed the three of them, though, Bree finally emerged from her room, bright blonde hair tousled.

"I need to pump some of that coffee right into my veins," she announced, and Bellamy grinned.

"Rough night?"

"Not exactly," Bree replied. "I mean, I think I slept well enough. But something about this place felt...off...I guess. Or maybe that was just my imagination filling me full of stuff about vortexes."

Marc glanced over at Bellamy, whose expression had immediately turned thoughtful. "Maybe it was just that...or maybe not. But let me get you some coffee."

She went to the cupboard and got out a mug, then filled it. No offer of milk or sugar or anything like that; no, she handed the mug directly to her cousin, as if she already knew that Bree drank it black.

A few breaths on the liquid in a cursory

attempt at cooling it down, and then Bree helped herself to a few swallows. "Much better," she said. "Now I feel like I can think." She paused there, and glanced down at her baggy tank top and yoga pants. Had she slept in the ensemble, or had she just figured it was the bare minimum she needed to put on before she let herself be seen in semi-public?

"Feel any different now?" Bellamy asked. Marc could tell she was trying not to sound too hopeful.

A shrug, and Bree sipped some more coffee. "Well, I'm more awake, that's for sure. But it's not as if it feels like my magic is trying to burst out of my body or anything."

"That's all right," Bellamy replied at once. "I honestly didn't feel any different, either. It was only when I first heard the voices that I realized something weird was going on."

"Then I suppose we should just go ahead with our morning and see what's up with that cactus after we're all showered and dressed," Marc said. "Bree, are eggs and toast okay for breakfast? We kind of ate all the bacon yesterday."

"Sourdough?" she asked hopefully, and Bellamy smiled.

"Is there any other kind of toast?"

They all kind of grinned at that comment, and then—even though Bree offered to help with breakfast prep, an offer Bellamy quickly declined, saying her cousin was their guest—Marc and Bellamy got their quickie breakfast together. Sure, she did the bulk of the work, since she was the one making the scrambled eggs, but he kept an eye on the bread, pulling it out of the toaster right when it was peak golden-brown and before it got too dark.

Afterward, they sat at the table in the kitchen nook and ate their meal while they watched a flock of Gambrel's quail assemble in the courtyard, drinking their fill from the fountain before they headed off to search for food. He wondered why Bellamy hadn't put anything out in the courtyard for them to eat, then guessed she was probably trying to avoid making a mess, since this wasn't her house.

No doubt she was already pushing things by having both him and her cousin Bree stay here, even if the arrangement was strictly temporary.

Once they were done with breakfast, they put their plates in the dishwasher and headed off to their respective bathrooms. This time, he and Bellamy showered together, with her telling him that she didn't need to wash her hair today, and besides, this would allow them to get ready faster.

True enough, but even though they goofed around a little, teasing each other without progressing into full-on foreplay, they both understood they needed to keep the morning moving so they could see if the inflow vortex at the ranch had had any effect on her cousin.

That was why they all assembled at the front of the house a little before ten, the bright desert sun already hot, beating down on Bree's damp hair. Clearly, she'd thought she needed to wash it today, although she'd still gotten ready fairly quickly.

The cactus planted here all looked happy and healthy, although any flowers they might have sported would have come and gone in May or June. Now that they were inching toward mid-August, those flowers wouldn't return until late next spring.

Well, unless you had a green witch with you…or at least, someone who could call on green witch powers when she needed to.

However, Bree was looking doubtful, hands on her hips as she stared down at the innocuous cactus, a plump thing about eighteen inches high.

"I'm not so sure about this," she said. "Like I said earlier, I don't feel any different."

"And, like I told you, neither did I," Bellamy returned. It seemed pretty clear she wasn't about to let this go.

How could she, really? If it turned out the vortexes really could be instrumental in enhancing witchy powers, they might become their secret weapon when it came to dealing with the Collector.

"Okay," Bree said, and pulled in a breath. "So…cactus flowers."

She held out a hand, in almost the same pose used by the Jedi in the Star Wars movies when they were invoking their powers.

And then….

Small buds appeared all over the surface of the cactus, buds that rapidly opened into cheerful, bright yellow flowers. They paused at the peak of their bloom rather than shriveling back down to nothing again, and Bree looked over at him and Bellamy, her expression more one of shock than anything else.

"It worked," she said, her tone wondering. "I've never been able to do anything like that before."

"Never?" Marc asked. It wasn't that he didn't believe she was telling the truth, but it never hurt to ask.

"No," Bree said, emphatic. "So it sure looks to me like your inflow vortex worked."

"It does," Bellamy agreed. "But maybe you should try something else, just to be sure."

"Something relatively harmless," Marc added, figuring it probably wasn't a good idea for Bree to try summoning a tornado or a swarm of bees, or whatever.

Her blue eyes glinted with amusement. "I think I can manage 'relatively harmless.'"

And she spread her arms and a rainbow appeared over the house, arching from the court-yard to the patio off the room where she was stay-ing. It hung in the air for a moment before it disappeared.

"Just an illusion," she said. "There's not enough water vapor in the air to support a real rainbow. Still, that's the first time I've ever made an illusion that big."

Bellamy set her hands on her hips, looking pleased. "It sure seems to me as if the energy here did something. I guess we'll need to see whether your powers get stronger after you've spent a second night here at the house."

At once, Bree tilted her head, as if she didn't look completely convinced. "I was thinking about that earlier while I was in the shower," she said. "Don't you think it would make more sense for me to be at home tonight and then see whether my powers are still strengthened tomorrow morn-ing, or whether whatever the vortex did for me has already gone away? If we did that, it might help us figure out whether this vortex energy is going to be much use in the long run, or whether it's more of a parlor trick than anything else."

Bellamy's lips pursed, but Marc could see the merits of Bree's argument.

"I think she's right," he said. "I mean, you heard the voices at the Devil's Bridge strongly enough the other day, Bellamy, and you didn't sleep here the night before. So that would give us another data point."

Although she still didn't appear completely convinced, she seemed to decide that they might as well roll the dice and see what happened.

"Also," Bree added, "I'm playing a gig at 1912 Winery in Uptown on Friday night, so if you wanted me to come back here and see what that does for my powers, it'll give me an easy place to crash rather than driving all the way back to Jerome."

"Okay, it's a plan," Bellamy replied. "I guess just send me a text if you notice anything unusual or if anything changes." Her cousin nodded, and she went on, now looking at Marc, "I suppose we'll find out tonight what the outflow energies will do for you."

And hope like hell it wasn't anything weird.

17

Bree left not too long after that, taking her overnight bag with her and promising once again that she'd contact Bellamy if her powers started acting up in strange ways. It didn't sound as if she had a gig that night and would probably just be hanging out in her apartment, and for that, Bellamy could only be grateful.

The last thing any of them needed was some kind of strange phenomena busting out in public that would need to be covered up…and quickly.

With her cousin gone, Bellamy knew she had a decision to make. Her boss had given her some grace and allowed her to take Tuesday and Wednesday off, but now it was Thursday morning, and that meant she was supposed to be at Sedona Vines at noon. She still had a few hours, but she couldn't put this off indefinitely.

Especially since she knew she'd look like an even bigger flake if she waited until 11:45 or something to make the phone call.

"You seem worried about something," Marc said as they went back inside after walking Bree to her ancient Suburban.

"It's work," Bellamy replied. "I'm supposed to be there in less than two hours."

His mouth tightened. "Well, we don't have much going on today. What if you just went in?"

The idea was tempting, even though she didn't much like the idea of leaving Marc to fend for himself while she spent all day at the wine bar. He'd have to check in at the Sky Ranch Lodge without her, which she supposed wasn't the end of the world, but still.

And those were minor complications compared to all the unknowns that lurked in the equation. What if the Collector or one of his lackeys decided this sleepy August day was the perfect time to go on the attack? What if her powers decided to flare up and cause a scene? True, they'd been pretty quiescent after her experience at Red Rock Crossing the day before, but since they had no real idea what they were dealing with here, she knew she couldn't discount that possibility, either.

Staring off into space and delivering wind-driven prophecies probably wouldn't be a very good look for Sedona Vines' assistant manager.

"I should call," she said, doing her best to hold back a sigh. "We don't know what's going to crop up next, and the last thing we want is for me to be stuck at work if something major goes down."

Worry was clear in Marc's dark eyes, but he only said, "Do you think it's going to be a problem?"

The thing was, she just didn't know. Jack had seemed pretty mellow about the whole situation when she called him on Monday, but she'd only been asking for two days off, not a sabbatical of unknown duration.

She shrugged, the only response she could really give. "I guess I'll find out in a few minutes."

Marc put a sympathetic hand on her shoulder, then leaned down to kiss her softly on the cheek. "I'll be here, no matter what happens."

That was the only good thing about this whole mess. Some part of her would have been all too glad to have never discovered the real effect Sedona's vortexes had on the witch population, but on the other hand, she wouldn't have passed up meeting Marc Trujillo for the world.

His presence gave her the strength she needed to pick up her phone and call Jack. Not at the wine bar, because it was way too early for him to be there, but on his personal cell, the number he'd given to all his employees in case of emergency.

Bellamy supposed this could be considered one. With her having to bow out for the Goddess only knew how long, her boss would be scrambling to cover her shifts, especially with the weekend coming up.

But she knew she couldn't avoid this. The witch world hadn't interfered with her life before now, and she guessed it was just making up for lost time.

Jack's voice at her ear, already sounding suspicious. "Bellamy? Aren't you supposed to be in at noon today?"

Which was still an hour and a half off. Would Marcy be able to take her hours today, or would Jack have to watch the place by himself?

One could argue that Thursdays in general weren't party central at Sedona Vines, but all it took was one unscheduled tour bus to upset the apple cart.

"I am," she said, then made herself to take another breath. "Or at least, I was. This mess with my family has kind of blown up, and I honestly don't know when I'm going to make it back to work."

There, she'd said it. Now all she could do was let the chips fall where they may.

A pause on the other end of the line. Then

Jack said, "I'm sorry to hear that your family's having a difficult time. But I need someone I can rely on, Bellamy. I can't go on indefinitely getting different people to fill your shifts." Another hesitation, longer this time. "I'm afraid I'm going to have to let you go. You can come in sometime next week to pick up your final paycheck."

Well, there it was. In a way, it had been almost a relief to hear Jack utter those fateful words, because at least now she wouldn't have the problem of what to do about work hanging over her head.

No, she was utterly fancy-free.

"I understand," she said calmly. "You have a good rest of your day, Jack."

And she touched her finger to the phone's screen to end the call.

Only a foot or so away, Marc was watching her carefully. "Well?"

She sent him a limp smile. "I got fired."

"Oh, Bellamy."

At once, his arms were around her, holding her close, and she let herself relax into the embrace, glad of the strength and reassurance and love she could practically feel flowing from him, giving her the support she needed.

Was that sensation her gift expanding even more, or just the subtler energy of two souls who'd somehow managed to find each other despite everything?

Either way, she thought she was okay with it.

"I'm all right," she murmured into Marc's shoulder. "And it's going to be fine. There's no way I could have gotten through all this stuff with the vortexes and the Collector and put in eight hours a day at the wine bar on top of it. I've got my stipend, and I've got what Ike's paying me every month to watch the ranch. It's not as if I'm going to be out on the street or anything."

A fate that never befell those of witch-kind anyway, just because there was always a relative to take you in if you happened to fall on hard times.

Which were generally few and far between, because even though not everyone had the gift of luck like Lucas Wilcox did, witches and warlocks tended to be a bit more fortunate than the civilian population, with odd little windfalls popping up here and there when they least expected it.

"Of course not." Marc let go of her, but only so he could take a step back and entwine his fingers with hers. "You're sure you're all right?"

She looked up at him, at the dark eyes under their emphatic brows, at the finely sculpted mouth she just loved to kiss. With Marc around, she couldn't be too worried about the future.

"I'm fine," she said, and realized she meant it. After they got past this stuff with the Collector and the vortexes, then she'd have to sit down and figure out what to do with herself, but she'd worry about that when the time came.

"You're more than fine," Marc said, then kissed her gently. "You're the most amazing woman I've ever met."

Bellamy had always thought she was pretty ordinary—well, at least as witches went—but if he wanted to think she was the greatest thing since sliced bread, she wasn't going to disabuse him of that notion.

"You're pretty amazing, too," she replied, then gave his fingers a squeeze before letting go. A smile touched her lips, and she added, "Well, now that we have most of the day free, what should we do with it?"

He smiled back at her. "I can think of a few things."

They didn't spend all day in the bedroom, of course, and went out for a late lunch down in the Village of Oak Creek, ostensibly so he could experience the outflow energies at Bell Rock, but mostly, he guessed, so they'd be far enough away from Sedona Vines that Bellamy wouldn't have to worry about running into any of her erstwhile co-workers…or worse, her boss.

But they had great barbecue at a place called the Colt Grill, which she told him also had another branch in Old Town Cottonwood, and afterward, they walked the Bell Rock trail to get a feel for the place. It was a very easy stroll, not really a hike, although he could tell if you stayed on it, the going would get a lot tougher the higher you climbed.

That wasn't their intention, though. The early parts of the hike should have been enough to allow him to feel something, but although the spot was beautiful—if hot—he didn't think he sensed anything different.

He told Bellamy as much when they paused at a spot where the massive rock formation cast enough shade that they could stand comfortably in its shadow. The place wasn't deserted, but at this time of year, not too many people braved the trails at three in the afternoon when the August heat was at its peak.

They'd taken things slowly, though, and had bought some bottled water at the Ace Hardware store right next to the Colt Grill. Because of that, neither of them was overheated, although Marc was very glad of the shade that sheltered them now.

Her expression thoughtful, she said, "I've been thinking about this a lot. I really believe that we have to sleep on or near a vortex for our powers to get enhanced. Otherwise, every time a witch or warlock came here to shop or go to the movies or whatever, they'd get a juice boost, so to speak."

He had a feeling she was right about that. Of course, the real test would be tonight—or rather, how he felt tomorrow morning when he woke up after sleeping basically on top of the powerful Airport Mesa vortex.

"Do you think the McAllisters and the Wilcoxes realized that, too, all those years ago?" Marc asked, and Bellamy pursed her lips.

"I don't know. As far as I can tell, none of the McAllisters who first settled here ever mentioned anything about it. And although I can't speak for the Wilcoxes, it doesn't seem as if they talked about it, either." She glanced up at the red rock formation that towered about them, still looking as if her mind was going a mile a minute. "I think some of the people in my family would probably want to say that if Jeremiah Wilcox had known about the vortexes way back when, he would never have entered into that kind of agreement, since the Wilcoxes were always about grabbing whatever power they could. But…."

"But…?" Marc prompted. His clan had had very few negative dealings with the Wilcoxes, just because their territories were located on opposite ends of the state, and they also had the McAllisters as a sort of buffer between them. However, even he'd heard of how grasping, how amoral, some of the Wilcox *primuses* of the past had been.

Bellamy took a swig from her bottled water, then said, "But my friend Devynn traveled to the past and met Jeremiah Wilcox, so I know he's nothing like the old horror stories that used to get handed around back before Angela and Connor broke the curse and united our clans. I really think that if Jeremiah had known about the vortex power, he would have brokered that deal just to make sure no one would exploit those energies."

Maybe that was what had really happened. But since all those negotiations—whatever they'd been—had taken place more than a hundred and fifty years in the past, Marc supposed they'd never know for sure.

Well, unless Devynn McAllister used her gift to go back to the past again, which he had a feeling wasn't going to happen. Bellamy hadn't gone into a lot of details, but it seemed to him that Devynn had no intention of using her time-travel ability any time soon, especially with the amulet locked up and no way to use it to help her enhance her magic so she'd be able to guide herself exactly when she needed to be.

"I can see that as a possibility," he allowed. "And I suppose in the end, the important thing is that the two clans agreed on that one thing.

Otherwise, your shared history might have been even messier than it already is."

Bellamy gave a thoughtful nod, then drank some more water. "It sounds like we mostly stayed out of each other's hair after those early days, which had to be a blessing. Sure, the McAllisters didn't trust the Wilcoxes a bit, but with all those miles of open land between our territories, it was easy enough to just…stay away from each other." A glance up at the sky, and she added, "It's well after three. Do you want to head back so you can check into your hotel room?

"We'll have to swing by the ranch first to pick up our stuff," he reminded her, and she just smiled.

"No worries. It's probably a good thing if I drop in and out when I can, just to make it look as if I haven't abandoned the place."

Her expression was still cheerful enough, but he could tell she was slightly worried about the situation. After losing her main job, she probably didn't want to do anything that would jeopardize her caretaker gig at the ranch.

Marc kind of doubted that would happen, since she'd already told him the owner was in the Far East somewhere. Maybe he had spies among his neighbors, but the houses in that area were set far enough apart that he thought it would be pretty hard to tell whether Bellamy was sleeping at the ranch.

Besides, the most she'd be gone was two nights. After their test with Bree's gifts and the inflow vortex at the house off Dry Creek Road, he guessed he'd only need the one night at Sky Ranch Lodge to determine whether the masculine energy of that particular vortex had any effect on him, but he figured he might as well go with the worst-case scenario.

"We'll check on everything and make sure the alarms are on before we leave," he assured her.

Those words seemed to cheer her slightly, and she said, "Sounds like a plan. Let's get going."

They made their way down the path to the parking lot, which was mostly deserted on this hot Thursday afternoon. Bellamy didn't show any signs of overheating, luckily, probably because they had plenty of water and they'd done their best to stick to the shade where they found it. Marc, of course, wasn't too bothered by the heat —it might have been in the mid-nineties here, but it would be ten degrees warmer than that in Tucson, and he was more than used to hot weather.

Still, it felt good to get in his truck and start blasting the air conditioning, and to head north on Highway 179, which would take them back to the heart of Sedona and 89A, the only real east-

west route through town. Traffic wasn't too bad—
although people tended to be over-cautious whenever they hit one of the roundabouts that dotted
the highway—and he figured they'd be at the
ranch in twenty minutes at the most.

Everything looked the same when they got
there, along with the incongruously blooming
barrel cactus near the gate to the courtyard.

"I wonder how long those cactus flowers are
going to last," Marc commented as he pulled into
the driveway and turned off the engine.

A hint of a smile played around Bellamy's
mouth. "I have no idea," she replied. "I suppose I
need to get some stories ready about this new
super-fertilizer I found, just in case anyone asks."

He didn't know whether that would be too
much of a concern—he hadn't seen a hint of the
people whose properties abutted the ranch, so
either they weren't even here or they just didn't
choose to be friendly—but he only nodded. "I
suppose it's always good to have an explanation
lined up."

After that, they went inside, where he
returned the few belongings he'd brought with
him to his overnight bag, while Bellamy got out
the bag she'd used when staying at his Airbnb and
filled it with a few necessities and a change of
clothes. It seemed clear that she didn't think she'd
need anything more than that, not when they

were going to be staying only a few miles away from the ranch.

Once they were done with their minimal packing, they drove over to Sky Ranch Lodge, which, as advertised, was perched on top of Airport Mesa. In fact, the Sedona Municipal Airport was only a stone's throw away, along with a restaurant called the Mesa Grill, a place he thought would be a good venue for dinner. That way, they could stay up here and absorb as much of the vortex energies as possible.

Or maybe not, if Bellamy's theory that the vortexes only affected them while asleep turned out to be true.

The room was spacious, if a little dated. However, since it looked like the hotel had been built sometime in the mid-twentieth century, he knew the room must have been remodeled since then, because it had luxury vinyl plank floors and quartz countertops in the bathroom, rather than grody old carpet and Formica or something.

But the grounds were gorgeous, as he and Bellamy discovered when they ventured outside. Walkways traversed the property, some of them sporting bridges that crossed over small streams which happily burbled away underneath, and when they got to the overlook at the western edge of the gardens, they found a spectacular view of West Sedona and the countryside beyond, with

Mingus Mountain and the rest of the Black Mountain range a bluish-purple smudge on the horizon.

"This place is fantastic," Bellamy said. "I think Connor and Angela got married right here." And she spread an arm to indicate the green lawn behind them, which Marc guessed would accommodate seating for at least a hundred people, maybe more.

And to have wedding photos with that spectacular vista behind them?

He couldn't think of a better place.

The briefest flash in his mind of Bellamy in a white dress and a lace veil, one that vanished almost as quickly as it had appeared. Was that the vortex working on him, or merely wishful thinking?

Possibly a little of both.

They'd gotten a pair of drink vouchers when they checked in, so, after lingering at the overlook for a moment longer, they headed off in search of the bar, which proved to be right around the corner from the hotel office. The vouchers got them a couple of glasses of wine, and they wandered the grounds until they found a spot with a garden bench in a secluded section away from the buildings and the more popular paths.

"This feels good," she said, after they clinked their plastic cups together and took a sip. "I don't know if it's the vortex or what, but I like being up here."

"Maybe it's the vortex…or maybe it's just the fresh air and the feeling of being up above everything."

She nodded, gaze moving past the little grotto where they sat toward the west, even though they couldn't really see much of a view from up here.

"It does seem like we're kind of away from it all," she agreed, then sipped some more of her chardonnay. Because it was so warm, they'd both opted for white wine, which felt cool and very welcome. "And I could definitely use some of that now."

The faintest of sighs escaped her lips. Rather than drink more of her wine, though, she only sat there with the cup cradled in her hands, her eyes still seeming to focus on something far off in the distance.

"I'm sorry about work," he said softly, and her shoulders lifted.

"Well, I couldn't expect Jack to keep me on after this, especially since I was still in my probationary period. I'll figure something out, though. I mean, there are a ton of tasting rooms around the Verde Valley, and they tend to have a lot of turnover because you get people coming here for the total Sedona experience, and then they leave when they realize the reality doesn't meet their expectations."

"It seems like a pretty amazing place to me," he said.

Bellamy shifted on the bench, now facing him. "Oh, it is," she replied. "I mean, it's one of the most beautiful places in the world. But it's also expensive and filled with tourists. There's a lot of competition for housing. And although Cottonwood and Clarkdale—and even Camp Verde and Rimrock—take some of the overflow, a lot of people insist on living right in Sedona no matter how much it costs and just make it tougher on themselves."

He supposed he could see that. After spending a couple of days here, though, he thought he'd be happy to live anywhere in the Verde Valley… although he could already tell that dealing with the ebb and flow of tourists and traffic in Sedona itself might get a little old after a while.

And that didn't even take into account the vortexes—if they even had any effect on him at all.

Well, they'd find out soon enough.

18

FOR ALL THAT MARC DID HIS BEST TO ACT natural at dinner—which they had at the Mesa Grill, and got an amazing sunset view for dessert —Bellamy could tell he was on edge, not sure what to expect from sleeping right on top of an outflow vortex.

To be fair, she didn't quite know what was going to happen, either. The increase in her powers had been so subtle that she hadn't even realized what was going on until that unsettling episode at the Devil's Bridge. She still didn't understand why she'd been in a near-trance when she heard the voices that time, although she was beginning to have her suspicions.

Maybe the boost to her powers had already been starting to fade after she'd spent the night before at Marc's Airbnb, and the voices had put her in a slightly altered state of consciousness so they could still get through to her. Although she didn't much like the idea of outside forces having that kind of an effect on her mind, she thought that theory might be the right explanation, even if she couldn't completely say how the voices had done it.

Or who…or what…the voices actually were.

However, Marc's obvious unease hadn't prevented them from making love before they went to sleep—slow, gentle, different from some of the more intense sessions they'd shared over the past couple of days. That was all right, though, since Bellamy could tell he wanted to confirm the connection between the two of them, that she'd be there next to him, no matter what happened.

That was for sure. She wasn't going anywhere.

Several times during the night, she awoke when he shifted position, but because he settled right back down, she had to believe it was all just the normal sorts of movements anyone might make when they were dead asleep. And each time she'd adjusted her own position as well and then fallen into slumber almost immediately.

After all, it had been a very long day, with some ups and downs she would have preferred to avoid.

But a little after four—she knew that because she instinctively looked over at the clock on the nightstand to check the time—he sat bolt upright in bed, staring out into the darkness.

"The cave," he whispered, and she stared at him.

Was this a normal dream…or a vision?

And was it like sleepwalking, when you weren't supposed to startle the other person or do anything that might make them wake up?

She'd also raised herself to a sitting position, but gently, so the bed wouldn't squeak too much. Marc was still staring at nothing in particular… although she noticed how his gaze was fixed to the north and east of their current location.

His hands were curled in the sheets, tightly clenched, and his breathing came so fast, it sounded as if he'd just completed a heavy-duty rock climb rather than merely sitting there in bed.

"Have to…." The words trailed off, and his chest rose and fell as he continued to pant.

Bellamy hated to stay still and not respond, but she honestly didn't know what to do. It sure seemed as if he was having a vision of some kind —or at least some sort of spectacularly bad dream —but if she disturbed him in any way, would he lose the thread of the vision and not be able to remember any of it when he awoke?

That would sort of defeat the purpose of this whole experiment.

Then his eyes opened even wider, and he let

out a heavy gust of a breath. He sat there like that for a moment before something about his body appeared to sag. Whatever he'd been staring at didn't seem to hold his attention any longer, because she could just barely see his brows pull together before he looked over at her.

"It worked," he said.

"The outflow vortex?" she responded, and he nodded.

"I had a dream…but it wasn't a real dream. It was a vision."

Bellamy didn't exactly sag with relief—she was too concerned about Marc, about what having that dream-vision might have done to him. "You said something about a cave."

He released his grip on the sheets and instead rubbed his palms on the covers. "That's what I saw. A cave somewhere deep in the red rock wilderness. Our thief is staying there."

Well, that was one way to avoid notice. If the person had some kind of hidey-hole out in the middle of nowhere, then it wasn't as if anyone could have used occupancy records from the various hotels in the area to track them down. Sure, that was Forest Service land and you weren't supposed to camp there except in designated areas, but Bellamy sort of doubted their would-be magical thief cared too much about that kind of thing.

"Did you see them?" she asked, and Marc nodded again.

"Sort of. I didn't see their face, but they were tall and had sort of dreadlocked hair pulled back in a ponytail."

"They were Black?" she responded, now a little surprised. As far as she knew, you'd have to go far to the south and east to find any witch clans that were African-American. How would someone from one of those families have even ended up in Sedona?

For a second or two, Marc hesitated. Then he said, "I don't think so. I think it's a white person with that kind of hair."

There were several regulars in Sedona and the surrounding areas who affected dreadlocks as part of their crunchy-granola personas. However, Bellamy knew they were all civilians, so there was no way they could be the Collector's minion.

"Well, that'll make them easier to identify," she said, taking care to keep her tone light, "even if you weren't able to catch a glimpse of their face."

"Do you have any idea where a cave like that might be located?"

She didn't even have to stop to think about it. "Probably out in the Secret Canyon wilderness somewhere. We were on the edges of it when we went on the Devil's Bridge trail, but it goes much deeper than that. It's all been mapped, of course, and we can use an app to guide us around. Still, it's a good thing that you and I are both experienced hikers, because it can get pretty rough out there."

Marc must have picked on the implications of that comment right away, because he said, "You think we should go out to the Secret Canyon wilderness and find this person?"

Although neither of them had turned on a light, and the only real illumination was from the clock on the nightstand a few feet away and maybe a little glow from the landscape lighting outside that had slipped past the blackout curtains, Bellamy thought she could still see enough of his expression to know he was frowning.

"The vision came to *you,* didn't it?" she said simply, and he gave a reluctant nod.

"I guess it did."

"We can do this," she went on. She couldn't say for sure whether the confidence building inside was false bravado, or whether some deeper, subtler instincts were at work.

Maybe the voices still whispered on the wind, only this time so softly that she heard them with her soul and not her ears.

"Who else?" she said, when it seemed Marc was all right with merely sitting there and listening to her argument rather than trying to comment. "I suppose Levi wouldn't have a problem hiking out there, and maybe Connor and Angela wouldn't, either. Sure, they can teleport, but not when they don't know exactly where they're going. No offense, but I don't think your grandmother could manage a hike like that, and I know Allegra Moss sure as hell couldn't."

Definitely not Allegra, who some days seemed as though she could barely get up the stairs of her front porch. More than once, people had tried to convince her that she should sell the house to someone else in the clan and move down the hill to a more manageable home in the 55+ community in Clarkdale, but she always adamantly refused. She'd lived in that house for more than fifty years, raised her children there…sat at her husband's side as he moved beyond the veil and on into the next life…and she wasn't leaving until they carried her out on a stretcher.

Her prerogative of course, but she also was not a candidate for hiking around in some of the roughest terrain Sedona had to offer.

And Tricia seemed to be in decent enough shape, but she was also getting up there and probably shouldn't be put in a position where she might fall and break a hip, or worse.

No, it definitely seemed as if Bellamy and Marc should be the ones to handle this.

"If we go out there and don't find anything," she continued, "then sure, we'll pass along everything we know and see if Levi or Angela or Connor can figure out how to track down this person. But it just seems to me that if you had the vision now, then we should act as well."

For the first time, Marc smiled, teeth flashing in the darkness.

"Do you think we could get a couple more hours of sleep first?"

Bellamy couldn't help smiling in return, and leaned over so she could give him a kiss. Not the kind of deep embrace that would signal she was open to other activities, but one that, she hoped, would tell Marc she loved him and would always be there for him.

And that she would also listen to him when he was intimating that they didn't need to go running off half-cocked. Yes, the sun rose early at this time of year, but she knew if they woke up around six-thirty and got ready quickly, then they could still be out in the Secret Canyon wilderness less than an hour later.

After that?

Well, she supposed they'd just have to see.

~

They went to sleep again, although Bellamy had reached for her phone and set an alarm. If they were going to go traipsing around the back of beyond, they needed to be up early enough that they could beat most of the heat.

It started beeping away at six-thirty, and she sort of reached over to swat the thing, almost knocking it to the floor.

"I'll get in the shower," she said, leaning over to kiss Marc before she pushed herself out of bed.

A quick one, since she was out of the bathroom ten minutes later, already dressed, her coppery hair pulled back into a ponytail. "It's all yours," she announced as she started rummaging through her overnight bag.

"On it," Marc replied, and swung his legs over the side of the bed so he could get up. The vinyl plank floor was cool against his feet, and he hurried over to the bathroom, which was still warm and steamy from Bellamy's brief shower.

He did his best to be as quick as she had been, and decided he didn't need to worry about shaving today. Most of the time, he'd let a few days pass before he broke out the razor again, since he preferred to be a little scruffy, but he should have tackled the task today.

Oh, well. Hopefully, Bellamy wouldn't mind the way the scruff was about to become a beard if he let it go much longer.

A comb through his damp hair and that was it. She hadn't washed her hair, either, because time was of the essence this morning. Marc had to hope their quarry would have no idea they were coming and would stay hunkered down in the cave he'd seen in his vision, but if he—or she—didn't, then better to go chasing after them before temperatures climbed out of the eighties.

However, even though he hadn't seen the unknown thief's face, he'd gotten the impression it was a man. Maybe that supposition would turn out to be totally wrong, since there were plenty of tall, broad-shouldered women out there, but the feelings he got from his visions were usually correct.

Bellamy was already dressed in shorts and a tank top and hiking boots, and was rubbing sunblock on her arms when he emerged from the bathroom. "Almost ready?" she asked, and he nodded.

"Just about," he replied. "Let me get some clothes on, and then I'll probably want some of that sunblock, too."

He moved fast, however, and they were both out the door just a little after seven, well ahead of schedule. The little breakfast area adjacent to the reception desk had coffee and Danish out, though, so they paused just long enough to pour themselves some go-cups and pick up a couple of pastries before heading over to his truck. A bit of dew sparkled on the roof, telling him that humidity levels had come up a bit. The sky was clear, but he still wondered if they might be in for some storms later today.

An inquiring glance at Bellamy, and she tilted her head up at the pale morning heavens above.

"The wind is from the east," she said. "So yeah, we might get some more monsoon action."

Which could be good or bad, depending on how you looked at it. Sure, a sudden downpour would help with the August heat, but gulleys and dry creek beds filled up fast in those sorts of conditions. The last thing they needed was to get swept away in a flash flood.

"All the more reason to get this over with," he said, touching the fob to unlock his truck.

Her lips pressed together, but she didn't say anything as she got inside. Instead, she directed him to take much the same route they would have if they were going back to the Enchantment resort, except this time they'd turn right and park at the Boynton Canyon trailhead.

"From there, we can head back into the Secret Canyon wilderness," she explained. "But I wanted to ask if this was the cave you saw in your vision."

She held up her phone, which showed an image of a cave mouth, clearly taken from inside, since it looked out onto a spectacular vista of red rocks.

Because he was letting the truck drive itself, Marc didn't have to worry about looking away from the road so he could study the photo.

At once, he could tell it wasn't the place he'd seen in his dream. "No," he said. "That one is a lot bigger. The place I saw was barely big enough for a tall person to stand upright. I'd probably hit my head against the ceiling if I tried that."

Bellamy didn't look too disappointed. "Well, it was worth a shot. I had a feeling this one couldn't be the cave you saw, though, just because the Birthing Cave is a popular destination for hikers, even if it's kind of hard to get to. So I suppose we'll just have to keep looking and let instinct guide us."

He nodded, then said, "It's a little better than that. At the beginning of my dream, it was almost as if I was watching a drone fly over the landscape before it zeroed in on the cave where the thief is hiding out, so I'm hoping what I saw will be enough to get us where we need to go."

At once, her face lit up. "That's great news. I think we'll really be able to do this."

Marc didn't want to say anything to dampen her enthusiasm, but, even though he'd agreed to go along on this expedition, he couldn't help feeling they were taking an enormous risk. They still had no clear idea as to what the Collector's minion was even capable of, and it wasn't as if his magical talents were the kind that would allow them to mount any kind of real offensive.

But he did have his shield magic, which he hoped would be enough to provide some kind of protection for the two of them. True, cowering in a corner while the thief threw fireballs or lightning bolts at him and Bellamy didn't seem like the best way to handle such a confrontation, and yet Marc couldn't think of what else he could possibly do if the unknown warlock...or witch...went on the attack.

If they even found the person at all. His vision of the night before had provided some decent clues, and yet, they were still heading into pretty rough country. It seemed all too likely that their prey would elude them, and they'd have to go to the elders and Connor and Angela and say, sorry, we tried, but it looks like the big guns should have handled this in the first place.

Marc didn't voice any of those doubts to Bellamy, though. She looked utterly hopeful about the outcome of their expedition, and he wasn't sure whether that was over-confidence in the sort of intel he'd be able to provide, or maybe a tendency to underestimate their opponent. The thief had gotten past the wards in Angela and Connor's house and had also attempted to break into the library at Zoe's home in Scottsdale, an indication that they were good at stealth and unraveling wards, at the very least.

If it was even the same person who'd committed both crimes, something no one seemed to be very sure of yet. The winds had told Bellamy that the Collector had many servants, so they had no idea how many of them could be lurking out there.

For all they knew, the dreadlocked thief he'd seen in his dream could have an accomplice somewhere nearby, which would make this whole confrontation a lot more dangerous.

Quite a few cars were parked at the trailhead, so many that Marc counted himself lucky to snag the last available spot.

Would having this many people around make their mission that much more difficult?

"Don't worry," Bellamy said in an undertone after she came over to join him on the driver's side of his Nissan truck. "Most of these people are probably headed toward the Birthing Cave, or maybe the Three Sisters, which is a rock formation about a mile down the trail. We're going much farther than that."

Marc supposed he should be glad that they wouldn't be tripping over hikers while they were trying to apprehend the thief. All the same, he still found himself hoping they wouldn't have an audience during that magical confrontation.

Trying to cover it up afterward would be a real nightmare.

But he and Bellamy were prepared, with lots of bottled water and a couple of Kind bars she'd slipped into her overnight bag when she was packing.

"You never know," she told him as she handed one over so he could put it in his pack, and he couldn't help smiling.

He liked a woman who was prepared...and who understood that, while the pastries they'd snacked on during the drive over here were tasty, they weren't exactly the sort of meal to sustain them during an extended hike.

"No, I guess not," he said, then settled his backpack a little more firmly on his shoulders. A pause as he let himself take in the landscape, the red rock formations on all sides, the scrubby junipers and cholla cactus and other native plants that helped make the trail harder to see.

"Let's do this."

19

THEY HAD TO PACE THEMSELVES, SINCE neither of them knew exactly how far into the Secret Canyon wilderness they'd have to venture before they found the cave Marc had seen in his vision. At least they'd gotten out here early so the morning air was still cool and mild against her cheeks, although Bellamy knew it wouldn't take long before the sun was high enough in the sky to really start raising the temperatures.

She had been able to tell right away that he knew what he was doing, since he kept his gaze fixed on the trail and moved steadily, negotiating rocky patches with ease and maintaining sure footing the entire time. Yes, he'd told her he hiked a lot, and she'd already seen him in action while they were heading out to the Devil's Bridge, but now that they were past the Birthing Cave and moving into a section of the trail that wasn't nearly as well-traveled, she could only be glad that he was her hiking companion today and not someone with a lot less experience.

His dark eyes kept scanning the landscape from behind his sunglasses, and she knew he was trying to see if he recognized any landmarks from his dream. So far, that didn't seem to be the case, since he didn't appear inclined to leave the main trail and move onto one of the smaller, fainter ones that branched off every once in a while.

The Secret Canyon wilderness was huge, though, and she knew they'd only hiked about a mile so far. It made sense that the thief would want to conceal themselves way back here, in a place where few people—locals and tourists alike —rarely traveled.

Which sort of begged the question of how they came and went. Did they have a vehicle hidden somewhere, maybe a dirt bike because it would be a lot less suspicious? These trails weren't designated for motorized vehicles, but rules never stopped some people.

Especially people who seemed to think it was no big deal to break into a house warded six ways from Sunday and owned by the *prima* of a witch clan.

Bellamy and Marc hadn't spoken much, but she was fine with that. She knew he was concentrating on the landscape, doing his best to see if anything from his dream jumped out at him. Besides, she'd never been much for chatting while hiking, just because she came out to these isolated spots to be alone with the rocks and the trees and the hawks and ravens that occasionally circled overhead, not to talk about silly inconsequentials that could have waited until they were back in civilization.

Actually, that had been part of the reason why she and one of her previous civilian boyfriends—John Brooks—had split. The guy never wanted to shut up, even when surrounded by the kind of beauty that should have made him want to be quiet so he could drink it in.

Marc, on the other hand, didn't seem to have a problem with silence, as though he knew all they needed was one another's company, whether they were talking or not. From time to time, he glanced over at her so he could give her an encouraging look…or maybe to check and see how she was doing…but he remained quiet.

Not that he needed to have any worries about her. She was keeping up just fine, and could do this all day if she had to. Of course, she'd prefer not to, just because in a few hours, it would be truly hot instead of comfortably warm, but she'd manage as long as the water held out.

But then he paused so he could take a swig

from the bottle in his hand, and Bellamy did the same, glad of the cool liquid trickling down her dry throat.

"Nothing yet?" she asked, and Marc shook his head.

"Not so far." He went quiet then for a second or two before adding, "But all my intuition is telling me we're on the right track. We just haven't gotten to a place yet where it feels right to go off the main trail."

Which meant they could be hiking for hours still. She was less than thrilled with that idea, even as she told herself she was the one who'd pushed for this. Marc had wanted to talk to the elders, and possibly Angela and Connor as well, and maybe they could have come up with a better plan.

Or maybe not. Sometimes it felt as if the *prima* and *primus*—and Levi, too—had the powers of gods, but the situation wasn't quite that cut-and-dried. As she'd pointed out to Marc when he woke up from his dream, even they couldn't teleport themselves into a place they didn't know. They would have been forced to trudge out here like ordinary mortals.

Just as she and Marc were doing.

Another ten or fifteen minutes passed, and then he paused on the trail, pointing toward a barely visible path that branched off toward the west. "There," he said.

"You're sure?" Bellamy responded. Yes, she'd be more than happy to move off the main trail and into a place where they might be getting closer to their quarry, but she also didn't want them to take a wrong turn and have to retrace their steps.

His head lifted toward the red rocks, eyes narrowing slightly, as though he was comparing them to what he'd seen in his vision. "I'm sure," he said, and the words sounded confident enough. "I recognize that formation over there, the one that sort of looks like a rooster head."

She followed his gaze. Yes, that odd little formation with the jagged top and the funny protrusion off to one side did look kind of like a rooster.

Well, if you squinted, anyway.

"Then lead on," she replied, even as her heart began to beat a little faster. Yes, she'd signed up for this—had even pushed Marc into it, when he'd obviously thought it would be better if they got some advice from the older generation first—but now that they might be getting close, she found herself wondering if maybe going off half-cocked had really been the best plan.

You can, whispered on the wind, and she went stock still.

"What is it?" Marc said. He'd begun to take a step down the new path but had paused, clearly catching something in her expression.

"I heard them," she replied.

"The voices?"

"Yes. They said, 'You can.'"

His mouth curved upward at the corners. "Well, I'd say that was a vote of confidence. Ready?"

What could she do except nod?

He began walking down the trail, not moving too fast, still conserving his energy since they didn't know how far they would need to go. Bellamy followed in his wake, ears straining to see if the winds had anything else to say, but they seemed to believe they'd done enough by delivering that one encouraging message and were now content to sit back…if they were even the kind of beings who could sit…and see what happened.

It was much rougher here than the ground they'd covered already, the trail riddled with rocks, some of them big enough that they had to detour around the things before they could continue on their way. Most likely, these trails were only maintained once a year, if even that. She was sure the people with the Forest Service did their best, but of course they would focus on the paths hikers tended to use the most.

Because although it was beautiful out here,

with the clear blue sky overhead and the red rocks soaring above them in almost every direction, there were plenty of other spots around Sedona that weren't quite so off the beaten path and probably showcased more important rock formations, the sorts of landmarks people would want to show up on their Instagram feeds and their TikTok videos.

But because Marc kept forging ahead, Bellamy knew she couldn't do anything other than that as well. The sun climbed higher as they walked, now beating down on their heads in earnest. He didn't seem to mind too much, but she slid her pack off her shoulder and pulled off the foldable field hat she'd stored in there earlier, then zipped up the backpack and hoisted it into place again.

As her dad Jordan had said on multiple occasions, being outdoorsy was great…as long as you protected yourself from the sun and didn't allow it to turn you into a wrinkled little raisin.

Bellamy had no wish to shrivel into anything, and she knew the fair skin she'd inherited along with her red hair meant she needed to take more precautions than most people. Maybe the hat looked kind of silly, but it did the job.

After all, she knew she didn't have to worry about impressing Marc anymore.

Now he'd stopped a pace or two in front of her, again with his head up as he surveyed their surroundings. She didn't see anyplace where the path branched off again, but it didn't seem as if he was too concerned about that.

"Over there," he said, this time pointing to their right, which she thought was roughly northwest.

"There isn't a path," she replied. And okay, she knew she sounded dubious, but wandering from even the faint trail they'd been following seemed like a recipe for disaster.

"No," he said. "But I can tell someone's come this way. See all those bent stalks in the dry grass?"

And he pointed toward the place where he'd been looking.

Sure enough, it did seem as though something had come through here, something big enough to bend the grass. And when she squatted down to look at the dry red earth, she saw something else.

"Footprints," she said briefly. "Hiking boots, I guess, because I doubt anyone's stupid enough to come out here in tennis shoes."

Marc flashed a smile at her, then leaned down to look at the prints in question. "You'd be surprised. I've seen people trying to scale rock walls in flip-flops. But you're right—the tread on these does look more like hiking boots."

"So…what now?" Bellamy asked, even though she thought she knew the answer.

He straightened, then settled his pack more

firmly on his shoulders. "We find out who left those tracks."

The going was harder than he'd thought it would be, just because he had to keep stopping and peering down at the ground to make sure he hadn't lost the elusive trail of those hiking boots. Also, whoever had gone this way hadn't walked in a straight line, but had looped back and forth, sometimes backtracking, sometimes wandering to either side before returning to their original route.

An attempt to throw any pursuers off the scent?

Marc was inclined to think so, even though they hadn't seen a single soul for the last forty-five minutes and he guessed no one other than the thief…minion…whatever you wanted to call them…had left these tracks.

Or maybe that was too easy. For all he knew, they were following the trail of someone who'd come out here to commune with nature and would be rightly annoyed to have their spirit walk interrupted.

But his instincts were telling him that wasn't the case at all. More and more landmarks appeared, the same ones he'd seen in his dream. Not just the "rooster" rock, but one that almost looked like the hoodoos in the Bisti wilderness in New Mexico—no, he'd never been there, but he'd seen pictures online—with a rounded rock sitting on top of an impossibly thin column, seeming as if it was going to topple over at any moment. Or there was the one with the sheer, fluted face, looking almost like the red rock version of Half Dome in Yosemite.

All this reassured him that they were headed where they needed to go, even if it felt as though the journey was taking forever. Sure, he'd guessed that their quarry would be hiding out in the middle of nowhere. He just hadn't understood exactly how far out in the middle of nowhere it would actually be.

Behind him, Bellamy plugged away, following him over the rocky terrain without a single word of complaint. She'd pulled a floppy army green hat out of her pack and put it on her head, probably doing what she could to fend off the sun, which grew hotter and brighter by the minute. The thing made her look absolutely silly and positively adorable at the same time, and he wanted to pull her into his arms and kiss her and tell her again how much he loved her.

He didn't, though, because the same instinct that was driving him forward was also sending the signal that he needed to remain focused. Plenty of time to kiss Bellamy—and a whole lot more—once this was all done.

The ground rose steadily as they walked toward a large rock formation, one that was almost its own small range of hills. Even from this distance, he thought he could see shadowy spots on the red rocks.

Caves?

Sure looked like it to him, although the ones he'd spotted were shallow enough that he guessed they wouldn't provide any kind of real shelter. Still, if the geological conditions here had allowed for the formation of small caves, then it seemed to him there might be bigger ones somewhere among those rocks, places where a person could hide themselves for days if necessary.

He stopped and pointed at the closest of the caves, barely more than a carve-out in the sheer rock face. "See that?" he said, although he kept his voice down. Yes, it seemed as if he and Bellamy were utterly alone here, but that wasn't any reason to take chances.

"I see it," she said in a similar undertone.

"None of the caves on this side of the formation are probably big enough to be hiding our thief," he went on. "That's why I think we should circle around to the west and see what we find over there."

"Do the tracks go that way?" Bellamy asked.

Her voice wasn't quite doubtful, but he got the feeling she didn't want to go marching off into even more nothing without some kind of indication that they were going in the right direction.

He hadn't checked, but when he looked down, he saw the faint boot prints curved around to the north of the giant formation. "Yes," he said. "Harder to see because the brush is even taller here, but I think I should be able to find them."

"Then lead on, MacDuff," she told him, then grinned in response to his blank look. "You never did *Macbeth* in high school English?"

"*The Merchant of Venice*," he said briefly, and she tugged at the brim of her floppy canvas hat.

"Well, that was probably more fun. Anyway, let's get going."

He tilted his head in acknowledgment, then kept plugging away, following the tracks as best he could, sometimes having to double back and check again when it seemed they were going astray. The only good thing was that it seemed the thief had given up on obscuring his trail, because, although it followed a meandering course as it avoided clumps of cholla and clusters of juniper, it wasn't looping all over the place the way it had been a little farther back.

From time to time, Bellamy would send a wary glance up at the sky. Marc wasn't sure why, since he hadn't even spotted a hawk this far out, but maybe she was just worried about the two of them being so exposed. Their clothes were in natural colors, khaki green and light tan, so it wasn't as if they were wearing bright pink or something that would stand out against the landscape—especially now that Bellamy's coppery hair was mostly covered by that silly hat —but still, they were the only two people out here. If their prey was standing up on that rock formation someplace where they couldn't spy him, he'd probably be able to see them pretty easily.

But they'd already set out on this course, so there didn't seem to be much point in turning around. Either they'd come all this way for nothing…or they hadn't.

Right then, Marc wasn't sure which option was less appealing.

But he kept plugging away, doggedly following the faint trail the thief had left behind. As they walked, he noted how another red rock formation gradually came into view, not as tall as the one they'd been using as a landmark.

However, this new hill—or whatever you wanted to call it—was pocked with even more caves, several of them much deeper than the ones he'd spied earlier.

"He's in there," Bellamy said, coming to stand next to him.

Marc glanced down at her, a little surprised. "How do you know?"

"I just know."

"Did the voices tell you that?"

At once, she shook her head, although her face, shadowed by her hat, showed nothing but confidence. "Not in so many words. But I think they would have told me if we'd gone astray, so I'm pretty sure we're on the right track."

From your lips to God's ears, Marc thought, although he didn't say anything. He knew the McAllisters were pagan and seemed to give most of their allegiance to the goddess Brigid, while the de la Paz clan was still firmly Catholic even hundreds of years after emigrating from Mexico. His parents had been nominally religious at best, although they dutifully took the clan to midnight mass on Christmas Eve and to services on Easter —probably to appease the elder ranks of the family more than anything else.

He nodded, and they continued on their way. Even if the voices hadn't directly told Bellamy that their thief was hiding somewhere in those tall, jagged, red rocks, her certainty helped boost his spirits a little, especially since only a few minutes before, she'd been looking pretty dubious about the route they were taking. And this path felt a little more protected, thanks to the way junipers grew on either side, shielding them from unfriendly eyes.

With any luck, those shields would hold until they could get the jump on the guy.

Wishful thinking, maybe, but Marc had a feeling that was about all they had to go on right now.

So they'd keep going until they found him… or he found them.

20

BELLAMY WASN'T SURE WHY SHE FELT SO upbeat right then, unless it was the way the voices had whispered in her ears a while back.

You can.

Two simple words, but in this case, maybe they would be enough.

The sun was higher in the sky now, beating down on them, but off to the south and east, she could already see thunderheads building, fulfilling the promise of the dew earlier that morning. Most likely, the storms wouldn't arrive for hours yet.

Still, if it rained, the hike back to Marc's truck might not be as blazingly hot as it would be if the sun continued to rule uncontested in the heavens.

On the other hand, she recalled how they'd crossed a couple of dry creek beds on their way out here. Those creeks wouldn't be nearly so dry if they got a good downpour, and they might be forced to wait on this side until the waters subsided.

The rocks that were their destination grew steadily closer. Despite that sensation of certainty from earlier, unease crept its way down her spine, telling Bellamy that at least part of her wasn't quite so confident about this confrontation as she wanted to believe.

But she had Marc with her. He walked a few feet ahead, clearing the way as best he could, and the set of his shoulders and the lift of his chin let her know he wasn't going to back down from whatever confrontation might be looming.

And that meant neither would she.

The ground began to slope upward as they grew closer to the big pile of red rock with its assortment of caves. Now that they were nearer to the formation, she thought she could see a barely visible path zigzagging its way upward.

"He practically left out the welcome mat," Marc said with a grin as he pointed at the trail in question, which he must have spied right around the same time she had. "That'll make it a lot easier to figure out which cave he's holed up in."

Bellamy had to agree with that assessment... even as she thought they were going to be awfully exposed climbing up those rocks.

But they were almost there, and it wasn't as if they could turn back now.

Or rather, while someone else might have thought they'd gathered enough information that they could take back to the elders and Connor and Angela and let them decide how to deal with all this, Bellamy knew neither she nor Marc was about to do such a thing.

Not when they'd come this far.

When they got to the rocks, she was glad of her sturdy hiking boots, since she didn't think any lesser footwear could have managed to maintain a purchase on the slippery, gravelly soil beneath her feet. And it was a damn good thing that both she and Marc had experience with this sort of activity, or she had a feeling they would never have managed to keep following their quarry's trail.

But even though they weren't in much danger of sliding down the hill, she couldn't help but wince at the amount of noise they were making, with small rocks tumbling off the path no matter what they did. The sounds seemed loud as thunder to her, even as she tried to reassure herself that it wasn't too bad, and if the thief was close by, maybe he'd think it was only a wild animal, a coyote or a javelina or even a deer.

Not that she thought any of those animals would be stupid enough to come up here where there were barely any plants for them to forage.

They kept going, however, and if Marc was worried they were giving their position away, he didn't show any sign of it, everything about his posture clear that he intended to see this through to the end.

No matter what.

The only good thing was the way the rock formation had so many funky outcroppings and half-formed caves and other geological features, so they weren't quite as exposed here as she'd feared. Yes, one slip and she'd probably fall at least twenty or thirty feet before she hit another shelf where she'd be able to stand, but so far, they were both hanging in there, moving quickly enough to cover a decent amount of ground while doing every-thing they could to maintain their footing.

They passed between two tall rock spires and then out into an open, flat area partially shaded by a rock ledge far overhead.

Tucked up against the back wall of the opening —Bellamy couldn't really call it a cave, not when it only had rock overhead and to one side—was a sleeping roll, a large rucksack, and a camp stove.

"Do you think that stuff is his?" she asked in a whisper, and Marc straightened his backpack, even as his eyes narrowed, taking in the rough encampment.

"Could be," he replied, also keeping his voice

low. "Or someone who just wanted to camp way off grid." He stopped there and looked around. "I don't see any sign of him, though."

Maybe he went off to pee behind a bush, Bellamy thought, and fought the incongruous urge to chuckle.

There wasn't anything funny about their situation.

"Do you think he might be setting snares for rabbits or something?" she asked, still in an undertone. "Doing what he can to supplement any food he might have brought along?"

Marc surveyed the campsite. "I suppose it's possible. He's got a camp stove, so he could definitely cook something like that."

During this *sotto voce* conversation, they'd moved slowly toward the makeshift little encampment. Now that they were closer, Bellamy could see the rucksack was stained and worn, sporting patches from various national parks that she guessed were partially there to cover up tears and holes.

"You'd think if the Collector was paying him to do his dirty work, he'd make sure his lackey was a little better outfitted."

About all Bellamy could do was give a puzzled lift of her shoulders. Something about this didn't feel quite right, and yet….

"Or maybe 'he' just doesn't care about shit like that," came a new voice from behind them.

She and Marc both whirled at almost the same moment, which she also guessed might have looked amusing to an outside observer. However, with the way her nerves suddenly started thrumming and her stomach wanted to pull itself into knots, she knew she didn't find anything particularly funny about the way the thief had materialized right there without them even noticing.

As Marc had described from what he'd seen in his dream, the stranger was tall and skinny—not as tall as Marc, true, but still probably just scraping six feet. His mid-brown hair was heavily dreadlocked and pulled back away from his lean face with a leather cord, and sharp blue eyes stared at them from a deeply tanned face.

Her ears rang for a brief second, signaling her that they were definitely in the presence of someone who was witch-kind. And since Marc hitched his shoulders briefly, she guessed he'd experienced the tingle or whatever it was that told him the other man was a warlock.

"Which 'he'?" Marc said, sounding remark-ably calm, considering the thief had just sneaked up on them as if that kind of stealth wasn't any big deal. "I can't really believe that about the Collector, not when he was having you try to steal from both the McAllister and the de la Paz *primas*."

The thief didn't seem too moved by that argument. Looking at him, Bellamy had a hard time trying to determine his true age, since, while he had a few creases around those supernaturally bright eyes and cutting down from his nose to the corners of his mouth, he still could have been anything from thirty to fifty.

"What the Collector wants has nothing to do with material wealth," he said. "It's all about making sure those magical artifacts have a safe home."

"They're safe where they are," Bellamy put in.

The man only smiled. He had very good teeth, considering how disheveled the rest of him was. "Are they? After all, I didn't have too hard a time getting into your *prima's* house."

Bellamy's eyes narrowed, even as Marc said smoothly, "Sure, you got in…but you didn't get back out with your prize. Was the Collector pretty pissed off about that?"

No response at all to this barb. The thief only stood there, watching them carefully…

…and then he was gone.

Bellamy let out a startled breath, even as Marc blinked and looked all around them, obviously trying to figure out where the man had disappeared to.

"Do you think he can teleport like Devynn's fiancé Seth?" Bellamy asked, backing up to Marc so they were almost touching. It just seemed much safer for them to stand like that so at least the thief couldn't teleport directly behind either of them.

"Not exactly," the man said, appearing out of nowhere next to his rucksack. He knelt down and opened it, then pulled out something.

Oh, shit.

Not just a single something, but a pair of hunting knives, one for each hand. He straightened and sent them an evil smile.

"Nothing personal," he added. "But I can't have you telling anyone about me...or the rest of us."

The knives flew through the air, glinting as they caught the light that filtered into the enclosure. Bellamy started to flinch…

…but then Marc reached back and caught hold of both her hands, as though telling her she needed to stay put. At the same moment, a strange shimmer surrounded the two of them, falling into place just a fraction of a second before both knives hit the odd barrier and bounced off harmlessly, falling to the rocky ground underfoot.

A flash of annoyance crossed the thief's face. "Nice trick," he said, the irritated note in his voice belying those words. "But defensive magic isn't going to get you out of this."

"Maybe not," Marc said, still sounding strangely calm. "I can hold this barrier for hours, though. Nothing will get through it. Not your knives, not magic—not even a push from you. So I guess it's stalemate."

While Bellamy was very glad to hear that it didn't seem as if anything could affect the barrier he'd raised around them, she wasn't sure she liked the idea of standing here for hours. If nothing else, what if the thief got fed up and went to fetch the Collector?

It wouldn't change anything, she told herself. *Not if what Marc said about this barrier is true. No kind of magic is getting through it.*

The thief still stood several paces away. If the disgusted expression he now wore was any indication, then he'd also realized that bringing in outside help wouldn't do a lick of good.

"What does the Collector want?" Marc pressed. "Why are you working for him?"

Now the thief smiled. "You'll hear nothing of him from me."

Well, maybe not, but at least the scruffy minion had confirmed that the Collector was a warlock. They'd already mostly known that, since the voices had also referred to him as a "he," but still, Bellamy thought it couldn't hurt to have confirmation from someone who worked for the guy. Sure, there were exceptions like the Ludlow *prima* over in Northern California…and that awful woman in South Dakota…but in general, when someone from the witch community went bad, it tended to be a warlock.

At the same time, though, she knew she could trust the warlock who had his back pressed firmly against hers with her life. Marc was going to make sure they stayed safe, no matter what.

"And you say that your shield will hold against any kind of magic," the thief went on. "But I'm not sure it can hold against this."

He reached into his pocket and pulled out a small, round silvery object hanging from a silver chain, maybe a little smaller than the amulet he'd tried to steal only a few days earlier. "You see, while the Collector likes to keep his prizes safe, he also knows when it's time to send them out into the world to do their work."

After delivering those words, he held the object by its chain and began to whirl it around, faster and faster. And the faster it went, the more she could see the shield Marc had erected around them beginning to lose its brilliance. For the moment, it still held, but she knew it would only last a minute longer, if even that.

He gritted his teeth and scowled, trying to get it to stay in place, but she got the impression that all the magical will he was throwing against the problem wasn't changing anything at all. Soon enough, they'd be utterly unprotected…and who knew what else the thief was hiding in his rucksack? Some more knives?

A gun?

Some kind of magical weapon she couldn't begin to imagine? After all, if the Collector had the guy trying to pick up amulets and grimoires and the Goddess knew what else, what was to stop him from grabbing all the enchanted weaponry he could find?

A shiver of worry went through her, and then she heard it.

You are not defenseless.

The words came to her on the wind, gentle, almost chiding, as if the voices wanted her to know this was not the time for self-pity.

No, it wasn't.

It was a time for action.

She raised her hands, knowing they would emerge outside Marc's rapidly disintegrating barrier…but also knowing they only had this one chance.

Her kind of magic didn't need anything more than that. No invocations to the four quarters, no crying out to them to save her.

No, she only had to think of fierce breezes sweeping down the canyons, gathering strength, coming to protect the one woman in the McAllister clan who could hear their voices on the wind.

She called it to her now, imagining hurricane-force gusts, the sorts of frightening, swirling downbursts that came when the monsoon storms were their strongest. It was desert strength she needed now, born of Sedona's red rocks…and yes, its vortexes.

It came out of nowhere, tugging strands of hair loose from her ponytail. No, not at full strength yet, but she knew that, even if she was the one who'd summoned the wind, she still needed to treat it with the proper respect.

"Get down!"

She pulled Marc with her as she fell to her knees and then flattened herself against the floor of the not-quite cave. He didn't protest, as though he could tell she knew something he didn't…and that he had better go along with whatever she told him to do if he wanted to survive.

All this had happened quickly enough that the thief barely had time to react before the winds reached him, howling, hungry, certain they'd found their prey. He also dropped to his knees, but because he wasn't lying flat the way Bellamy and Marc were, the gale was still able to catch hold of him.

For a moment, it pushed him up against the rear wall of the protected space, splaying his limbs wide as if propping him up in one of those awful spinning carnival rides her cousin Roy had convinced her to go on when they were both little kids. But then the wind seemed to understand that wasn't the desired outcome and instead pulled him away from the wall, turning him over and over again as he rolled across the floor of the place where he'd taken shelter.

His fingernails scrabbled against the red rock, trying to find some purchase, trying to find something he could hang onto.

And then he disappeared again.

But Bellamy could still hear the horrible sound of his nails scritching against the rocky floor, and it came to her.

He couldn't teleport like Seth.

No, the thief was a warlock who could turn himself invisible.

A terrible scream hit her ears then, sounding far too high-pitched to have come from a man's throat. One moment of even more awful silence, followed by a thud that had a horrible note of finality to it.

Both Bellamy and Marc remained pressed against the cave floor for a moment longer, as if neither of them could quite acknowledge what had just happened. But then he pushed himself up to a standing position and looked around, brows pulling together.

"I think he's really gone," he said.

Bellamy got to her feet as well. "You're sure?"

He flashed her the smile she'd come to know and love so well. "Since no one's throwing knives at us right now, I have to believe your winds pushed him off the cliff."

Holding hands, they walked as close to the edge as they dared, then looked down.

No one was there.

How could he have survived a fall like that? Could the thief also fly as well as turn invisible?

Marc passed a thoughtful hand over his stubbled chin. "I think we're going to have to head down there and see what we can find."

From the ledge almost a hundred feet above, there hadn't been much to see. But down here, Marc could easily spot the clump of crushed manzanita almost directly below the place where the winds Bellamy had summoned had pushed the guy off the cliff.

And when he reached out, he could feel one sprawled arm…and the rest of the man's body.

"He's really there?" Bellamy asked, her voice barely a whisper, as if she was afraid the mere sound of it would be enough to bring the Collector's thief back from the dead.

"Oh, yeah," Marc replied. "But don't worry… he's not going anywhere."

Although she didn't reach out to touch the body—he guessed she wasn't willing to go quite that far—her expression was troubled. "It's weird that he didn't turn visible again when he died. I've never heard of someone's magic holding on after they were dead."

Marc hadn't either, but he knew there was a whole lot about the magical world he didn't know. Probably just a strange quirk of the thief's particular talent.

"What do we do now?" she said, worried gaze fixed on the crushed manzanita bush and its grisly burden. "I mean, I guess we should call the police?"

Judging by the way those words ended on an upward inflection, he had to believe she wasn't entirely sure that contacting the authorities was the best option.

And Marc knew that wasn't going to happen.

"What are we supposed to tell them?" he responded, hoping he sounded reasonable as he made the argument. "The guy's invisible, Bellamy. That's not the sort of thing we can easily explain away."

Her mouth pursed, and she gave a reluctant

nod. "I suppose so. But what…are you saying we should just leave him here? I don't know if I can do that."

Marc wasn't sure he could, either. Or rather, while he wouldn't report the man's death to the authorities, he wouldn't leave him to be pecked at by vultures, either.

Somehow he had the feeling they'd still find the body, even if it wasn't visible to the naked eye.

"We'll bury him," he said, and Bellamy now looked aghast.

"With what? It's not like either of us packed a shovel."

No, they hadn't, and despite the rain from a few days earlier, the ground was hard-packed and dry. On the other hand….

"There are plenty of rocks all over the place," he said. "We'll make a cairn."

She still didn't appear too thrilled by the suggestion, but because she couldn't really argue with him on that point—not when there were red rocks and other stones scattered pretty much everywhere you looked—she only nodded. "Okay."

First, though, they needed to get the body off that manzanita bush. Luckily, Marc always kept a pair of work gloves in his backpack, since you never knew what you might find along the trail.

However, he'd never expected to use those gloves to move a dead body.

Because the guy had been so thin, it wasn't as difficult as Marc had feared to lift him off the manzanita and lay him on the ground. Bellamy had already headed out to collect rocks, coming back with some likely specimens before ranging a little farther afield to grab some more.

And even though the last thing he wanted was to rifle a dead man's pockets, he knew he had to check to see if the thief had any I.D. on him. Probably a long shot, since he doubted the guy would want to carry anything that might identify him, but he still needed to check to make sure.

Assuming those things wouldn't also remain invisible.

No wallet, no driver's license, not even a library card. In one pocket, Marc found a folded twenty-dollar bill—one that appeared to him clear as day as soon as he removed it from the dead man's pants—and in another, a small, folded piece of paper.

When he opened it up, he saw it was a ticket for this past Tuesday's mega-millions drawing.

What in the world was a magical thief doing with a lottery ticket? Hoping for a big win so he wouldn't have to be the Collector's lackey anymore?

Marc couldn't begin to guess. Rather than

waste time on speculation, he stuffed the ticket in his pants pocket, figuring they could check the numbers later.

"What's that?" Bellamy asked as she set some more rocks on the ground next to the small pile she'd begun making.

"A lottery ticket," he replied, and she blinked.

"From our guy?"

He nodded.

A frown touched her brow. "He didn't seem like the type of person to be interested in material stuff like that."

No, he didn't, but people had their odd quirks. Maybe the guy just liked picking up a ticket every time he got gas, or something like that.

Marc shrugged. "True, but it's definitely a lottery ticket. The only other thing I found was a twenty-dollar bill, so I have a feeling he paid cash for it."

Which meant there wouldn't be any kind of paper trail to connect the man to the ticket. He hadn't signed it, so that made the ticket pretty much open season for anyone who found the thing.

"We can check the numbers when we get back in town," he said, and Bellamy sent him a wide-eyed stare.

"You're not seriously *keeping* it, are you?"

"Of course I am," Marc replied. "Look at it as compensation for having the guy throw knives at our heads and do his best to kill us."

That argument seemed to get through to her, because she looked down at the pile of rocks at her feet, rather than staring at him like he'd just suggested they knock over a bank or something. "Okay," she said. "I mean, it's just a worthless piece of paper, right?"

Considering the odds of winning the lottery were just slightly lower than getting struck by lightning in the same place at the same time two days in a row, he couldn't really argue too much. "Probably," he replied. "But let's get this finished."

She went off to gather more rocks but returned only a moment later, something silvery dangling from her hand. "I found this. I think it's that whatever-it-was he was using to mess with your magic."

Up close, the thing looked smaller than Marc had expected, about the same diameter as a half-dollar. It wasn't all silver, either, but instead was bisected around its equator, so to speak, with the lower half glass, or maybe rock crystal. Both the silver and the crystal were smooth and unmarked, with none of the runes that Bellamy had told him were engraved in the amulet Devynn Rowe and Seth McAllister had brought back from the past.

Remembering how it had affected his powers,

Marc was loath to touch the artifact, even though it looked harmless enough. "I suppose we can figure out what to do with it later. Can you put it in your backpack?"

"Sure," she said, and coiled up the chain before depositing the thing in one of the pack's outer pockets.

With that handled, he supposed they should return to the task at hand. Now that the man's body—still invisible, and apparently planning to stay that way—was now lying safely on the ground, Marc ventured out to gather his own pile of rocks. It took quite a bit more than he'd thought to have enough to create a cairn that would cover the dead man and protect his remains from wild animals and the elements. They were sweating and tired by the time they were done, but at least they'd made sure to treat the body with as much respect as they could.

"Should we say a few words?" Bellamy asked. She pulled off her hat so she could wipe some perspiration from her forehead, then set it back in place.

"I guess so," Marc replied, although he wasn't sure of the best way to handle this. He'd attended enough funeral masses that he could probably fake some kind of prayer, but he had no idea whether the dead man had been Christian at all, let alone Catholic. It seemed kind of disrespectful to lay him to rest using the words of a religion that wasn't his. "I'm not sure what to say, though."

Bellamy was silent for a few seconds, expression somber as she gazed down at the cairn that concealed the man's remains. "Be at peace, wherever you were," she murmured. Then she looked back up at Marc, face a little too pale for someone who'd just been laboring in the heat for the greater part of an hour. "I killed him, didn't I."

It wasn't a question…but Marc knew he was going to answer it anyway.

At once, he went over to Bellamy and pulled her into his arms. "You did *not* kill him," he said fiercely. "You called the winds to protect us, which is exactly what they did. And you wouldn't have even done that much if it hadn't been a matter of life and death. It was self-defense, nothing more."

She held on to him tightly for a moment. Then she let go and stepped away, face still pale but now almost resigned. "Maybe so. I still hate the idea of just leaving him out here."

"I know." Marc paused, wishing he could think of the right words to reassure her that there was nothing else they could have done, not when they couldn't possibly tell the authorities that an invisible man's body was lying somewhere in the depths of the Secret Mountain wilderness. "But you know his soul has moved on, right? This is just a…shell. That's all."

"That's what I've been told," she replied, then shook her head. "Okay, it's probably a little more than that, just because I know an afterlife exists, or Angela wouldn't be able to talk to ghosts."

Well, hopefully the man's spirit wouldn't see any need to linger in this desolate spot, and instead would move on to a new life with a new set of lessons to be learned.

Or, considering how he didn't seem to have done much good with this one, maybe a life where he needed to learn the lessons he'd ignored here.

Marc went over to Bellamy and took her hand in his, then squeezed it gently.

"Let's go home."

21

BUT WHAT WAS HOME, REALLY? BELLAMY KNEW Marc had probably just been talking about getting back to home base, which in this case would be the ranch where she was playing caretaker, but she thought she needed to examine the question more deeply than that. Sooner or later, her current gig would be over, and that meant she'd have to make some hard decisions about where to go once the ranch was no longer an option.

First, though, she probably needed to find a new job.

Or maybe burn as many candles to Brigid as possible as a way of assuaging her guilt.

Deep down, Bellamy knew Marc was right. If the man in the cave had turned visible again after he died, then maybe they could have thought of a way to report his death without involving either of them directly—say, by telling the authorities that they'd stumbled across his body while they were out hiking. There wouldn't have been any real physical evidence to connect them to him, not when it had been the winds that had made the man fall to his death, so she supposed that plan probably would have worked.

But with his body remaining stubbornly invisible the entire time they'd been gathering the rocks to build his funeral cairn, they hadn't been left with a whole lot of options.

Also, it wasn't as if the guy had seemed too worried about knocking off the two of them. No doubt he would have buried them in shallow graves and counted it a good day's work.

Just as they reached the parking lot, the clouds that had been steadily gathering overhead finally decided to let go. Thunder crashed, and rain began to pour down so quickly that Marc barely had time to unlock his truck before they both got soaked.

"Good timing," she said, knowing how breathless she sounded.

"Looks that way," he replied, then touched the ignition button. "I hate to think what would have happened if the storm had started while we were still out on the trail."

Worst case, they probably would have been trapped for a while if one of the dry creeks really began to flow. But that hadn't happened. They'd made it to the truck, and that meant they could drive to the ranch and shower, and then decide what to do next.

No matter what, though, she guessed they'd have to talk to the elders. They deserved to know what had happened—and she wanted to hand that silvery amulet or charm or whatever the hell it was off to them as well. Although she hadn't noticed anything weird when she picked it up, she thought it better to have the elders deal with the thing.

Maybe they could put it in the safe next to the bronze one that enhanced your abilities. It did seem as if the two artifacts were almost polar opposites from one another, with the silver orb taking away one's magic rather than strengthening it.

Or maybe it only affected magic that was currently operating rather than cutting it off at the source. She couldn't know for sure, and thought that better minds than hers could figure it out.

"Once we're cleaned up, we should probably call your grandmother," she said after they were back on Dry Creek Road and headed toward the ranch.

Marc let out a breath, but he didn't bother to contradict her. "Yeah, I'm not thrilled about that, but we shouldn't keep something like this from your clan's elders…or from Angela and Connor. And we'll need to hand over that orb, too."

At least he hadn't suggested that she should keep it. While she could see how possessing such a powerful artifact might give a witch or warlock a definite advantage, she was glad Marc also thought it would be much better in more experienced hands. The twenty-dollar bill and the lottery ticket were a different matter altogether, since it was clear they were ordinary, everyday items and nothing the *prima* of the clan needed to worry about.

The rain followed them all the way to the ranch. Because Bellamy had grabbed both the remote for the gate and the garage from her Fiat and thrown them in her pack, they were able to pull directly into the garage and avoid getting soaked all over again. Once they were inside, they headed right for the main bathroom, where they pulled off each other's filthy clothing and tossed it in the hamper before they got in the shower.

They kissed, and took turns massaging soap over each other's bodies, but they both seemed to understand things shouldn't go any further than that, not when they still needed to make contact with the elders…and probably get called to Jerome to discuss the whole mess in person. Some things just shouldn't be handled over the phone.

That turned out to be exactly the case when

Marc called his grandmother. No, he didn't go into a lot of details, but after he informed her that the Collector's servant wasn't going to be any more trouble, she told him flat out that they needed to come over as fast as possible.

"I'll have everyone else gather here," Tricia added, her voice coming clearly enough from the phone's speaker that Bellamy could hear her as well. "Well, not Connor and Angela. They're up in Flagstaff today to attend a Wilcox funeral. But we elders will pass along what you've told us, so you don't need to worry about waiting for them to get back to Jerome."

Well, that was something, she supposed. The mention of a funeral made guilt stab through Bellamy again, even as she did her best to remind herself that if she hadn't called the winds to defend herself and Marc, then both of them would probably be dead.

"All right," he told his grandmother. "We'll be there as fast as we can."

"I know you will."

He ended the call and returned the phone to his pocket. Dark eyes met hers, steady, telling her that he'd be at her side through all of this, no matter what.

"I guess we'd better get going," he said.

Bellamy had transferred the silvery orb to her purse after they were done with their showers, so there was nothing to delay them from getting in his truck and driving up to Jerome. And although some people might have used this time to get their stories straight, Marc knew he didn't have to worry about that. What had happened was straightforward enough, even if there was far more left unknown about the whole situation than he would have liked.

What was the identity of the thief, and what was his connection to the Collector?

Where had he gotten the orb? Was it something the Collector had given him in his quest to track down more magical artifacts, or had he stolen it recently and was planning to take it back to his master, and had died before he delivered his prize?

If that turned out to be the case, then Marc could see how the Collector might be extra pissed off to have lost one of his minions and a valuable item he'd found, all in one fell swoop.

When they were just on the outskirts of Old Town Cottonwood, Bellamy's phone beeped from within her purse. She pulled it out and unlocked it, then read the message on the screen.

Abruptly, her face fell.

"What is it?" he asked, alarmed. Was her former boss threatening additional actions besides just firing her? Had something happened to one of her fathers, or someone else in the clan?

She put on a weak little smile that didn't fool him for a second. "Oh, that was Ike. He said the house sold, so I'll need to be out of there by the end of the week."

Which was tomorrow, Mac supposed, since today was Friday.

"Wow," he said, since he wasn't sure how else to respond. "That was fast. Have there even been any showings since you started watching the place?"

At once, she shook her head. "No. Ike says the buyer is taking the place sight unseen. Cash offer, too, which means there won't be any lengthy escrows or anything like that." She was in profile to him, so he could see the way she swallowed before she continued. "I guess I need to be looking up Airbnbs, too. Either that, or move back to my dads' apartment."

The reluctance in her voice was obvious, and Marc thought he understood why. Sure, it seemed as if she had a great relationship with her parents, but now that she'd had a taste of freedom, she wasn't too eager to return home and be their little girl.

"Well, there were plenty available when I looked," he said, trying to sound encouraging without being falsely upbeat.

She looked a little more cheerful. "That's something, I suppose. I guess I can do some research after we get past this meeting with the elders."

He wanted to tell her that they could look for a vacation rental together, since he had to be out of his in a few more days anyway. But maybe that was asking too much.

Or maybe not. They might not have pledged to be together for all eternity yet, but he knew he couldn't imagine a single day without Bellamy McAllister in it…and he hoped she felt the same way about him.

So he only said, "Sounds like a good idea," and they continued their way through Clarkdale and up the hill to Jerome.

All three elders were already waiting at his grandmother's house when Marc and Bellamy arrived, and there was a pitcher of lemonade and a set of matching glasses sitting on the coffee table.

"Thank you for coming over so quickly," Tricia said, her tone almost formal, as if she wanted to signal that she was going to be handling the current situation as a McAllister elder and not as his grandmother.

Which he figured was fair. Bellamy was one of their own, and although Sedona was supposed to be a neutral place, it was still far more McAllister territory than anything to do with the de la Paz clan.

"It wasn't a problem," he replied as he and Bellamy sat down on the couch. His grandmother and Allegra occupied the two wing chairs that usually faced the sofa, while Levi was sitting in a side chair that appeared to have been brought in from the dining room.

"All right," Levi said once they'd all poured some lemonade for themselves. "Why don't you tell us exactly what happened?"

Marc glanced over at Bellamy, and she gave him an encouraging tilt of the head, as though she was all too happy to let him provide the narrative of their last couple of hours.

So he explained their theories about the vortexes as best he could, and how Bellamy and her cousin Bree had clearly responded to the inflow type, while he'd only experienced their true effects after spending the night at the Sky Ranch Lodge up on the Airport Mesa outflow vortex.

The elders exchanged troubled glances at getting that particular piece of news. "I suppose that's why both the McAllisters and the Wilcoxes decided to stay away," Allegra said. "That kind of energy is just too unpredictable for any of us to handle."

Although Marc wasn't so sure about that... after all, he and Bellamy and Bree had had their powers enhanced, but not in a way they hadn't predicted…he decided now wasn't the time to argue that point.

Instead, he described the visionary dream he'd had while sleeping at the Sky Ranch Lodge, and how he'd seen the man who'd tried to steal the amulet from Angela and Connor's house. "Since we had an idea of where he was, we decided to go find him."

"That was not the wisest of plans," Levi said, golden-brown brows drawing together.

Maybe not, but Marc didn't want to argue the point. "We knew what we were doing. We're both experienced hikers."

Levi's frown remained in place. "That's not what I'm talking about."

Bellamy reached over and took Marc by the hand. Her touch made him feel a bit better—not only because he always loved to feel her skin against his, but that by doing so, she'd shown the elders that their relationship wasn't precisely a casual one.

"We thought about letting you know what was going on," she said. "But even Angela and Connor would have had a tough time teleporting into a place so unfamiliar to them. And we didn't know if any of you could have managed hiking out into such rough country. So we figured we might as well go ahead and do what needed to be done."

None of the elders seemed too happy with this observation, although at least Allegra appeared somewhat resigned, as though she knew deep down that her nearly ninety-year-old knees and back could never have gotten her all the way out to that lonely rock formation where Marc and Bellamy had found the thief.

His grandmother's eyes narrowed, but it seemed as if she also had realized she could never have kept up with a couple of fit twenty-somethings.

And since neither Tricia nor Allegra seemed compelled to argue the point, Levi also refrained, even though he was probably the one with the most reason to.

"We hiked for almost two hours just to get out there," Bellamy put in. "The place was really in the middle of nowhere. I have no idea how the guy even found it."

"Some kind of magic, maybe," Allegra suggested, but Bellamy only gave a small lift of her shoulders.

"I suppose that's possible, even though the only real magic we saw him display was a gift of invisibility."

"Well, that explains why none of the security systems were able to record him," Levi said.

"And I think I have an idea of why he was able to get past the wards," Marc added with a nod toward Bellamy.

She pulled the silvery orb out of her purse and handed it over to Levi, whose eyes narrowed as he studied the object.

"Like the amulet, I can feel that it's very powerful," he observed. "But what is its particular magic?"

Marc explained how the thief had spun the orb around, and as he did so, the shield magic Marc had been employing slowly began to break down. "So I suppose it's possible he also used that thing to get past the wards. Luckily, they were strong enough that he still couldn't get the safe out of the house."

"Or it would have taken too long, and he realized the longer he stayed there, the greater the chance that someone might have detected him," Tricia said. "Either way, we were very, very lucky."

"I suppose that thing will have to go in the safe as well," Allegra added. "If it takes our powers away, we certainly need to make sure it's locked up."

Marc didn't know for sure if that was exactly what the orb did. To him, it had felt more like it was chipping away at the magic of his spell rather than attacking the gifts he held at the core of his being. However, since the end result was similar enough, he supposed there wasn't much point in arguing about it. Most likely, the elders would study the thing—maybe with some help from the Wilcox clan's more powerful witches and warlocks —and then realize Allegra was right, that it needed to be locked away and, with any luck, forgotten.

"So, you encountered the would-be thief, and he used the orb on you," Levi said then, clearly determined to stick to the narrative as much as possible. "What happened after that?"

Bellamy's lips tightened, and Marc gave her hand another reassuring squeeze. He knew she was beating herself up about the man's death, but she shouldn't. If the winds hadn't come to their rescue, he very much doubted they'd be sitting here in his grandmother's living room and relating the tale.

"I could tell we were in big trouble," she replied, "because the guy had knives with him, and maybe worse. So…I called to the winds, and they came to us and knocked him right off the edge of the cliff. And that was the end of it."

The elders exchanged another of those glances, and Marc got the impression they knew there was much more than that to the story.

"What about his body?" Levi asked.

"It stayed invisible," Marc replied. "We'd been thinking about calling the authorities, trying to give them some story about how we were hiking in the area and stumbled across the corpse. There wouldn't have been any sign of foul play, obviously. Any autopsy would have shown he died from a fall, which wouldn't have been so strange, considering where he was camped out."

"But then when he didn't turn visible again," Bellamy said, picking up the thread of the story, "we knew that wasn't going to work. So we gathered a bunch of rocks and built a cairn for him. Maybe someone will come across it one day, and maybe not. The place where we buried the guy is way off the trail, so I don't see any reason why anyone would even be out there."

All three elders were silent for a moment, as if none of them was quite sure how to respond to her tale. But then Allegra spoke.

"It sounds to me as if you did everything you could," she said, giving him and Bellamy an encouraging look. "And you brought the orb back, which can only be a good thing."

"It is," Tricia said briskly. "All the same, if you can give us the GPS coordinates of the cairn, we should probably have someone go out and make sure it's not something that can easily be found."

"I can do that," Marc replied. "I had my tracking app going the whole time."

The elders appeared satisfied with that response, although Levi said, "This thing with the vortexes…it's not something we'll want to advertise. Say nothing to anyone. I'll talk to Bree and make sure she understands how important it is for her to keep it secret."

Although Marc hadn't planned to go blabbing about the connection between witch-kind and the vortexes to anyone, he nodded anyway. "No problem. We both understand now why the McAllisters and the Wilcoxes wanted to make sure no one from a witch clan lives in Sedona permanently."

Levi's gaze shifted to Bellamy, who sent him a lopsided smile. "And you don't have to worry about me, either," she told him. "I heard from Ike, the owner of the place I've been caretaking, as Marc and I were driving over here. He just sold the house, so I couldn't stay there anyway. No more nights in Sedona for me."

This news seemed to relieve all three elders. However, Tricia sounded sympathetic when she said, "I'm sorry it didn't work out for you. But I'm sure we can find you someplace."

"Oh, it's not a problem," Bellamy replied. "I've already started poking around."

Which wasn't exactly true, since Marc knew she had been waiting until after this interview to look for Airbnbs or any other furnished rentals in the area. Still, it was close enough.

"I'm sure this whole thing must have been

an ordeal for you," Allegra said in her wispy voice. "Is there anything else you need help with?"

Marc glanced over at Bellamy, whose expression was carefully neutral. Although she was doing her best to hide it, he could guess that all she really wanted right then was to get the hell out of there.

However, it seemed she also wanted to make sure they weren't keeping any secrets from her clan's elders.

"We also found a lottery ticket and a twenty-dollar bill on the dead man," she said carefully. "Would you like to keep those as well?"

"Are they magical?" Levi asked at once, and Bellamy shook her head.

"Not that I was able to tell," she said. "But maybe you can see if you can sense anything from them."

She sent Marc a significant glance, so he pulled the ticket and the twenty-dollar bill out of his pocket and handed them over to Levi, who held them for a moment, his expression thoughtful.

"These are ordinary civilian items," he told her before he gave them back to Marc. "There's no need for the elders to watch over them."

Bellamy watched as he shoved them back in his pocket, her expression almost conflicted, as if she'd been secretly hoping Levi might take them off their hands.

"Just wanted to check," she said, then glanced over at the oldest elder, who'd watched the whole exchange with shrewd, faded eyes. "But thank you for asking, Allegra. I think what Marc and I want the most is to just put this whole thing behind us."

"I can understand that," his grandmother said briskly. "And it does seem as if you've done everything you could to make sure no civilians ever find out about what happened."

Levi's expression seemed to darken. "Still, I wish we could have learned more about the Collector."

That would have been nice, but mostly, Marc and Bellamy had just been concentrating on staying alive. "Well, we know for sure that he's a warlock, because the guy definitely referred to him as 'he.' And we also know they must not have had any kind of magical connection, or you would think the guy's boss would swooped in to save him."

"Or at least to collect the orb before it fell into our hands," Bellamy added, her suddenly grim expression an indication that she didn't think the Collector was too worried about the health and well-being of his servants. "But we didn't see any sign of the man."

"I suppose that's a good thing," Levi said. "I would hate to think he's omniscient. As it is, it seems we can go on with our lives without having to do much beyond being a little more cautious."

Marc thought he could manage that.

"But thank you for coming and speaking with us," Allegra put in. "I think your grandmother and Levi and I have plenty to discuss."

That seemed to be the signal that the meeting was over, which was just fine with Marc. He let go of Bellamy's hand and rose from the couch, and she did so as well, sliding her purse strap over her shoulder at the same time.

"Just let us know if you think of anything else you need to ask us," she said, and then they headed outside and over to the spot at the curb where Marc had left his truck.

They climbed inside, and he looked over at her. "Want to get out of here?"

"Hell, yeah."

When they reached the bottom of the hill, rather than head down into Clarkdale or veer to the right so they'd remain on 89A, Marc instead pulled into the gas station that had sat at the roundabout there ever since Bellamy could remember.

"You need a charge?" she asked. Most of the fuel pumps had been replaced by quick-charge stations, although a couple remained for those holdouts—like Bree with her ancient Suburban—who'd refused to get rid of their internal combustion engines.

"No," Marc said with a grin, and fished something out of his pocket. "I think we should check this."

In his hand was the crumpled lottery ticket he'd found in the thief's pocket, the one that Levi had inspected just a short time earlier. Bellamy stared at it blankly for a second or two, then said, "That's yours."

"No, it isn't," he replied, still smiling. "Sure, I found it, but considering we'd both be dead if it hadn't been for your talent for calling the wind, I think you deserve it way more than I do. Go ahead—check the numbers."

For a second or two, she only continued to look down at the ticket. Because the man hadn't signed it, the thing was basically like cash, which meant anyone who found it could turn it in.

Still….

"It's probably worth five bucks, if even that," she said, and Marc only shrugged.

"Maybe so. I have a feeling, though."

She felt her eyebrows lift. "A vision?"

"Not exactly," he replied at once, which she

probably should have already realized. As far as she'd been able to tell, his visions only came to him when he was asleep. "I know we've been through a lot," he continued, his expression now earnest, "and maybe this is just a waste of time. Something is telling me you should check the ticket, though, so the only way to find out for sure is to go inside and have the clerk run the numbers for you."

This was crazy, wasn't it?

However, since it looked as though Marc wasn't going to budge on this one, she decided not to argue about it, especially since she wanted to find a quiet table at a restaurant in Cottonwood and have a late lunch.

And maybe a glass of wine. Sure, she and Marc had managed to hold it together after the confrontation in the cave, but her nerves still jangled and she knew she'd probably feel better after she'd done something to calm them down.

"Okay," she said, and got out of the truck and walked into the convenience store. It had racks filled with all kinds of junk food and the usual sunglasses display and a few shelves of car-related items, like tire-pressure gauges and mobile quick chargers.

The most important thing about the place, though, was the guy standing behind the counter, who sent her a speculative gaze as she approached.

He was probably in his middle thirties, sort of gangly, and she really hoped he wouldn't laugh at her when she handed over the ticket to have it checked.

"Can you run these numbers for me?" she asked, glad that at least she sounded normal enough. "I forgot to check online."

Luckily, the clerk didn't seem to see anything odd about her looking up her lottery numbers at an out-of-the-way service station in Clarkdale, and obligingly smoothed out the ticket before putting it in the machine behind the counter. A second or two passed, and then the man let out a low whistle.

"Good thing you checked," he said. "I heard the winning ticket had been sold at a convenience store in Prescott, but no one's claimed it yet."

"W-winning?" Bellamy stammered, trying to figure out if the guy was pulling her leg or whether he was only telling her the simple truth.

"Oh, yeah," he said with a grin. His teeth were a little yellow, and she wondered if he smoked or vaped, even though those vices weren't very common anymore. "You got all six, plus the bonus number. A hundred and fifteen million."

This couldn't be happening, could it?

How was it possible that their thief had somehow possessed a winning lottery ticket?

Well, someone had to win, she supposed,

although she knew weeks often passed when no one did and the money just rolled over to the next drawing.

As to why the dreadlocked stranger had bought the ticket in the first place, she still couldn't hazard a guess. Maybe it was a ritual of his, a way of rolling the dice before he set out on the next mission the Collector had assigned him.

"It's still early enough to get to Phoenix," the clerk went on, and she stared at him as if he'd just told her to prepare for a trip to Mars or something.

"'Phoenix'?" she repeated.

In answer, he rummaged around under the counter and then pushed a brochure across the worn laminate. "This has the address to the lottery center in Phoenix," he explained. "With such a big win, it's just better if you get that ticket turned in as soon as possible. And sign your name on the back—you wouldn't want to have someone steal your millions, would you?"

Probably not. She smiled shakily as the clerk handed over a pen, and then she signed and dated the back of the ticket. The whole time, she felt like even more of a fraud, but since Marc had insisted the ticket was hers and its original owner sure as hell didn't need it anymore, there wasn't much else she could do.

"Thanks," she told the man as she got out her

wallet and tucked the ticket inside, then put it and the brochure back in her purse. "I guess I'd better get going."

"For sure," he replied. "You've got until five o'clock."

And it was almost two o'clock now. The drive down to Phoenix would probably take about two hours, maybe more, depending on where in that huge urban sprawl the lottery office was even located.

She hurried outside and climbed into Marc's truck. The monsoons hadn't quite made it out here yet, so the day was still blazingly hot and the air conditioning felt heavenly as she closed the door behind her.

"Well…?" Marc asked.

"It's a winner," she said briefly, and his eyebrows lifted.

"For real?"

"For real," she replied. "One hundred and fifteen million. The clerk said we should drive straight to Phoenix to turn it in at the lottery office there."

Marc had kept the engine running the whole time, but he didn't seem inclined to pull out of the parking lot quite yet. "That's…crazy."

"I know," she said. "And I'm sure the elders won't be thrilled about it. We're supposed to be keeping a low profile, you know?"

"Oh, I know." His head tilted slightly. "But lottery winners can request to be kept anonymous, right?"

"I'm pretty sure they can," Bellamy replied. That knowledge steadied her a little. No one outside the clan would even have to know that she'd won millions of dollars.

Well, until she turned around and bought herself a Rolls Royce or something.

She knew she wouldn't do anything like that, though. Her little Fiat convertible suited her just fine…although she thought maybe it would be nice to get a Wrangler, something with real four-wheel-drive so she and Marc could explore the back country whenever they liked.

Of course, that assumed he planned to stick around. With all that had happened over the past couple of days, discussions about their future had sort of been put on the back burner.

But with the threat of the Collector still out there somewhere and no one exactly sure what that mysterious warlock might try next, Marc wouldn't leave her alone…would he?

He'd finally gotten the truck moving, heading to the right so they could stay on 89A. That made sense, because they needed to get to the intersection with Highway 260, which would take them down to the interstate through Camp Verde and then all the way into Phoenix.

The craziest thought danced in her mind. She had absolutely no idea how long it took for the people at the lottery to disburse the funds, but even if it was more than a month, that couldn't stop them from shopping, could it? After all, she would need a permanent place to land at some point, even if her current plan had been to find a short-term rental while she got her life sorted out. And people wouldn't think buying property would be nearly as out of character for her as acquiring a fancy car, since almost all the McAllisters eventually settled down in a house of their own.

Might as well go for broke, she thought, and see where she and Marc really stood.

She looked over at him, at his fine profile, at the dark scruff of beard that couldn't hide the strength of his chin and jaw. Maybe he hadn't been in her life for very long, but she certainly couldn't imagine a world without him in it.

"Want to go house shopping with me?"

A slow smile spread across his lips.

"Thought you'd never ask."

The Witches of Mingus Mountain series continues with Bree's story in *Demon Loved.*

ALSO BY CHRISTINE POPE
(SERIES WITH ASTERISKS ARE COMPLETE)

LEGENDARY (Urban Fantasy/Paranormal Romance)

Silver Linings

Lion's Share (October 2025)

Trial by Fire (January 2026)

VEGAS SLAYERS

(Urban Fantasy/Paranormal Romance)

Speak of the Devil

Devil in the Details

The Devil Went Down to Laughlin (September 2025)

Devil May Care (December 2025)

THE WITCHES OF MINGUS MOUNTAIN

(Paranormal Romance)

Stolen Time

Borrowed Time

Killing Time

Wind Called

Demon Loved

Christmas Past (November 2025)

PROJECT DEMON HUNTERS*

(Paranormal Romance)

Unquiet Souls

Unbound Spirits

Unholy Ground

Unseen Voices

Unmarked Graves

Unbroken Vows

Unholy Night

THE DJINN WARS*

(Paranormal Romance)

Chosen

Taken

Fallen

Broken

Forsaken

Forbidden

Awoken

Illuminated

Stolen

Forgotten

Driven

Unspoken

Hidden

Written

Given

Mistaken

FAMILIAR SPIRITS*

(Cozy Mystery/Paranormal Romance)

Spells and Spaniels

Cauldrons and Cats

Hexes and Hedgehogs

Charms and Chihuahuas

Runes and Ravens

LATTES AND LEVITATION*

(Cozy Mystery/Paranormal Romance)

Caffeine Before Curses

Muffins After Magic

Pastries and Prophecies

Eclairs and Ectoplasm

Sugar Skulls and Specters

Wedding Cakes and Wishes

HEDGEWITCH FOR HIRE*

(Cozy Mystery/Paranormal Romance)

Grave Mistake

Social Medium

Household Demons

Perpetual Potion

Jingle Spells

Wandering Monsters

Uninvited Ghosts

Prophet Motive

Ballroom Bits

Spell Check

Brew Confessions

Charm School (July 2024)

Higher Ground

Haunted Hearts

THE WITCHES OF CLEOPATRA HILL*

(Paranormal Romance)

Darkangel

Darknight

Darkmoon

Sympathetic Magic

Protector

Spellbound

A Cleopatra Hill Christmas

Impractical Magic

Strange Magic

The Arrangement

Defender

Bad Blood

Deep Magic

Darktide

Star Bright

THE WATCHERS TRILOGY*

(Paranormal Romance)

Falling Dark

Dead of Night

Rising Dawn

THE SEDONA FILES*

(Paranormal/Science Fiction Romance)

Bad Vibrations

Desert Hearts

Angel Fire

Star Crossed

Falling Angels

Enemy Mine

TALES OF THE LATTER KINGDOMS*

(Fantasy Romance)

All Fall Down

Dragon Rose

Binding Spell

Ashes of Roses

One Thousand Nights

Threads of Gold

The Wolf of Harrow Hall

Moon Dance

The Song of the Thrush

THE GAIAN CONSORTIUM SERIES*

(Science Fiction Romance)

Beast (free prequel novella)

Blood Will Tell

Breath of Life

The Gaia Gambit

The Mandala Maneuver

The Titan Trap

The Zhore Deception

The Refugee Ruse

STANDALONE TITLES

Hearts on Fire (Paranormal Romance)

Taking Dictation (Contemporary Romance)

Golden Heart (Gaslamp Fantasy Romance)

Night Music: A Modern Reimagining of The Phantom of the Opera (Contemporary Romance)

Ghost Dance: A Sequel to Gaston Leroux's The Phantom of the Opera (Historical Mystery/Romance)

Flight Before Christmas (Fantasy Romance)

* Indicates a completed series

ABOUT THE AUTHOR

USA Today bestselling author Christine Pope has been writing stories ever since she commandeered her family's Smith-Corona typewriter back in grade school. Her work includes paranormal romance, paranormal cozy mystery, fantasy romance, and science fiction/space opera romance. She makes her home in Arizona.

Christine Pope on the Web:
www.christinepope.com

facebook.com/ChristinePopeAuthor
youtube.com/@ChristinePopeAuthor